ACCLAIM FOR *BY THE WATERS OF KADESH*

With *By the Waters of Kadesh*, Carole Towriss once again crafts a story that immediately grips the heart and mind. From the dry and barren desert to the exotic land of the Canaanites, readers are swept into a world of hope and despair, love and hatred, righteousness and some of the most unimaginable evil experienced by man. Each scene and character is so real, so dynamic, one feels as if they were actually there, with the Israelites, when they encounter a land and people groups so contrary to themselves, all they can do is tremble. And praise God He, and not those living in darkness, is in control.

Jennifer Slattery
Novel Reviews

By the Waters of Kadesh is a heart-warming love story set in the midst of a gripping imagining of the twelve-man scouting mission into the Promised Land, Israel's rejection of God's plan to take the land, and their disastrous attempt to escape His judgment by invading after all. Carole Towriss expertly weaves romance, betrayal, intrigue, and adventure together to form a captivating story that you won't want to put down.

Elizabeth Maddrey
Grant Us Grace Series: *Wisdom to Know,*
Courage to Change, and *Serenity to Accept*

Once again, Carole Towriss does a fabulous job of connecting modern readers with the past and bringing to life Bible stories through her Journey to Canaan Trilogy. Those who have read *In the Shadow of the Sinai* will enjoy this sequel as they become reacquainted with familiar characters (such as Kamose, a former Egyptian soldier and Ahmose, his nephew) and are introduced to new ones (including Tirzah, an

Israelite widow, and her brother-in-law, Gaddiel). *By the Waters of Kadesh* is a delightful tale of romance and action that is sure not to disappoint. More than just an entertaining read, this novel delves into the topic of disappointment and leads readers to the One who can ultimately heal their heartache.

Heidi Glick
Dog Tags (Pelican Book Group)

Carole Towriss has done it again! Not only does she take a story we already know and make it into a page-turner, she yanks us into an intriguing plot with twists and turns that leave us breathless. We can't help but care about these characters that leap off the page and into our hearts. Well done, Carole! I'm looking forward to the next installment.

Sandi Rog
award-winning author of *The Master's Wall, Yahshua's Bridge,* and *Walks Alone*

A beautifully written Biblical fiction, characters who put God and others heroically before themselves, and a romance that makes me realize there is such a thing as happily ever after: All these fit together in one engrossing novel, *By the Waters of Kadesh.*

Anne Baxter Campbell
author of The Truth Trilogy: *A Roman's Quest; Marcus, Centurion* and *What is Truth*

Ms. Towriss writes with rich, descriptive narrative, that will put the reader into the wilderness with the Israelites, and enable them to taste the manna, to experience the putting up and taking down of tents, and walking miles every day, to the emotions, fears, and blessings the Israelites experience. If you like Biblical fiction, you won't want to miss *By the Waters of Kadesh.*

Laura V. Hilton
award-winning author of the Amish of Webster County series

By the Waters of Kadesh is a moving story of Tirzah, a beautiful young Hebrew widow, as she makes the long trek with her people toward Canaan during the exodus. She finds love and protection in the arms of Kamose, an Egyptian soldier who, like Moses, forsook Egypt and cast his lot with God's people. I was pulled into the story immediately and became an onlooker at every scene. The story twists and turns with surprises in every chapter.

Tension and conflict lurk on every page. The story is told against the backdrop of Yahweh's love and blessings, even amidst the broken pieces and frayed edges of life. I learned that Kadesh is as good as Canaan when God is there. Carole Towriss is a master storyteller.

Dr. Art Criscoe
Senior Editor, Christ to the World Ministries

Beautifully written ... a story of family, faith, and God's love for His people.

Tanya Eavenson
author of *Unconditional*

Carole Towriss's *By the Waters of Kadesh* is an excellent sequel to *In the Shadow of Sinai.* Many of the same, beloved characters return in this story that covers the next big phase in the journey of the Children of Israel from Sinai to the borders of Canaan, the land God promised to His people. Kamose, the captain of Pharoah's bodyguard who left all to follow Yahweh and His people into the wilderness, is asked to train the spies Moses chooses. But when his training is done, he no longer feels he has a purpose. Moses advises him to wait and Yahweh will reveal it to him. While he waits, he meets and falls in love with Tirzah—a beautiful widow with twin daughters—who also feels she has no value in Yahweh's sight. The beautiful story of God's love that results from these characters and their deepest longings is worthwhile reading. This is a biblical fiction author who is making an impact with her stories of God's love, grace, and redemption.

Marjorie Vawter
Freelance editor and author of "A Shelter from the Storm"
in *Sundays in Fredericksburg* (Barbour Publishing)

By the Waters of Kadesh

Carole Towriss

DEWARD
PUBLISHING COMPANY

By the Waters of Kadesh
DeWard Publishing Company, Ltd.
P.O. Box 6259, Chillicothe, Ohio 45601
800.300.9778
www.deward.com

By the Waters of Kadesh is a work of fiction. Names, characters, places, and incidents are either a product of the author's imagination or are used fictitiously. Any resemblance to actual persons, living or dead, events, or locales is entirely coincidental.

Printed in the United States of America.

ISBN: 978-1-936341-65-8

For my God,

who lifted me out of the mud and mire
and set my feet on a rock.

I will say of the Lord, "He is my refuge and my fortress, my God, in whom I trust."

Psalm 91.2

One

8th day of Ziv, Spring
Wilderness of Zin

Tirzah slipped out of the tent, her bare feet sinking into the warm, coarse sand. She dragged the flaps down and tied them together to shut out the fading evening light, and tiptoed away. She cast a look at Gaddiel sitting on the other side of the campfire as she sank to the ground and reached for a cold manna cake from the stack on the plate. The sweet, honeyed taste filled her mouth as she bit into it.

She glanced past the rows of tents at the barren sand surrounding them as she chewed. Not a single sign of life broke through the gravelly sand; nothing could endure the blistering sun or evaporating winds of summer. Very little had survived the long, dry season of her life, either.

The setting summer sun cast long, twisted shadows of the flames onto her tent. The fire danced and skipped. When was the last time she had that much energy? She was tired … so tired. She could barely hold her head up to take another bite. How did she get to this point? Why did Yahweh let things get this bad?

She shoved the rest of the cake in her mouth. At least she liked the taste of manna, unlike most of those around her. One more and then a little goat's milk. Maybe she could get some sleep tonight.

She closed her eyes and let her head fall onto her raised knees, her long hair tumbling about her shoulders.

A plaintive cry broke the stillness.

Naomi. Tears pooled in Tirzah's eyes. She delayed one more moment before putting her hand to the hot ground to push herself up.

Gaddiel glared at her, his dark eyes flashing from beneath bushy brows.

"I'm sorry. I'll quiet her."

Her brother-in-law rose and disappeared into his own tent, pitched next to hers.

She hustled into the tent. The child sat on her mat, eyes darting about, breathing raggedly, tears streaming down her face.

"Hush, *habibti.* Back to sleep."

"I'm scared." Naomi rubbed her fists into her eyes.

"I know. But it's all right. I'm here now. Back to sleep." Tirzah eased her back down and lay next to her. She pulled her close and rubbed circles on the little girl's tummy to comfort her until the child, not fully awake, rolled over and drifted off.

Her twin sister lay fast asleep on the other side of her, undisturbed by the noise and movement.

But Tirzah stared at the green stripe around the tent's roof for hours.

Again.

❧❦

Morning forced its way into the tent early. Tirzah peeked out and squinted as the sun bounced off the desert floor and into her eyes. A long-eared owl screeched as it returned to its nest after the night's hunt. She shaded her eyes and looked above her. The glowing cloud of Yahweh's presence hovered protectively over the camp, and the scent of burning wood and hot manna surrounded her. Sighing, she crawled out.

She gathered a few twigs of dry brush and started a small fire, just enough to boil water. After quickly gathering the day's manna, she tossed it into the pot and stirred it into a thick dough. She deftly formed it into cakes and placed them on a pan.

Keren stumbled out of the tent.

Tirzah turned from the fire and stretched out her arms. "Up first as usual, I see." She pulled her daughter to her. The best part of her day. "Your sister still asleep?"

"Uh huh. Should I wake her up?" Keren ran her hands through her hair, leaving it sticking out in several places.

Tirzah chuckled and tried to smooth Keren's locks, but the long, brown waves refused to stay behind her ears. "Yes, please. We have to go soon." She flipped the cakes over.

"Again?" Keren scrunched up her face and threw her head back.

"Don't whine, habibti. It won't help. You know we have to follow the cloud." Tirzah jabbed a finger at the sky with one hand and shooed Keren into the tent with the other.

Keren disappeared inside and a few moments later reemerged with her sister.

Naomi draped herself around Tirzah. "Morning, *Imma*." She pulled back and kissed her mother.

"Good morning, habibti. Did you sleep well?" She already knew the answer to her question. Naomi had awakened crying twice more.

"No. Had bad dreams again."

Tirzah pushed Naomi's hair from her eyes. "I'm sorry. Have some manna. We have to walk soon." She gave each girl a cake, wrapping their little hands around them. "I made them big again so you only have to keep track of one. Hang on to them. Both hands."

She stood to strike the tent. First she tossed out the sleeping mats and their other meager possessions, then the willow poles. Sounds of collapsing tents, braying animals, and crying children filled the air.

Thank Yahweh for the army tents Moses had appropriated for them at their first campsite fourteen months ago the night of the escape. Succoth was a large training ground for the Egyptians, stocked with tents and other needed supplies. There were more than enough tents for the Israelites, and they were easy to put up and take down, which was especially nice when no one was around to help. When the tent collapsed, she folded it neatly into a square and placed it into its pouch.

She loaded everything onto their donkey. "I don't know what I'd do without you, Benjamin. I couldn't possibly carry everything. I can barely keep up as it is." She stroked his neck and offered him water. When he finished drinking, she tied the bowl to the last pack.

The rest of her tribe had started without her, including Gaddiel. She breathed evenly, resisting the anger rising within her. It didn't do any good. He demanded she cook for him three times a day, but never once had he lifted a finger to help her. When her husband was alive, he never had either. Since Gaddiel inherited all of Jediel's property upon his death, she had to do his bidding just to be able to live in the tent and keep the donkey and one sheep. And he made it clear he thought he was generous with that.

Tirzah slipped the girls' sandals on their tiny feet, then picked up Keren and set her on top of the gear she'd strapped to Benjamin. She placed Naomi in front of Keren and the packs. "Hold on tight, girls." After checking the ropes attaching the sheep to Benjamin, she picked up his lead rope and began the long, hot walk.

෨෴

Kamose brushed the dust from his face, dust kicked up by hundreds of thousands of sandaled feet, hooves, and wooden wheels. He loosed the leather thong at the base of his neck and ran his hands through his thick hair; they came away covered in grime. Soldiers walked for hours without kicking up dust. Why couldn't these people learn to pick up their feet?

His stomach growled and his legs ached. Eleven months in a lush valley at the foot of Mt. Sinai had made his warrior's body soft, and now days of desert marching had taken their toll. He retied his hair and smiled as he recalled the place that had been his home for nearly a year.

Ahmose tugged on his hand. "Uncle Kamose, will you carry me? I haven't asked for two days. Just for a little while?"

He grinned at the boy. "How old are you now?"

"Nine. Just for a little while? Please?"

Kamose swung the child onto his shoulders and grabbed his dirty feet.

"Can't we stop yet? It looks the same as where we camped last night." Ahmose rested his chin on his uncle's head.

"We stop where the cloud stops, you know that. Where's your pack?"

"Bezalel traded some of the jewelry he made for a donkey. He put all the packs and tents on it so he can help Meri carry baby Adi. You can put yours on it, too, if you want."

"Sounds like a good trade for him."

More and more brush appeared under their feet, and soon tiny, yellow desert flowers sprang up here and there. Tall treetops appeared in the distance.

"I think we're almost there, *habibi*. I see date palms, and it looks like the cloud has stopped." He gazed up at the glowing, puffy gift of Yahweh, thankful for its protection from the blazing late summer sun. "We should check with Joshua."

Up at the front of the group, Joshua's lean form was a stark contrast to Moses's shorter, stockier body. But even at eighty years old, Moses had no trouble keeping up with his young assistant.

Joshua dropped back from Moses and fell in step with Kamose.

"Moses says we'll camp at Kadesh Barnea tonight. It's an abundant oasis with four springs. There will be plenty of water for everyone, and all the animals, too. From there we'll enter Canaan."

"I know it well. I headquartered there many times when I was in the army."

കം ∕ടി

Kamose and Bezalel tossed packs from the donkey as they waited for the Levites to mark off the outer court of the tabernacle. Several of the Levites laid down silver sockets in an enormous rectangle, and others followed, attaching the silver-plated acacia wood pillars. Behind them came still more Levites, connecting fabric to the tops of the pillars and stretching it out to the ground at an angle, forming a wall around the moveable dwelling that housed the presence of Yahweh.

"Ever tire of watching them build it?" Kamose glanced at Bezalel as they stood on the edge of the activity.

Bezalel shifted five-month-old Adi higher on his chest, then shook his head. "No. I am still amazed I had anything to do with it at all. I think my grandfather was right, that Yahweh planned this to be my life from the start, and that's why I spent so much of it enslaved as an artisan in the palace. I hated it, but I learned everything I needed to know." He smiled. "And I found Meri. And Ahmose, and you."

Moses's tent was on the first row, facing the tabernacle with the rest of the Levites and priests. Leaving room for a walkway between Moses's tent and the courtyard wall, Kamose pitched the tent he shared with Joshua and Ahmose with its back to Moses's. Another row was setting up facing theirs with room for campfires in between. All around the tabernacle, in vast rectangles, the tribes set up their tents in neat rows. Judah was directly east, with Issachar and Zebulon on either side. Reuben, Simeon, and Gad were to the south.

Benjamin, Ephraim, and Manassah camped to the west and Asher, Naphtali, and Dan settled north of the tabernacle.

Kamose snapped the willow poles into place and stretched the tent over them almost without thought. After doing it eleven days in a row, he could do it in his sleep.

He grabbed the corner of Bezalel's tent and helped him finish. "Are we putting up a tent for your mother this time?"

"Yes, but I'm not sure if she'll stay in it. She's been spending so much time with the midwives. I think she likes it there, likes being needed. She'll be around often enough, though. She can't stay away from her granddaughter very long." He laughed as he glanced at Meri, who sat nearby with baby Adi.

"Uncle Kamose!" Ahmose bounded up to him. His dark eyes sparkled, and some of his straight black hair had escaped its leather tie. "They said there's a spring! Can we go see?" The child bounced on his heels.

Kamose chuckled. Where did the young get their energy? "Yes, we can go see. Where is your pack?"

Ahmose looked from side to side. "I don't know. I put it down somewhere…."

Kamose folded his arms over his chest and waited. "When you find it and put it in the tent, we can go."

"Yes, Uncle." Ahmose scurried away and returned almost instantly. He threw his bag in the tent. "Now can we go?"

Kamose chuckled and tousled the boy's hair. "Yes, habibi, we can go." They walked north through the neat rows of tents springing up, then out of camp northeast, toward the sound of rushing water. The terrain around them grew greener the nearer they drew to the water.

A massive spring bubbled up through the desert floor. Date palms soared into the sky, bunches of round, brown fruit weighing down long branches toward the sand. Scruffy, gray-green broom bushes bordered the water on all sides. Brown babblers with curved bills and long tails bounced on tiny feet looking for insects, hopping around each other in an intricate dance. Petite scrub warblers hid in the brush, poking their streaked heads out for only a moment before pulling them back into the dull foliage.

Ahmose dropped to his knees at the edge of the spring and scooped handfuls of water into his mouth.

Bezalel grabbed him by the neck of his short tunic and pulled him back. "You'll make yourself sick. Slow down."

Kamose looked over his shoulder and pointed west. "There's another spring further west, then two springs south of here, to the east of camp. And several more on the south side of camp that are smaller and not as sweet that will serve the animals. Joshua says we'll be here only until we establish a camp inside Canaan."

"It's not as lush as Sinai, but it will be better than it has been the last two months." Bezalel wandered off toward the eastern end of the large pool. As he passed a broom bush, a group of babblers escaped from the shrub, and Ahmose chased them into the shallow edge of the water, their chirps mingling with his laughter.

Kamose smiled at his carefree nephew, then raised his gaze and scanned the horizon to the north. On the edge of the foreboding desert, slopes turned into hills, and those turned into mountains.

Bezalel returned. "There's a stream connecting this spring to the next one. It's not huge, but it's running water."

"Depending on the time of year, there's one running between all of them. This is a popular spot on several trade routes. It's been fought over for generations."

"Looks like the desert is coming to an end." Bezalel pointed toward the north.

Kamose nodded. "Yes, they'll have to choose wisely when they decide who will be first to go in."

Disappointment pierced his heart like a dagger. One thing was certain. It wouldn't be him.

10 Ziv

The shrill blast of the trumpet awakened Gaddiel after a restless night. He shook his head to dislodge the fog. His sister-in-law's annoying little girl had cried most of the night. Even in his own tent he could hear her. Couldn't they have called for a meeting some other morning?

One sounding of the trumpet. That meant only the tribal leaders were called to the meeting, not the entire assembly. Gaddiel sat up, stretched, then reached for the water skin. He took a long draw, tossed the nearly empty skin to a corner, then kicked aside the long-sleeved *thawb* he used for a light blanket, and crawled out.

Tirzah had already arisen and prepared manna. He grabbed a bowl and filled it with the warm meal. He stuffed it down, but the sweet flavor couldn't improve his sour mood.

On the way to the gate of the tabernacle he caught up with Eliab.

"Good morning, Gaddiel." Eliab's strong, deep voice belied his age.

Gaddiel looked down at the man. "Good morning, Elder. Do you have any idea what the meeting is about?"

"We are on the edge of Canaan. I assume we will discuss plans for entering the land Yahweh has promised us."

Couldn't Eliab walk any faster? Old age and short legs—not a good combination. Gaddiel wanted to get to the gate and find out why they had been summoned.

Palti of Benjamin and Shammua of Reuben joined them. From all directions, elders headed toward the tabernacle courtyard in the center of camp. Within moments, a crowd of seventy sat in front of the western gate. Moses and Aaron made seventy-two: six leaders from each tribe—a head elder and five others.

Gaddiel rubbed his beard as he surveyed the men. The head elders were generally at least as old as he was, except for Nahshon. When

Nahshon's father, Amminidab, died, the eldership of Judah passed to him. Nahshon had proved to be a strong leader at the battle over the golden calf at Sinai, and even at the age of twenty-one, all of Judah was willing to follow him. Of course the fact that his half-sister had married Aaron didn't hurt. Gaddiel scoffed. In ten years Nahshon might be a good leader, but now?

The other leaders were a varied group, some younger, like Gaddiel, some older. Together they ruled their tribes, settled disputes, and offered wisdom. Gaddiel was an elder, but only because of his lineage. If he were going to make a name for himself, this would be the time to do it. He needed to stand out. He shoved his way to the front.

Moses stepped out from the courtyard. He faced his leaders and smiled. His weathered face evidenced the struggles of eighty years as both prince and shepherd. "Generations ago, Yahweh made promises to Abraham. He promised to bless him, to make him the father of a great nation, to make his descendants as numerous as the stars in the sky and the sands of the seashore. He said He would give him the land of Canaan as an everlasting possession.

"Fourteen months ago, Yahweh kept the promises He made to Abraham. He heard our cries and redeemed us from slavery at the hands of Egypt. He made us His people at Mt. Sinai. And now Canaan awaits us just over those hills." Moses lifted his right arm, pointing his staff north beyond the tents of Dan, Asher, and Naphtali. "It has been a long journey, but it is nearly over. Yahweh has given us this land. All we must do is go in and take it. I have told Joshua to ready an army—"

"Wait, wait, wait!" Gaddiel stood and addressed the crowd, waving his arms.

Moses raised a brow at the interruption, but Gaddiel pressed on.

"We can't just go in there with an army. We have no idea what awaits us. We could be slaughtered. I insist we send in spies first."

Sethur jumped up. "I agree. I'll not let any Asherites attack without advance information."

Joshua rose, spreading his hands wide. "But Yahweh has already given us the land. There is nothing to fear. It doesn't matter what we find. Yahweh has promised us the victory. Remember what He has done for us already. Has He yet broken a promise?"

Murmurs of assent bubbled up around Gaddiel. "Joshua's right. We must trust. Yahweh parted the *Yam Suph*, killed the Egyptian army. He'll give us this land."

Gaddiel was not going to let Joshua—another child, like Nahshon—take over. Joshua had taken all the glory so far—at the battles at Rephidim and Sinai, going up Mt. Sinai with Moses, insinuating his way into prominence like a Nile viper. Even his tent was next to Moses's. Everyone in camp knew the name "Joshua," and Gaddiel had had enough.

"No!" He pounded his fist into his open hand. "We've been through two battles already. We all know what it's like to carry a weapon and use it on another man. We've all had blood on our swords, our hands, our clothes. If there is something we can do to minimize the fighting, the killing, the dying, why wouldn't we do it? Yahweh gave us the power to think and to reason. Surely He does not expect us to run in blindly and risk our lives, risk leaving our women and children widowed and fatherless. No, we must send in spies."

Eliab stood. "He makes sense. I stand with him. Zebulon will not attack without information from spies."

Nahshon took a spot near Joshua. "Judah stands with Joshua. We obey Yahweh."

Moses raised his hand. "That's enough. This will not be put to a vote. I must talk to Yahweh. Return to your tents until the trumpet sounds again."

The elders dispersed.

Gaddiel winced. Perhaps he should have kept his mouth shut. He had taken a huge risk. But then again, without risk, nothing could be gained … and the gain he sought was status.

No matter what it took.

Two

Kamose slid his dagger down the length of the willow branch a final time, removing the last of the twigs and knots, making it as smooth as possible. He ran his fingers down the branch, then took an end in each hand and flexed it. Satisfied, he tossed it in a pile with the rest of the replacement poles. Anything to keep busy.

Nahshon strode toward Kamose. "We need your help."

Kamose sheathed his blade. "Why?"

Nahshon picked up one of the poles. "I've just come from the assembly. It has been suggested we send spies into Canaan before we send in men to take the land."

Fists on his hips, Kamose studied his sandaled feet. It wasn't a bad idea. He would have made the same decision himself had he planned this conquest as a commander in Egypt. The problem was, he hadn't planned it. Yahweh had.

He returned his gaze to Nahshon, and saw the same dilemma in Nahshon's eyes.

"What do Moses and Joshua say?"

"Moses is bewildered. Joshua is angry."

Kamose smiled. Anger was exactly the reaction he expected from his young friend. "What do you need from me?"

"They want to talk to you."

"What can I do?"

"They want a professional soldier's perspective. And you're the only one we've got."

"Lead the way." Kamose followed Nahshon back to Moses's tent. "What do you think should be done?"

Nahshon shrugged. "I don't know. I'm glad it's not my decision."

They reached Moses's tent and Nahshon pulled back the tent flaps. Moses and Joshua sat waiting for them.

Kamose sat on a cushion facing them, next to Nahshon. "I thought Yahweh promised to deliver the land to you."

Joshua scowled. "He did, but the people are uncomfortable going in without information." He threw his hand in the air and blew out his frustration. "They will not trust Him."

Kamose turned to Moses. "What do you think?"

The strain of his decision showed in Moses's eyes, and he raked his hand through the white hair that barely touched his shoulders. "I didn't expect this reaction. I know the people have complained constantly since we left Egypt. But I thought once we reached here, where we can see Canaan, where we are two days from entering the land, that they would go in and take it as Yahweh said. I did not expect this delay." He rubbed his hand over his clean-shaven face.

Kamose chuckled to himself. Moses had to be the only Hebrew who shaved every day—a habit he still practiced from his life as an Egyptian prince.

Moses interrupted Kamose's thoughts. "What is your advice, Kamose?"

"Spies are a common military tactic. I have often been part of a scouting mission. But I cannot make this decision."

Joshua repeatedly flicked his thumb across the tip of his spear as he looked north toward the hills. "Do you think it would help?"

Kamose studied his friend for a moment before he spoke. "You may feel it is not necessary. But perhaps the people don't have the faith you do. You can see a future that does not yet exist. Most men cannot." He shrugged. "If you let them go and see the land first, maybe they will have the faith they'll need when it comes time to attack."

Moses sat silently for several moments. Then he stood, pulling himself up with the shepherd's staff he was never without. "We will send in spies. We must begin immediately. Kamose, I want you to train them."

Kamose nodded. "Who will go?"

"Joshua will be one of them. Any thoughts on the others?"

Kamose drew a deep breath. "I think you need to begin making distinctions among your elders between leaders and warriors. Joshua is a good choice. He is a fighter." He paused. "I would not send Nahshon."

"Agreed," Moses said.

Nahshon jumped up, eyes flashing. "Why not? I fought as well as any of you."

Moses crossed to him and put his hand on his shoulder. "You are a leader. Your people look to you for guidance. We need you here." He left the tent.

"It's not an insult, Nahshon." Kamose spoke quietly. "You are too important to risk."

Nahshon sat and huffed, resting his forearms on his knees.

Joshua leaned closer to Kamose. "I want you to tell us what we need to look for, how to get that information, and most importantly, how to survive."

Kamose nodded. "When do you want to start?"

"As soon as possible."

"Is there a way to meet the spies before training begins?"

Joshua shrugged. "Sure. But why?"

"Men act differently in the field, around other men. This will allow me to get to know them a bit before training starts. I can meet with each one tomorrow, and the next day is the Sabbath. We can start the next day. We'll meet north of camp."

Joshua chuckled. "This is exactly why we need you."

∽∾

Gaddiel paced in front of his tent. It could go either way. If Moses agreed to send spies, Gaddiel would look brilliant. It was, after all, his idea. But if not, he would appear a menace.

His thoughts were interrupted by the call of the trumpet. Judgment time. He headed toward the center of camp, willing himself to take measured steps.

He reached the entrance to the courtyard. Moses was not waiting. The time stretched out. Where was Moses? He called them here; he must have a decision. Sweat beaded on Gaddiel's brow. He clenched and unclenched his jaw, resisted pacing. His shoulders began to ache.

Finally, Moses emerged from the inner court. "I have spoken to Yahweh. I have considered the matter. I have sought advice." He paused—for far too long—and looked at the group assembled before him. "We will send scouts ahead."

Gaddiel bit his lip to keep from smiling too broadly. Tension flowed from his body.

"Each tribe will choose one scout, a leader. You will receive more instructions later."

One scout? The strain returned, wrapping itself around his body like a snake. Gaddiel cracked the knuckles of his right hand with his thumb.

Outside the tabernacle gate the seventy split into their tribes.

Gaddiel turned to Eliab, Jacob, and the others. "I should go from Zebulon."

Jacob snorted, fists on his hips. "Why you? Why not me?"

Gaddiel glared at him. "You have a young wife and a new baby.

What would Miriam say if you went home and told her you were going to spy out a land full of unknown dangers, and would be gone for who knows how long?"

Jacob folded his arms over his chest, lips pressed into a thin line. *One down. Four to go.*

Eleazar shook his head. "I don't want to go. My leg will not allow me to climb those cliffs."

Matthias agreed. "Nor I. I also have a new baby."

Two more out of contention. Eliab couldn't possibly want to go. Gaddiel tried to keep his face blank as he looked to his leader.

Eliab eyed Gaddiel. "It does not have to be one of us."

What? Gaddiel raised his hands. "Who else would it be? He said a leader! We are the leaders."

"There are others. It's a big tribe."

"No!" Gaddiel's voice rose in pitch with every word. "It should be me!"

"I worry you want it too much. Why is it so important to you? We only want to gather information."

Gaddiel took a steadying breath. He was going to lose this if he wasn't careful. *Keep calm, keep this focused on the mission, on the land.* "I just want to make sure we get all the facts we need. This is our only chance. We need to do it properly."

Eliab stared at him for what felt like hours.

The screech of a hawk overhead echoed in Gaddiel's ears as he awaited the answer that would define his future.

"All right. You may go. If Moses approves." Eliab stepped closer. "Be sure that is your only goal."

Gaddiel put his arm around Eliab's shoulders as they made their way toward Moses. "Of course, Elder. What else would I want? I seek only the good of Israel."

∂◌᷍

The morning sun burned off the night's chill as Tirzah pulled the pot of cooled manna off the dying fire and set it in the sand. She grabbed a spoon and ladled the mixture into three bowls.

After banking the fire, she turned to kneel in front of the girls, placing her hands on their shoulders. "I'm going to check on Benjamin, so I want you to stay here and eat your manna. Don't move, understand?"

"Can't we come, too?" Keren stuck her bottom lip out.

"No. It's a long walk, and I can't carry you both."

"Please, Imma? Please?" Four big brown eyes pleaded with her. Eyes she couldn't refuse.

She smiled. "All right. Eat your manna first. But I will not carry you." She scrubbed the pot with sand while they ate. Then she reached into the tent to put it away, grabbed their sandals, then laced them on her daughters.

The trio set off south through the tents of Zebulon toward the smaller springs that fed the animals. She felt eyes on her, heard whispers. She kept her gaze straight ahead.

They reached the flocks of sheep and goats, donkeys, even a few camels, and scanned the area for her beloved Benjamin.

"There he is!" Keren clapped her hands. "Over there." The little girl pointed toward an older donkey, watching them, his long ears pricked up at the child's voice.

Keren started to run but stopped short and looked over her shoulder. "I can't run, can I?"

Tirzah shook her head. "You might scare the sheep. Walk."

The girls approached the animal, Tirzah behind them. She let them greet the donkey first, but they grew bored quickly and sat to play in the sand. The docile flock ignored them.

Tirzah stroked the donkey's nose. "At least Gaddiel let me keep you. Otherwise, I think we'd still be stuck at Mt. Sinai." She combed her fingers through his mane, straightening the short hair. She drew her hand down his shoulders, his ribs poking up under her palm.

"Soon, Benjamin, soon. We're almost there. All the grass you can eat. And you will never carry anything, ever again."

Benjamin nuzzled her, his warm nose digging into her cheek.

She grasped his mane and led him to the water, pushing her way through other animals and taking him closer to the edge, nearer the softest, greenest grass. Fat, spotted sandgrouse scattered when his feet touched the water. "You need to be more forceful, Benjamin, or you will die of thirst." She leaned toward him to whisper into his long ears. "You won't do that, will you? I guess I'll have to come here every day to make sure you get some water and grass. Until we get to Canaan, anyway."

She waited long enough to make sure he drank his fill and ate some soft grass, and then turned back to the girls, who had dumped sand on each other's head, and now sat giggling. It would take forever to get it out. She groaned. Then she took a deep breath, grasped their hands, and headed for her tent.

After combing out the sand, making three trips to get water, washing tunics, sweeping out the tents—hers and Gaddiel's—cooking the midday meal, and cleaning up, Tirzah propped Naomi on her hip and grasped Keren's hand as she headed east, looking for the meandering river she'd heard connected all the springs. Lined on both sides with date palms, grass, and soft sand, there were a number of places perfect to rest in the shade and escape the worst of the day's heat. The river was scant enough the girls could wade in it without danger. On the other side of the water, the remains of a rock fall in the distant past were apparent in the felled trees and large rocks lodged up against them.

She dragged and shoved some crumbling fallen logs into a large, misshapen half-circle bounded by the water so the girls could run without getting out—she had no more energy to chase them today. They had napped after the meal, but she had too much to do. She leaned against a log and closed her eyes.

Squeals of laughter jolted her awake. A boy, about eight or nine years old, she supposed, chased butterflies with her girls.

They ran toward her, pointing at tiny flying creatures. "Imma! Look!" Naomi didn't pay attention to where she was going, tripped over a fallen limb, and went flying.

The boy dashed to Naomi's side before Tirzah reached her. "Are you all right?" He searched her knees for an injury. She touched a spot on one knee, and he placed a gentle kiss on it. She raised both arms to him, and he picked her up and carried her off to her sister.

Tirzah stood there, mouth open, as a little boy cared for her children. Who was he?

"'Mose! 'Mose, come here!" Keren waved him over to another log. They peered inside a hole, and Keren poked it with a stick.

"Ahmose!"

The unfamiliar voice startled her. Tirzah turned to see a dark-haired young woman with a baby in her arms.

"I'm so sorry if he is bothering you. He makes friends with everyone he sees. And he loves little children." The visitor shifted the baby to her other arm.

Tirzah returned to her spot by the log. "Actually, he's been a blessing, to tell the truth. I must have fallen asleep. I have no idea how long he's been playing with them."

"I'm glad, then. I'm Meri. May I join you?" She stepped over the log and sat down.

Tirzah studied the girl as she settled herself and the baby. Her slightly darker skin and sharper features revealed she was Egyptian, but she dressed like an Israelite. She spoke decent Hebrew but had a thick accent. "I'm Tirzah. These are my twins, Naomi and Keren. They seem quite taken with …" She gestured toward the boy.

"That's Ahmose. He's sort of my husband's brother."

"Sort of?"

Meri giggled, her dark eyes shining. "My husband, Bezalel, lived in the palace. Ahmose was a slave there and was often beaten. One day he was beaten so badly Bezalel took him home. Now he lives with us, and with Rebekah—Bezalel's imma, and with his Uncle Kamose, too."

"Bezalel, he's Israelite?"

"Yes, he is. He was a slave in the palace as well."

"And you, how did you meet your husband?"

"I … worked in the palace, too. I escaped and we married in Elim. This is Adi, our daughter."

"She's beautiful." Tirzah touched the baby's face. "Lovely name."

"Bezalel chose it. I'm still learning Hebrew, if you can't tell." She giggled again. "He's an artisan. So a name that meant jewel seemed appropriate."

Tirzah thought back to Mt. Sinai for a moment. "Bezalel—he's the one who built the tabernacle?"

"The furnishings. Oholiab made the tent and all the cloth articles. And they both had hundreds of helpers. I helped with the anointing oil. I learned to make perfume in the har—, in the palace." Meri spread a lambskin on the grass between them and laid the baby down.

Adi cooed, then sucked on her fist.

Tirzah yawned, covering her mouth with her hand. "Pardon me."

"Don't worry. I know the feeling."

"I don't sleep well at night, I'm afraid. Naomi wakes up a lot."

Meri glanced at the twins. "Really? She seems old enough to sleep all night. How old are they?"

"They were born three summers ago. She should sleep. But ever since we left Sinai, she seems to be plagued by bad dreams. She had them occasionally before that, but now it's almost every night." Tirzah studied her hands, playing with her fingernails.

"Can't your husband help?"

"He died at Sinai."

Meri's hand flew to her mouth as a soft gasp escaped.

"Imma! Bug!" The girls ran toward Tirzah with Ahmose close behind.

The boy held his hands cupped tightly together. When he caught up with them, he peeled them open. Inside were several round red bugs with black dots. He held one hand flat, and the creatures crawled on his palm.

The girls squealed with delight, fists waving. Petals from Keren's handful of wildflowers flew everywhere.

"Meri, look." He moved one hand toward her while he pointed with the other.

Meri poked at the insects. "They're beautiful, Ahmose. Who are you playing with?"

"Oh, this one's Naomi, and that one is Keren." Keren had already raced off again.

Meri touched Tirzah's shoulder. "This is their mother, Tirzah."

Ahmose dipped his head. He smiled and looked at her from beneath long lashes. "Is it all right if I play with them?"

"Of course. It helped me, actually. I didn't realize I had drifted off to sleep. You may play with them anytime you wish."

"I can?" His eyes widened.

Tirzah chuckled. "Yes. After the midday meal they usually sleep a while, but after that, like today, they'd love to play with you, I'm sure."

Ahmose grinned and ran off after Keren, Naomi scampering after them.

"He's really good with them, isn't he?"

Meri giggled. She seemed to giggle a lot. "Yes, he's very attentive. We can hardly keep him away from Adi. He just adores her. He has many other friends he plays with, but he seems to have a soft spot for younger children."

"So he grew up in the palace?"

"Until about two years ago. How he managed to keep such a cheery attitude, with everything that happened to him, I will never know."

"He's a sweetheart. And if he wants to play with the girls, he is always welcome. I'm exhausted all the time. I can't keep up with two of them, let alone getting water, cooking, washing clothes, gathering manna.… When Naomi wakes up all night, I never get any sleep." She frowned. "I'm sorry, I'm not usually a complainer. I'm just tired."

"Don't worry about it. I can barely deal with one little one. I can't imagine two of them, with no one to help." Meri looked up from her baby, a huge smile on her perfect face, framed by perfect, long dark hair.

Because your life has probably always been easy. Tirzah glanced to the west at the sinking sun. "It's nice of you to say so, anyway. I had better go back and prepare the evening meal." She stood and beckoned to the twins.

"I hope to see you again. I'd love to have someone to talk to. A lot of people don't like to talk to me."

Tirzah considered the girl. "Why not?"

Meri shrugged and made a face. "I'm Egyptian."

"Well, a lot of people don't like to talk to me, either. We'd make a good pair."

"Why wouldn't they talk to you?" Meri gathered Adi into her arms.

"I'm a widow."

"That's not your fault."

"Yes, but the fact I'm still unmarried is." Was it wise to mention this to her, this girl she might never see again, who couldn't possibly understand? It would bring up more questions than answers.

"I don't know what you mean."

"If we see each other again, I'll explain. For now, I have to go."

Tirzah settled Naomi on her hip, grabbed Keren's hand, and set off for her tent without looking back.

Three

11 Ziv

With the camp arranged by tribe, it wasn't terribly difficult for Kamose to find each scout. *Might as well start in my own section.*

Judah's spy was Caleb. A few inquiries led him to the man; he was obviously well known—and well thought of—in his tribe.

Caleb appeared to be a few years older than Kamose, yet still had a full head of dark hair and a strong build. He stood as Kamose approached his tent. "You must be Kamose. Joshua mentioned you."

"He asked me to train you before you leave for Canaan."

"I think that's an excellent idea. Please walk with me." Caleb strolled down the pathway in front of his tent toward Issachar, his hands clasped behind his back. "Joshua told me a little about you. Tell me more."

"I have been a soldier my entire life. I joined when I was very young. It's the only thing I've ever wanted to do. I was a charioteer, a foot soldier ... I was even on a ship for a while, but I hated it."

Caleb laughed.

Kamose continued. "I've been on many advance missions in several lands. The basics are always the same, no matter the terrain or purpose. It's not complicated as long as you follow a few simple rules."

"It sounds like you could be of great value to us."

Kamose thought about his young friend. "Joshua does not seem to share your enthusiasm for the mission."

Caleb laughed again, a hearty laugh that seemed to come easily and from deep in his chest. "Joshua is young and full of faith. He will one day be a great leader, but he needs to learn patience with others. I, too, believe Yahweh has given us the land, but the men are not as confident. It will do no harm to acquire information. And if we are going to do this, we may as well do it properly. So, what can you teach us?"

"You will need knowledge of the people, the land, and the cities." Kamose counted on his fingers as he talked. "Egypt has not warred in Canaan since Ramses was a young pharaoh, but at that time at least some of the cities were walled. Maybe more of them, now."

Caleb scratched his beard. "That will be a challenge."

"Yes, but there are always ways to find out what you need to know." Kamose cast him a sideways glance. "Do you know the other scouts?"

Caleb gave a pensive nod. "They are all leaders of their tribes. Most will give you no trouble. A few think more highly of themselves than they ought."

"I'll find that out soon enough. For now, I have eleven more spies to meet."

෫⚮

Kamose had traveled all the way around the camp and the last on his list was the spy from Zebulon, camped on the south side of Judah. When he found Gaddiel's tent, he was greeted by a tall woman with long, wavy brown hair that fell loosely about her shoulders. She balanced a small girl on her hip, while another sat at her feet.

"Does Gaddiel live here?" he asked.

"He does. He should be back soon." She looked him over, a fact that amused him, as most Israelite women were not quite so bold around men they had not met. "May I offer you water?"

He nodded.

She set the child down and stepped inside the tent, returning with a cup of water.

He downed it in one gulp, surprised to find it cool. "Thank you. Do you bury your water?"

"Yes. Keeps it a little cooler, but not much."

He returned the cup.

"There he is now." She pointed to a man approaching then ducked inside the tent, pulling the children behind her.

Kamose tore his gaze from the woman to Gaddiel.

"Who are you?" The man halted before him, his arms folded across his chest. He appeared young and strong, but his frown and the glare in his eyes ruined what might otherwise be a pleasant face.

"I'm Kamose. Joshua has ordered that I give you training before you enter Canaan. We will meet tomorrow morning at the head of the spring."

"Joshua ordered?" Gaddiel glowered.

"Moses has put him in charge of the mission, along with Caleb of Judah."

"We don't need any training. Especially not from you."

Kamose suppressed the urge to sigh. This wasn't the first time today he'd heard this, but this man's attitude was the most openly hostile. "It's tougher than it looks. Have you ever gone on a mission?"

Gaddiel snorted. "As a slave? In Egypt?"

"I've been on several. Come or don't come; it's up to you. But if you are caught, you will be killed."

He strode away toward Judah quickly. His stomach wanted food and his body needed rest. It had taken most of the day and all of his patience to meet eleven scouts. He only wanted to help. Why was it so difficult?

He held a long broom bush stem in his hands, repeatedly pulling it though his fingers. His mind returned to the same thoughts that had been plaguing him for weeks. He would give anything to be part of the contingent that would attack Canaan. He could almost taste the dust, the blood, the tension, the strategy. But this battle was not his.

If he was no longer a soldier, what was he to do for the rest of his life? He'd made peace with his decision to leave Egypt. He was, in fact, convinced it was the only decision he could have made. His life there was over. He could no longer continue as captain of the royal guard. The prince was dead. And while there was nothing he—or anyone else—could have done to prevent that death, he was responsible. The Egypt he knew, had loved and served his entire life, no longer existed. Yahweh had destroyed it.

He hurled the branch to the ground. He had given up everything to live a soldier's life. And he'd been a very good one. From charioteer to squad leader to division leader. Stationed in many lands. Head of the army and captain of the palace guard. There was nothing he had not done, no award he had not earned.

Now everything he'd ever wanted was gone. His glorious past was over. The present was uncertain. His future was … empty.

☙ ❧

Gaddiel yanked at the tent flap. "Tirzah! Get me something to eat."

His sister-in-law emerged with a plate of manna cakes and a skin of water.

He growled. "I should have been the leader. Instead, that child Joshua has been put in charge of the mission. Now I have to listen to an Egyptian tell me how to spy! I know more than all of them."

"Well, then perhaps the best course of action is to show up, listen, and wait for an opportunity to show them how much you know. If you stay here, how will they know how clever you are?" She filled his cup and wandered away with her babies.

Gaddiel paced in front of his tent. The water did nothing to quench the burning inside him. Caleb and Joshua. Joshua and Caleb. Why must it always be those two? Moses always played favorites. He would have sent his brother Aaron if he weren't so old. But he couldn't seem to see past the few people around him that flattered and wooed him. Gaddiel was above that. He was every bit as good a leader as Caleb, and much better than Joshua. Joshua was barely old enough to be considered a man! What was he? Twenty-three? Twenty-four? He wasn't even married yet. Gaddiel had killed more Amalekites than either of them at Rephidim. Moses only appointed Joshua commander of the Israelite army because his family was slaughtered by the Amalekites. What kind of logic was that? So he'd fought one more battle. A short one, at that, and he'd lost.

Joshua did a passable job commanding the army, but Gaddiel could have done better. He'd been one of the foremen of the brick-making teams in Egypt until they promoted a younger man. He knew how to manage men. Before the Hebrews were all kicked out of the place, he'd been a servant for a retired soldier. He knew a few things about spying. But none of that mattered to Moses. Only his precious favorites were rewarded.

This turn of events would complicate his plan immeasurably. He thought through everything again. He had assumed they would meet in a day or two and choose a leader together, and he had a speech ready. He'd planned to find out who the others were and visit them beforehand, get them all on his side. But that snake Joshua had used his connection to Moses to get himself named leader before the first day was even over. Gaddiel should have known. Now he was behind before the journey had even begun.

Tirzah was right, though. She was fairly intelligent, for a woman. He wolfed down his food, gulped the water, tossed the plate on the ground, and headed for his brother's tent farther down the row. He had to come up with a plan. His brother would help—he was good at that sort of thing. He poked his head in the tent. "Nathaniel?"

"Gaddiel. Why so angry? What happened?"

"You heard we are sending spies up to Canaan? And I am one of them?"

"Yes. Is that not a good thing?" He gestured for his brother to come in and sit down.

Gaddiel dropped onto a cushion. "Of course. Very prudent. But Joshua is the leader. And Caleb."

"Caleb? Of Judah? Why is it always Judah?" Nathaniel's mouth dropped and his voice rose in pitch as he offered Gaddiel a cup of cooled goat's milk.

Not much took Nathaniel by surprise, but apparently even he hadn't counted on this.

Gaddiel waved the cup off. "I know that Egyptian had something to do with it. I don't trust him. And—hear this—he's training us."

"That's insulting." Nathaniel's upper lip curled.

"I know." Gaddiel pondered a while. "I've got to find a way to discredit Joshua. He has been Moses's favorite for far too long. If we plan to be rulers once we reach Canaan, we have got to remove him from leadership, one way or another."

"Agreed. Any ideas?"

Gaddiel rested his chin on his fist, his elbow on his knee. "I hoped you might have some. I'm too angry at the moment. Tirzah says to go along, find a chance to show them how smart I am."

"Not a bad idea. She's pretty clever herself." Nathaniel stroked his well-trimmed, light brown beard. His light gray eyes, the same color as Gaddiel's, twinkled. "She still hasn't asked you to marry her?"

"No, and I don't want her to. Women aren't worth the trouble."

Nathaniel grinned. "Just because you had a bad one …"

Gaddiel shoved his finger in his brother's chest. "I'm glad she died. And the baby she carried. Saved me a life of pain."

"I wish she would ask you, so you could refuse and it would fall to me."

Gaddiel scoffed. "Like she would have you!"

Nathaniel spread his hands. "Why not? I'm as good as you. Maybe better."

"It doesn't appear she wants anyone." Gaddiel shrugged. "Which is fine with me. I keep Jediel's sheep, and she cooks my food, and I don't have a nagging woman in my tent."

"Maybe she'd have me if she knew you would say no."

"Leave her alone. I like this arrangement. I'm older and I say leave it alone. You're young. Find a bride of your own."

20 Ziv

Kamose walked back and forth before the twelve men who stood before him. His gaze quickly took in each one. He'd already met them and taken account of each. Most were young, quick, and strong—just what they needed. Caleb was a bit older, and brought wisdom and an ability to handle the others. Then there was Gaddiel. He was surly, arrogant, and divisive.

Kamose faced the scouts. "You have three jobs: to learn about the men, the cities, and the land.

"One. What kind of men inhabit the land? Are they many or few? Are they farmers? Are they warriors? What kind of resistance will they give us? Yahweh has given us the land, but we must still take it.

"Two. What kind of cities are there? Are they walled, or guarded in some other way? How many are there? How far apart are they?

"And three. How is the land? Is it fertile? Will it support us? What kind of crops does it bear now? What kind of livestock will it support? Moses asks that you bring back samples of the fruit of the land on the return journey.

"The journey will be difficult. You will sleep in the open. If you are found out, you will likely be killed. Everything you do and see will be new to you. You must be on your guard at all times. Never be complacent. Never forget you are part of a team."

He reached down to a pile of daggers, each with a belt and sheath, and passed them out as he talked.

"You've all fought out in the open, been in battle at Rephidim and at Sinai. Remaining unseen is altogether different. I'll teach you. How well you learn determines whether you stay alive."

He led the men to the first rise to the north of camp. "Most cities will be at the top of a hill since that's the best way to defend against attack. If the city is fortified, the main part will be walled in, at the crest. The dwellings will be inside and the crops, animals, and anything else will be outside. Everything will be brought in at dusk and the gates shut. I know Hebron had walls the last time Egypt fought Canaan. I don't know about anywhere else."

"If it's at the top of a hill, how can we possibly see anything without being discovered?" Palti asked.

"The land has many dips and rises. There will be places you can hide to view the city during the day. Then, at night, you can get closer to get more information. Now, you." He gestured at four of them.

"Down on your bellies. Close your eyes."

Gaddiel and three others dropped to the ground.

"Four more, go down on the other side of this ridge. Tell me if you see these men."

Shammua, Gadi, Ammiel, and Geuel sprinted to the other side of the rise.

"Now, you four, crawl to the top, but keep your heads down."

Gaddiel and the others crawled to the edge of the hillock.

Kamose strode to the top of the ridge and straddled it so he could see both sets of men. "When you reach the top, try to peek over to see the others without being seen."

Palti poked his head over the top. "I see th—"

Shammua shouted. "I see him!"

"Palti, you're dead. Out of line."

Gaddiel looked at the other two.

Igal tried next. Same result.

"Igal. Out of line."

Was anyone going to try anything different?

Gaddiel backed up a bit and crawled sideways until he was below a broom bush. He scooted up and raised his head behind the shrub. "I see Shammua, Gadi, Geuel, and Ammiel."

No one beyond the rise called out.

Kamose nodded his approval. "Excellent, Gaddiel. You get to stay alive."

25 Ziv

A dry wind blew through the leaves of the date palms. Tirzah leaned back against the trunk of one of them and watched the branches sway, the gentle movement vaguely soothing. She closed her eyes.

Moments later, the girls squealed with delight. "'Mose!"

Ahmose bounded over a log.

Meri followed him, carrying Adi wrapped in a blanket. She stepped over the fallen tree and settled in the sand next to Tirzah.

Tirzah drank the last of the sweet sheep's milk in her cup and offered the skin to Meri, who smiled as she accepted it.

The girls splashed in the shallow river, closely guarded by Ahmose.

Tirzah held out her arms to take the baby.

Meri gave her the babe. As she stretched her arms, three vertical rows of blue-black dots peeked out from the bottom of her short sleeve, ending just above her elbow.

A tattoo? Why would Meri have a tattoo?

"What a lovely spot. It's so much cooler here." Meri finished her milk and returned the skin. She eyed Tirzah for a moment. "Can you explain what you meant when you said you are sometimes shunned because you have not remarried?"

Tirzah shifted her weight against the tree and recrossed her ankles. She couldn't tell the girl everything. She'd never understand. "It's just not very acceptable for a widow to remain alone. She's expected to remarry again soon. So they see me as a troublemaker, a woman who chooses to flaunt generations of custom. I'm considered a rebellious woman."

"Isn't it hard being alone?"

Tirzah blew out a long breath. How to explain it? "To everyone else, my husband, Jediel, seemed kind and generous. But he was cruel. I hate to say it, but life has been much easier—and nicer—since he is gone."

"So you didn't know he was so cruel before you married him?"

"I didn't know him at all."

Meri blinked. "What do you mean? How could you choose him if you didn't know him?"

"I didn't choose him. Fathers arrange the marriages."

"Why would your father choose such a man for you to marry?"

Tirzah played with Adi's blanket, adjusting and readjusting it as she studied the mountains in the distance. "Jediel was very good at appearing kind to others. Only in our own home was he so cruel. And to be fair, it was my stepfather, not my father who chose. I took care of my mother when she was ill, and by the time she died, I was older than most brides. And I am taller than men usually prefer their women. So he married me off to the first one who paid the bride price."

Meri gaped at Tirzah with her mouth open, eyes as wide as pomegranates.

Tirzah touched Meri's arm. "It's not as bad as I've made it sound. Almost all fathers give their daughters a say. Many girls marry the one they love. I just didn't have a father who cared."

Meri let the silence sit for a moment. "Why didn't you leave him?"

Tirzah furrowed her brow. "Leave him?"

"Yes. Divorce him."

"Wives can't divorce."

"They can't?" Meri grasped Tirzah's hand. "Tirzah, I am so sorry."

Tirzah smiled. "Thank you."

Naomi skipped up with a handful of purple flowers. "For you, Imma." She pulled a few out and gave them to Meri. "You, too."

Meri watched Naomi run away. "Your girls are beautiful, Tirzah. "

"I don't know what I'd do without them." She closed her eyes and sniffed the flowers. Time to change the subject. "How did you end up working in the palace?"

Meri fingered the blooms. "Like yours, my mother died, but I was much younger. When she was alive, we were very happy. I adored her. But after she died, there were too many of us. My father couldn't manage. He couldn't take care of the farm and all of us. One year, the grain taxes were due. We went to the temple, and a priest came and talked to him. I was told I was to go work in the palace. When I arrived, I found out I had been sold into the harem to pay for five years' taxes."

"Oh, Meri, that's terrible!" Tirzah touched the dots on Meri's arm. "Is that what this means?"

Meri fingered the tattoo. "Yes. The mark of a concubine." Her face paled for only a moment. "It was a terrifying time. But to skip to the end, that's where I met Bezalel. He had been brought to the palace and forced to live there as a child. That's where he learned to make such beautiful works of art, and where he learned everything he needed to know to craft the tabernacle. I escaped with him, we married in Elim, and now we have this beautiful baby."

"I wish my story could have such a happy ending, but I don't see how it can. Anyway, now I am all alone, with these two little girls. They are exhausting, but they are the lights of my life. I thank

Yahweh every day for them. I may have nothing else, but at least I have them."

Meri shifted to face her more directly and grabbed her hand. "I don't think this is the end of your story. I've seen Yahweh change too many people's lives to think that. I thought my life was over when I found myself in the harem. I was alone. No one there would even talk to me. But I found Bezalel. Bezalel spent his life in the palace away from his family, his people. He felt abandoned by Yahweh, but Yahweh had a plan all along. He had been chosen to build a dwelling for Yahweh, and Yahweh had just been preparing him. You can't say it's over already. I think you have a lot to look forward to."

Tirzah pulled her hand away and shook her head. "Not me. This is all there is to my life. There will never be any more. Maybe there was for you. Maybe for Bezalel. Not for me. Not now. Not ever."

28 Ziv

Kamose called for the evening meal break and reached into his bag for the manna cakes he brought with him.

He looked over the group of scouts before him. They were not professional soldiers, but they would have to do. If he could just get enough information into them to keep them alive, he'd be satisfied. They didn't have to learn too many intricate espionage skills to bring back the knowledge Moses had requested. Anyone with a bit of common sense could find out whether the land was arable, the cities were fortified, and the people were armed. And Caleb and Joshua were more than capable of finding out far more than that. No, all he was worried about was whether or not they could keep their heads down and not be seen.

Kamose had not fought in Canaan himself. Those wars had ended before he was born. The most famous battle was fought on the very ground they now camped on. But the legends endured. Legends of giants. Cities with walls that climbed into the sky. Iron chariots. Weapons never before seen. He could only pray to Yahweh for safety.

He noticed the wives bringing dinner to their husbands. The sweet kisses and whispered endearments before they returned to their tents.

Then there was Gaddiel. He snatched the bag from the woman with the beautiful, wavy brown hair and the girls who clung to her. He barely acknowledged her, let alone kissed her. She glanced at the desert floor as he snapped at her, then turned to go. Kamose stared a beat longer than he should have at another man's wife, and then he diverted his gaze, pulling it to the cliffs past the rolling hills at the edge of camp. They'd spent today working on climbing the steep limestone bluff west of camp. A lifetime on a delta did not prepare one for rock climbing.

One more run at the cliffs tonight, and training would be complete. Kamose had done everything he could in ten days. Tomorrow the scouts would leave for Canaan. He could only hope he had taught them enough to keep them alive, to bring them all back to the wives and children they were leaving behind. He'd seen enough soldiers leave and never come back.

He didn't want it to happen here.

Four

29 Ziv

After ten days of training, except for one Sabbath's rest, Gaddiel's muscles screamed. Even the backbreaking work of the brickfields and unending days of marching had not strengthened his body enough for what Kamose had put the would-be scouts through. Long mornings of physical training, hot afternoons learning strategy, and barely cooler evenings climbing the cliff walls to the west.

Kamose had better know what he was talking about. He bragged often enough about his exploits as a great Egyptian soldier. Gaddiel was sick of hearing about it. The man never let up. Never seemed to break a sweat, either. Just constantly barked orders as if they were soldiers in his private army.

The former commander strutted before them, the jeweled gold armbands on his biceps glistening in the sun. Did he not realize he was no longer captain of the guard? He didn't need to keep wearing the symbols of his previous office. He could put a tunic on, too, instead of walking around wearing only that shenti tied around his waist. If he wanted to dress like that, he should have stayed in Egypt.

"If you remember everything I taught you, you will live, and bring back the information you need to successfully conquer Canaan."

Could that man take any more of the credit for himself?

"The first town you will encounter is Arad. The next is Hebron, an ancient city, older than most in Egypt, and probably walled. After that, it is unknown. Moses wants you to go as far north as possible. Caleb will lead the mission, and Joshua will be his second-in-command."

Joshua. Kamose probably had a hand in that decision as well. Joshua was his friend. They shared a tent. Kamose would want him to have the glory since Kamose couldn't grab it for himself.

Well, Gaddiel wouldn't let that happen.

The gray light of dusk clung to the sandy floor. Twelve families huddled at the edge of the desert north of camp. Gaddiel watched the other spies kiss their wives and hug their children. Tears flowed as husbands consoled their wives and promised a quick and safe return.

Not Gaddiel. He stood apart from the rest, pack already on his back, anxious to get underway. He had no time to waste on sentiment.

Tirzah approached, carrying a bag of food and skins, probably milk and water. As usual, one of the girls skipped around, but the other buried her face in her mother's shoulder and never raised her head to look at him. Tirzah needed to stop coddling that child.

"Why don't you make her walk? She's not a baby anymore." Gaddiel snatched the offering from her hand. "And you're late. We are about to leave."

She dropped her gaze and studied her sandals.

The wives pulled away from the men and returned to camp.

Gaddiel opened his bag. He expected to find manna cakes, but Tirzah had also added several handfuls of dates. It looked like she had given him her portion of tonight's manna as well. He tossed her a glance as she headed toward the tents, trailing far behind the other families. She knew he despised her, and he knew she felt nothing for him either. Why the extra effort? He shrugged and slipped the bags into his pack.

Off to the side, Moses waited with Kamose. The officer stood as if he were in charge, feet apart, hands folded over his chest, watching every move the spies made. When would he learn he wasn't a soldier anymore?

Caleb took the first step. He got about five strides ahead before Gaddiel decided he would be next. He couldn't let Joshua be second. Gaddiel stepped out into the desert.

It had begun.

ॐॐ

Moses's strong voice startled Kamose.

Kamose pulled his stare away from the cliffs. "I'm sorry. I didn't hear you."

"I said you're going to kill that bush if you don't keep at least some of the leaves on it." Moses nodded toward the pile of shredded green at Kamose's feet.

Kamose grimaced, and dropped the tattered leaf in his hands. He slapped his hands across one another to clean them.

"You want to be out there with them, don't you?"

"What makes you say that?"

The older man studied Kamose's face. "You seem ... restless."

Kamose blew out a frustrated breath. "The training is complete, and I don't know what to do next. It's an odd feeling."

Moses strolled through camp, beckoning Kamose to follow. They were silent for quite some time, until Moses spoke. "In many ways, you are like me. Or like I was at your age."

Kamose glanced sideways. "How is that? You were a prince. I am—was—but a soldier."

"Yes, I was a prince. I had the best of everything. Excellent tutors, the finest food, the softest linen tunics, servants for my every wish, more gold than I could wear. Ramses and I competed in every way possible. He was always jealous of me, although I was never quite sure why. He was the crown prince, and I was an adopted cousin, at most. There was nothing to envy."

Kamose scowled, bitter memories flooding his mind like the Nile flooded the delta. "Ramses has never made sense. He doesn't have to."

Moses chuckled. "Yes, I suppose as his personal bodyguard you would know that better than anyone, wouldn't you?"

"But none of that sounds like me."

"I was a prince of the most powerful nation in the world, and then suddenly it all was gone. I was hiding in the desert with nothing. I left with only what I was wearing. Everything I knew was stripped away."

Kamose closed his eyes for a moment as he recalled his own flight from Ramses. "What happened?"

Moses halted as they reached a flock of sheep. "I saw an Egyptian murder a Hebrew. I killed him—I thought in secret, but I was seen. I fled, as far from Egypt as I could." He picked up a lamb and stroked its head, hooking his staff in the crook of his arm. "I wandered in the desert for a while. Ended up tending sheep to stay alive. I went from a prince to a shepherd, from a soft bed in the palace to sleeping on the ground."

"Then what did you do?"

Moses shrugged. "Tended the sheep. What choice did I have? Every day I awoke and took care of the sheep. I led them to water, to fresh grass, kept them from predators. I did a job a boy could do. I thought I had wasted my entire life, that I was starting all over again. None of what I was, what I had learned, what I had accomplished, seemed to have any place or relevance in my new life. I felt completely lost for years. And a little angry as well."

"At whom?"

Moses set down the lamb. "At El Shaddai. I wasn't exactly sure who He was then. I'd been taught about the Egyptian gods in the palace. My mother taught me about El Shaddai before I was sent back to the palace—"

"Your mother?" The story kept getting more complicated. So much about Moses he didn't know. He'd known the basics—Moses was raised as an Egyptian prince, but left as an adult, then came back to free the Israelites. The rest of this was new, and totally unexpected.

"Yes, my real mother raised me for several years after the princess found me as a baby. She talked incessantly about El Shaddai." Moses waved a hand. "After I returned to the palace I forgot most of it, but on those long nights alone in the desert, I began to remember what she told me. I believe Yahweh was speaking to me, teaching me about Himself, bringing to my memory what she had placed there, and then expanding on it."

"How long were you in the desert?"

"Forty years."

"Forty years?" Despair hit Kamose like a blow to the chest.

"Yes." Moses leaned on his staff and stared into the distance. "I know now Yahweh was preparing me for this task. As a prince, I spent endless hours training on the field at Succoth. I learned military strategy, weapons, evasion, provision, leadership— all I needed to know to bring my people out of Egypt. I realized everything I had learned was not a waste. Far from it. Then my father-in-law taught me how to survive in the desert as a shepherd. I learned all the trade routes, the location of the Egyptian fortresses as well as the oases, how to find food when it looks like there is none. I see now each part of my life has led up to this mission."

Kamose clasped his hands at the back of his neck. He glanced at the glowing cloud above them. "But you didn't always know that."

Moses returned his gaze to Kamose and smiled. "Exactly."

A hot breeze stirred the leaves of the tall date palms. The bulbuls seemed to call to him from the treetops as thoughts jumbled through Kamose's mind.

He dropped his hands to his hips. "So … what should I do while I'm waiting?"

"Tend sheep."

"Excuse me?" He blinked at the bleating animals. What did he know about shepherding?

Moses laughed. "I don't mean actually tend sheep. That's what it meant for me. You should do whatever Yahweh puts in front of you at the time. For you, I guess it means take care of little Ahmose, train spies when necessary, whatever He sends your way. Maybe later there's a huge task waiting for you, like mine. Maybe something more mundane. But whatever it is, it's just for you, and it's important. And when you find it, or it finds you, you'll know." Moses put his hand on Kamose's shoulder for a moment, then turned back toward camp.

Kamose watched the old man trudge back to camp. For all Moses had been through, he was remarkably content. He'd learned to take life as it came. Kamose tried to control life, change it, bend it to his will like Bezalel molded gold.

He wanted to learn to face life like Moses.

He hoped it didn't take him forty years to do it.

Kamose considered Moses's words as he ambled toward his tent. He'd skipped the midday meal, instead talking to Caleb and Joshua, going over the last details of the mission, and now his belly was empty and his head was far too full of unwelcome thoughts. He wanted hot food, friendly conversation, and the warmth of family.

The sun almost touched the horizon as Kamose stepped between his tent and Bezalel's. The sweet smell of manna baking over thousands of desert campfires filled the evening air. An unfamiliar laugh came from the campfire. A captivating, female laugh—not Meri's, not Rebekah's. Not even Sheerah's, Nahshon's wife. Who else would be at their fire? The laugh drifted by again.

He waited a moment before stepping into the walkway, then strode to an open spot around the fire next to Nahshon and Sheerah.

"Uncle Kamose! Where were you?" Ahmose handed him a few manna cakes and a handful of dates. "Look, we have guests. This is Tirzah, and her daughters Keren and Naomi."

Kamose nodded to the woman. Gaddiel's woman. Next to her sat two small girls, duplicates of each other. They shared their mother's dark hair and pink lips. One hid behind Tirzah, but the other waved and smiled.

Meri placed her hand protectively on Tirzah's back. "Her brother-in-law left on the mission tonight. When I heard Gaddiel was one of the scouts and realized she'd be alone, I invited her to join us."

Brother-in-law? So he's not her husband. That explained a good deal of the odd behavior he'd seen from Gaddiel. Kamose managed a polite smile. "I'm sorry you are alone."

"At least I don't have to wait on him all day." Tirzah laughed, the sound of the tinkling of a tambourine when gently shaken.

Tirzah looked his way and her eyes held his for a moment. Heat crept up his neck and his throat went dry.

"We thought we could keep her company while he's gone. She has no other family." Bezalel pointed toward the Zebulon section of camp, next to Judah. "She's on the edge of Zebulon, not too far from here."

"Ahmose has been helping me by playing with the girls. They adore him."

One of the girls stood and tugged on Ahmose's arm. "Come with us, 'Mose. Let's go play."

Ahmose looked at Tirzah. "Is that all right with you?"

"For a while. Then they have to go to sleep. Can you play with them while I go get water? You'll have to stay close, because it's already dark."

"Sure."

Tirzah patted Ahmose on the head. Her hair fell forward into her face, and she tucked it behind her ear. She turned to go as Ahmose and the girls scampered off.

"Wait, we'll go with you." Meri handed Adi to Bezalel. Sheerah left the fire for her tent, and Meri disappeared for a moment to retrieve their skins, then the women walked toward Tirzah's tent.

Kamose watched them go. Tirzah's thick, wavy brown hair hung loosely down her back. She was head and shoulders taller than Meri, and her long legs had to move slowly to keep from getting too far ahead of Meri, making her hips sway seductively.

"She's quite beautiful, isn't she?" Bezalel's comment drew Kamose's attention back to the fire.

"What?"

"Tirzah. She's lovely, isn't she?"

Kamose swallowed past the lump in his throat. "I hadn't noticed."

Bezalel laughed so loudly Adi flinched and cried softly. "Sure you didn't." He put his hand on the baby's back and she settled instantly at her father's touch.

"You've been staring at her since you sat down." Nahshon chuckled.

No use denying it. Bezalel could see right through him. Kamose threw the stick he'd been holding into the fire. "I'm going for a walk."

He could hear Bezalel chuckling as he threaded his way between tents toward the desert.

Why was he so glad to find out she was not Gaddiel's? It had been a long time since he'd had any feeling for a woman. He'd always stamped out any hint of interest as soon as it surfaced. When he served in other countries he had formed relationships of a sort with local women, but he had never let himself feel anything for them, knowing he would soon leave. If one began to show signs of attachment, he broke it off instantly. He didn't want anyone getting hurt, didn't want to leave any broken hearts behind.

But this woman did something to him. If he were still a soldier, he could immerse himself in his work. Bury his emotions. Avoid her. But how could he steer clear of her when apparently she was going to be around his tent all the time?

Another dilemma this new, purposeless life had brought him.

ๅๅ๏๙ฅ

The meal over, water skins filled, Tirzah returned to her tent, Naomi on her hip and Keren in tow. She set her daughter down and poured milk into cups for the girls.

"Is he gone?" Naomi looked toward Gaddiel's tent as she asked the question.

"Yes, he will be gone for many days."

The girl's face brightened. "Good. I don't like when he yells at you."

"I don't either. But there will be no yelling for a while." Tirzah dropped her arm around Naomi's shoulders and drew her close. "Finish your milk, then go to sleep."

After the girls lay sound asleep on their mats, Tirzah sat in front of the flickering flames and leaned back on her hands. She glanced to her right, at Gaddiel's empty tent. A smile crossed her face, and closing her eyes, she looked to the moonless night sky.

She contemplated the next several days, maybe even weeks. A sweet freedom swirled around in her mind. No barks from him in the morning. No cleaning up his stinking tent and washing his soiled clothes. No insults, glares, or snarls.

She gathered her hair and worked it into a loose braid, then tossed it over her shoulder. Gaddiel was gone, but so was any measure of support or protection he might have offered. She shouldn't need any, but a widow was always in a precarious situation. It probably wasn't a smart idea, but she would think about it later and enjoy the next few days of freedom. Once they reached Canaan, she would have to do something, but for now, there was at least the manna.

"Tirzah." A familiar but unwelcome voice broke her moment of peace. "So nice to see you. How are you this evening?"

Tirzah lowered her gaze to see Jediel's youngest brother making himself at home in front of her fire. "I'm fine, Nathaniel. What do you want?"

"I came to check on you. Did you see Gaddiel leave?" He stretched his long legs out and crossed them at the ankles. He arranged his thawb neatly over his tunic and brushed away some stray ash. He might look very much like Gaddiel but at least he was tidier. Probably from being pampered as the youngest in the family.

She sat up straight. "Of course. I notice you didn't. He is your brother, after all."

"I thought it more important that you be there." His smile made her stomach turn.

"I'm not his wife."

"I noticed. When do you plan to remedy that?"

"I don't see it as a situation needing to be remedied."

Nathaniel waved his hand across the campsite. "Perhaps not here, in your little tent, with manna falling from the sky every day, but when we reach Canaan, how do you plan to feed yourself and your children? You will have no land and no way to grow anything or even feed your sheep to get milk."

Tirzah tightened her jaw and said nothing.

"I see. For such a clever woman, you haven't thought very far ahead. Well, I can see how you would not be interested in Gaddiel. He is rude, and cruel, as was Jediel. But I can assure you, if you claim your right of *yibbum*, Gaddiel will decline, and the... obligation... will fall to me. I, of course, would never refuse such a beautiful woman as you." His cold gray eyes held hers.

Tirzah stood and pointed her finger at the man seated across from her. "Nathaniel, I will never marry Gaddiel, or you. I would rather starve than marry a man like you. When I reach Canaan I will figure something out, but you can be assured it will not involve you. Now leave."

Nathaniel stood slowly.

Tirzah nearly bit her tongue off trying to hold it.

Nathaniel stepped away, then turned back to her, smiling one of his oily smiles. "I am an unusually patient man, Tirzah. You will eventually marry me, of that I am certain."

Tirzah shivered as a cold fear crept up her back. Of all that had happened to her, marrying Gaddiel, or worse, Nathaniel, would be unbearable.

But she could think of no way around it.

ॐ✑

The sun was gone and the moonless, star-filled sky had replaced it. Gaddiel's hands were raw, his knees skinned, his ankles swollen. His forearms and shoulders burned with every move. They'd practiced the climb, but never for more than an hour at a time. Kamose had only taught them the mechanics of getting up the mountain. And no matter how many times he had said, "And you'll keep doing this for hours," it hadn't sunk in. Until now.

At least they were a great deal more than halfway finished. The plan, according to the mighty Caleb, was to reach the cliffs beyond the desert and complete the ascent tonight, rest until morning, then hike toward Arad. As if they had another choice. They couldn't very well stop part way up the wall, and they would be too tired to go any farther once they reached the top. It didn't take a great military mind to come up with that plan.

He needed to establish himself as a leader alongside Joshua and Caleb, and soon. But how?

Pain shot through his forearm as he put his hand onto a sharp rock. Crimson stained the limestone when he lifted his hand.

They had a lot of ground to cover in the long days ahead. Maybe they should split up. Then he could lead one of the smaller groups. That would set him apart, set him up as equal to Joshua and Caleb.

He banged his knee into a protruding piece of the mountain. Maybe for now he should pay attention to the climb.

At the top of the cliff, Gaddiel dragged his aching body onto the mercifully flat land and tried to calm his breathing. He laid his head on his bruised arms and waited for his thighs to stop burning.

After a few moments, he picked himself up and made his way toward Caleb and Joshua. At least he made it before any of the others, although it galled him that Joshua beat him again.

He laid out his mat and blanket and gingerly lowered himself to the ground. He looked at the twinkling stars above him. They had chosen this day to leave so the moon would be full by the time they reached the heart of Canaan, giving them better light as they spied on the cities by night. He touched his palms to each other. The flesh was nearly ripped off in several places. His knees and biceps were on fire. His stomach begged for food, but he was too exhausted to pull the food Tirzah had sent with him from his pack. His belly would have to wait a bit. He untied the skin of milk from his belt, took a long drink, and lay back on his pack.

The stars flickered above as he tried to shut off his mind long enough to fall asleep. He concentrated on Caleb's deep breathing next to him, allowing the rhythmic noise to soothe his fractured nerves. Finally the dark and the exhaustion took over, and he slipped into sleep's oblivion.

Five

30 Ziv

Gaddiel groaned and rolled on his stomach. Overlapping voices—talking, laughing, joking—drifted toward him. Perfect. Last one up. The savory aroma of roasted meat wafted through the air, and he raised his head to find the source. Joshua had six sandgrouse on stakes leaning over a campfire. Gaddiel hated to admit it, but the boy took good care of the men.

Gaddiel rose and lumbered toward the nearby stream, his muscles protesting every step. He stripped off his tunic, knelt, and dunked his head in the water. The sudden coldness shocked him wide awake. He jerked back up, the water from his soaked hair dripping down his back. Pulling his tunic over his head, he struggled to slip it over his wet skin. No matter—the unforgiving summer sun would quickly dry both the cloth and his skin.

He trudged back to the fire and slumped to the ground, accepting half a bird from Palti. He tore a leg from the carcass. Sinking his teeth deep into the soft flesh, he ripped it from the bone. Juice dribbled down his chin and he drew the back of his hand across his mouth. The substantial taste of meat, something to actually chew, something that would last in his stomach more than a meager hour—he closed his eyes and suppressed a moan. It tasted better than anything he could remember ever eating. He was sick of manna. Just the thought of it made him gag.

"How long has it been since we ate meat?" Palti spoke around a mouthful of bird.

Gaddiel swallowed first. "Over a year. Feels like longer."

"You forgot about the quail. We had quail twice, once at Sinai and once just a few weeks ago."

"I didn't forget about it. I didn't count it. There was what, about five bites to a bird? It was hardly worth the work it took."

Palti glared. "Yahweh provided that meat. Perhaps you shouldn't dismiss it so."

Gaddiel shrugged. "Perhaps He should have provided better meat."

"Anyone think the giants are still in Canaan? The ones our grand-parents told stories about?" Igal's gaze flitted from man to man.

Palti laughed. "They're probably just legends. Don't even really exist."

"Are you sure? Sure we won't find any?" Igal threw a bone over his shoulder.

"There may be some very big people, but I think the stories grew over the years, as legends tend to do." Sethur's voice was unchar-acteristically calming. "I don't think there are people as big as the myths say—towering over us, legs as big as tree trunks, chests like a hippopotamus. They'll just be taller than we are."

"Igal, relax. It will be fine," said Gaddiel. "You'll see."

Closer to noon, the sun radiated heat over his shoulder. Gaddiel pulled his thawb from his pack and wrapped it around his head, using the arms to secure it. He craned his neck and looked up at the sky. The protective cloud had remained at camp, and after more than a year under its protection, without it his skin was already turning bright pink. The heat made it hard to think, and he had to be clearheaded. He needed this time to come up with a plan to take down Joshua.

The easiest way would be to discredit him. That would be an extremely difficult task. Joshua was held in such high regard. To convince everyone he had lied would take a great deal of work. Perhaps Gaddiel could be sent ahead with Joshua, then he could disagree with Joshua's report. Or he could simply tell everyone Joshua was saying something he wasn't really saying.

Maybe he didn't have to convince everyone. Just a few. Palti had been a close friend for years. He would side with Gaddiel no matter what. If there were any kind of disagreement or challenge, Palti would back him up.

Sweat dribbled down Gaddiel's neck and under his tunic. He rubbed his neck and pulled away a wet hand.

Maybe he could just injure Joshua, take him out of action for a while. It would be hard to do unnoticed. He could trip him. No, that would probably be noticed. He could kick a rock in his path, make him stumble. Probably not enough to cause a fall, though. Unless they were on a downhill.

Maybe combine the ideas. Make him fall, get hurt, then when Joshua claimed Gaddiel caused the fall, deny it. Who would believe he would do that to their leader? For no apparent reason?

But first, he would have to appear to be Joshua's biggest supporter.

3 Tammuz

"Kamose, could you go find Ahmose? He's been gone a long time."

Kamose studied his friend. Bezalel rarely worried about Ahmose. The boy was old enough to take care of himself, and he was comfortable with all their neighbors. And he was more Kamose's responsibility than Bezalel's now. "Does he need to come home?"

"No, I just want to make sure he's not bothering anyone, or hasn't fallen in the spring, or isn't hurt."

"Why don't you go look for him, if you're worried?"

"I'm busy."

"You're holding a baby."

Bezalel held Adi out. "Do you want to hold her?"

He'd rather face an Amalekite. "Not really. Where's Meri?"

"She's resting. Can't you just go look for him?"

Kamose narrowed his eyes. Was that a flicker of a smile crossing Bezalel's face?

"If he's not at the big spring… see if he's with Tirzah."

Tirzah. Of course. He would check the spring first, although he would bet Ahmose was with Tirzah, and that Bezalel knew it.

Warblers darted among the broom bushes, and the date palms cast long shadows over the north spring. Kamose surveyed the area, but as he suspected, no Ahmose.

He'd managed to avoid her the last several days, but as he strolled toward the area Tirzah favored, he smiled. She was beautiful, he had to admit.

Beyond the trees, the girls squealed as Ahmose chased them with a palm branch.

Kamose called to him.

"Uncle, can't I play a little longer?"

He glanced down at Tirzah, resting against a log, her legs curled to one side. "Are you sure he's not bothering you?"

"On the contrary, he is a huge help. Would you like to sit?" She gestured to a spot in front of the log.

He should really go. He had no reason to stay. He hesitated, then sat on the log, several steps away from her, resting his arms on his knees. While Ahmose and the twins splashed in the shallow river, Kamose tried to avoid staring at the lovely woman relaxing on the ground near his feet.

Her long hair was the color of cedar, meandering over her shoulders and down her back. She seemed only a few years older than most women with small children, but she also appeared to carry the weight—or sadness—of one who had lived much longer.

He cleared his throat. "So, Gaddiel is your brother-in-law. I thought he was your husband."

Tirzah nearly choked on the milk she sipped. "Whatever gave you that idea?"

"When I first met him you were in what I assumed was his tent. You brought him food when he was training. You came to see him off."

Tirzah scoffed. "Gaddiel was my husband's brother. When Jediel died at Sinai, everything passed to him, so I have to stay near."

"Why? Didn't you get anything?"

She traced the edge of the cup with her finger. "In Israel, everything revolves around the tribe, and the men in it. Since I have no son, it all went to his brother in order to stay in the family. He let me keep the tent, our donkey, and a sheep. In exchange, I cook and clean for him."

Kamose's anger at Gaddiel collided with his astonishment at her unquestioning acceptance of her situation. Every time he thought he understood how things worked in Israel … better change the subject. "Your daughters are adorable. How old are they?"

"They were born three summers ago."

"They look just like you."

"Oh, no, they don't. They're beautiful."

Was she just fishing for compliments? No, she continued to watch her children, smiling. She didn't even look up. His gaze moved from her to the girls and back. How could she not see the resemblance? Surely she had seen her reflection. Polished bronze mirrors were common in Egypt, even among the peasants and slaves.

The girls laughed and called to one another and to Ahmose. Keren clambered over a log, fell down, scrambled up, and ran off. Naomi squatted in a clump of wild desert flowers, her nose stuck deep into one.

"They are not very similar, are they?" Kamose said.

Tirzah laughed. "No, they're not. It's hard to believe they're twins sometimes. Or even sisters. But they are very good to each other. Keren takes care of Naomi, since Naomi tends to be more fearful."

"She's a good sister." Kamose picked at the log with his thumb. He was used to orders, commands—either giving them or following them. Not conversation with no purpose. "Do you have any sisters? Brothers?"

"I have a sister and two much older brothers."

"What's your sister's name? What's she like?"

"Her name is Hannah. She's always been the pretty one. She's younger than I am, but she married first, which is not our tradition. But she was so lovely, and clever, everyone wanted her. She had so many young men after her, she had difficulty choosing."

"Did you get along?"

Tirzah was quiet for a moment. "She was a good sister, too. Actually she was my half-sister. My father died the summer I was five. My mother married again, and Hannah is my stepfather's daughter. We had many happy times together, until..."

"Until...?"

Her eyes blinked rapidly. "Until all the boys started competing for her. Then she had no time for me. I was just... left behind. But part of it was my choice."

"How so?"

"I chose to care for my mother. She was quite ill by then. My father was gone, and my brothers... I couldn't bear to lose her, too. I didn't make myself very available to anyone. I stayed inside with her." She picked at her tunic. "Most of the boys wouldn't have known I was around, even if I had been pretty and charming, like Hannah."

If?

Tirzah looked up, over her shoulder. "What about your family?"

Ahmose's mother flashed through Kamose's mind. "I had one sister and many brothers. My parents are still alive." He paused. "At least they were when we left Egypt."

She twisted around to face him more squarely. "I'm so sorry. I didn't think before I asked." Her honey-colored eyes held his.

"It's all right. We've all lost someone. It always hurts."

"Not always." Tirzah lifted one shoulder.

Strange reaction. Why would it not hurt? What could she mean by that?

Tirzah brought herself to her feet in one graceful motion and adjusted the sash around her tunic. "I think it's time for us to return to our tent. I need to prepare our evening meal." She smiled—a sincere smile, but still guarded. "Thank you for letting Ahmose play with them again. It really is very nice for me, and they enjoy it, too. There aren't many children allowed to play with them."

Kamose stood as well and called to Ahmose.

The boy came running, the girls behind him. He had two handfuls of dates. "We picked these for you." Holding his hands out, he beamed at Tirzah.

"Thank you, habibi. That's very thoughtful. You are such a delight." She kissed the top of his head, and his cheeks colored. Then she nodded to Kamose and started for her tent, girls trailing behind.

He couldn't begin to understand the beautiful woman with the long brown hair. He'd never known anyone so cautious, so detached, except perhaps himself. But he'd trained hard to be that way, and for good reasons. Emotion was dangerous in battle.

What could have caused her to be so wary? The only one she seemed to respond to was Ahmose. Then again, Ahmose brought that out in everyone.

For now, Bezalel said they needed to look after her while Gaddiel was gone, and Kamose would do what his friend had asked. It was all he knew to do.

He smiled. At least it would be a pleasant task.

4 Tammuz

The flames settled down, and Tirzah used a stick to nudge the rocks around the fire closer together before she set the pot on them. She sat back and stared at the water as she waited for it to boil.

"Tirzah? May I join you?" A few strides away, Meri waited with a broad smile. She was much too cheerful for this early in the morning.

"Of course. Did you already eat?"

"Yes, Adi was up before the sun." Meri dropped to the ground next to Tirzah.

"Where is she now?" Tirzah yawned.

"Bezalel has her."

"He seems like a good husband." Tirzah poured the manna into the bubbling water.

"He is. When I first came to the palace, I never thought I would end up with anyone like him in my life."

Tirzah frowned and pointed a finger at her new friend. "Don't start."

"Start what?"

"The 'Yahweh has a plan' speech again."

Meri grinned. "All right, I won't."

Tirzah pushed her hair behind her ear. "But you still think He does."

Meri shrugged. "I heard Kamose came to visit you yesterday."

"He did."

"And what do you think?"

"Of…?" Tirzah stirred the manna.

"Of Kamose?"

"What about him?" She avoided looking at Meri.

"I think he might be interested in you."

Tirzah stopped stirring and looked Meri in the eyes. "Why would he be?"

"Because you're pleasant to talk to, you're very pretty, you're nice …"

"I'm certain he could find any number of much prettier and fascinating girls who would be happy to return his attentions."

Meri frowned. "So, you're not interested at all."

"Of course not. Besides, I'm quite sure you're wrong."

Meri bent her head as if to catch Tirzah's gaze. "About what? That you are interested in him, or that he is interested in you?"

"Both. Now please, find something else to talk about." *The girl never gives up.*

"All right. How is Naomi doing?"

Tirzah sighed and rested her forearms on her knees. "About the same. Still waking up several times most nights."

Meri placed her hand on Tirzah's shoulder. "I'm sorry. Is there anything I can do?"

"I don't think so. I keep hoping she'll just grow out of it."

Meri gasped. "I have an idea."

Tirzah looked up. Meri was sitting with her hands clasped at her chest, eyes wide and bright as a child given a new toy. "Why don't you move into Rebekah's tent? She's always with the midwives, and even if she comes back it's only for a night or two, and she'd be delighted to stay with you and help. Then you won't be all by yourself, and we can all help you with the twins. It will be wonderful." Meri beamed.

Tirzah shook her head. "Why would you do that?"

"Why not?" Meri spread her hands.

Tirzah shook her head again. "No. I appreciate the offer, but I don't think that's a very good idea."

Meri's face fell. "Why?"

"We'll be moving again when the spies come home, the girls are settled here, and I don't want them to get close to a bunch of people they'll just have to say good-bye to. They've already gotten so attached to Ahmose, I don't know how I'll tell them they'll never see him again once we get to Canaan."

"But how can you be sure of that?"

Could she really not see it? Tirzah took Meri's hands in hers. "Meri, you know they're dividing the land by tribe. I am part of Zebulon, and you are Judah." She stared at the girl until she was certain she understood.

"I know." Meri's voice was so soft Tirzah could barely hear her.

Keren stumbled out of the tent, with Naomi only a few steps behind.

Meri pushed herself up. "I guess I'll let you feed them. Will I see you later?"

"I hope so." Tirzah waved as Meri walked away backwards. She tried to smile, but it was halfhearted at best.

After a few steps, Meri turned around and trudged toward Judah, head down, shoulders slumped.

Tirzah's stomach cringed a little, but it was about time that girl realized not everything worked out for the best.

❧❧

"By tonight we should reach Arad. Depending on its layout, we can get close enough under cover of darkness to see what lies inside the city. As soon as we see dwellings, we stop and wait until the sun sets. Everyone understand?" Caleb looked around the group, waiting for assent from each one.

Gaddiel barely nodded.

"Pack up. We move now." Caleb stood and kicked sand over the fire.

Gaddiel stuffed the last of the sandgrouse in his mouth and threw the bones into the dying flames. He slung his pack over his shoulder and started north, not waiting for Caleb or Joshua.

Later, as the day drew to a close, Gaddiel crawled on his belly and shouldered a spot between Caleb and Joshua, who peered at the city through a pair of low bushes.

Caleb shoved Gaddiel's head to the ground. "Are you trying to get us all killed?" Caleb backed away, Joshua following.

Gaddiel surveyed the city on the hill before him. Wheat, barley, and beans grew in the valley before it. Earthen dams collected water for olive orchards. Goats, sheep, and cattle grazed freely on abundant grass all around.

But beyond the grass and fruit trees, livestock, and children running and laughing, Arad itself lay inside a wall that looked to be wider than Gaddiel was tall. Towers loomed above at regular intervals. Two gates stood open but were well guarded. His heart sank within his chest like a load of mud bricks.

Palti and Shammua joined him.

"Keep your heads down," he whispered.

A caravan spilled from the city. Traders with camels piled with cloth goods, traders carrying produce, traders with baskets of who knew what, filed out of the gate. The sun ducked behind the horizon. The gates shut like a huge maw, securing the inhabitants of Arad safely inside.

But as he nurtured his frustration, Gaddiel saw a way in. He backed down the rise and rushed over to Joshua and Caleb. "I know how we get more information."

Caleb peered over his shoulder. "How's that?"

"We go in disguised as traders. We just saw a huge string of them come out. They obviously go in some time during the day and are expelled at night before the gates close."

Joshua rolled on his back and pursed his lips. "We don't have anything to trade. We don't look anything like traders."

"Some had produce. We passed grape vineyards, and I don't see any grapes growing outside the city. We can get some. We combine clothing to look more like traders."

Caleb nodded. "Very well, Gaddiel. Take five men with you. Gather the grapes and whatever else you think we can sell. Return quickly. We'll try to ready the clothes."

"Fine. I need everyone's packs."

Caleb emptied his pack and handed it to Gaddiel. Joshua did the same.

After an hour of walking, Gaddiel found the grapes. He reached up and sawed at the biggest vine. Heavy and sagging with grapes, it broke before he finished and collapsed, knocking him to the ground.

Palti burst into laughter.

Gaddiel shoved the vine off his chest. "Shut up, Palti."

Palti offered him a hand up, still chuckling. "But it was funny."

"I suppose." He grabbed a piece of fruit. "Look at these. They're twice the size of any grapes we ever saw in Egypt. But it's these clusters—they grow so large. We'll have to break them up." He bit into a grape and the juice ran down his chin. "They're delicious, too. We should get a good price." He laughed as he wrestled with the lengthy vine bursting with grapes. Loaded with all the fruit they could carry in packs and on their shoulders, the spies turned back to camp.

An hour later, Gaddiel dropped a few grapes into Caleb's open hand.

Caleb laughed and clapped him on the shoulder. "Excellent. We've arranged the disguises, enough for four of us. You, me, Joshua, and one other. Do you have a choice?"

"Palti."

"Very well. Get some sleep. We don't know when the traders enter, so we have to be ready at first light."

Gaddiel dropped onto his mat, suppressing a grin. Joshua and Caleb had done what he said, almost without question. It was a powerful feeling.

❧ ❧

Joshua shook Gaddiel awake early, and they ate quickly. The four trader-spies each carried three packs to hold all the fruit. Geuel had brought an extra robe, which they ripped up to make belts. When they tied the belts over their thawbs, they looked very much like the traders they had seen entering Arad.

In dawn's gray light, the four journeyed south to a rise near the road. From here they could watch the city and the road, and see any visitors as they approached.

As the sun climbed higher, Gaddiel was losing hope. "It's nearly midday. We've been here all morning, without a sign of any traders. Maybe they come only once a week."

"We'll wait until after the evening meal, then we'll go back to the others. They may have a circle of places they visit each day." Caleb lay back with his arms under his head, his eyes closed.

How could Caleb relax at a time like this? Gaddiel stared at the city, then back at the road. Back and forth, back and forth.

As Gaddiel stuffed a piece of dried meat in his mouth, a puff of dust rose into the sky far to the south. He blinked and looked again. The cloud grew bigger and duskier. Figures emerged. A camel. Then another. A man to the side of the camel. A pair with a donkey. More and more men. The traders!

"If you're caught, you'll be killed." Kamose's words rang in his ears. Could he remember everything he'd learned? If only Joshua weren't coming. Joshua irritated him. And unnerved him.

They waited until the line passed them, then jumped off the rise and sprinted to fall in behind the last trader. Gaddiel's blood pounded as they stood in line at the main gate to Arad. Would they be caught? The sun stood high in the southern sky, raining down heat. Sweat ran under his tunic, cloak, and the heavy packs on his back. Dust choked his throat. He cracked his knuckles—first one hand, then the other. Next to him, Joshua seemed annoyingly calm.

The guard frowned as Gaddiel stepped up to the doorway. He peered in his packs, all three of them, and said something in a language Gaddiel did not understand. Gaddiel frowned and shook his head, and the guard motioned to another who was leaning against the wall.

"Grapes?" The second guard spoke in Egyptian. "We haven't had grapes here in weeks. The other traders said the harvest was over."

"Obviously not. Perhaps they were just too lazy to carry them. They are quite heavy." Gaddiel shifted the load on his back.

"You may enter. Out by sunset."

Gaddiel shoved his way past Joshua and Caleb and entered first. One road, broad and crowded with residents and traders, hugged the circular walls. Caleb studied the road leading to the center of the city.

Away from the south gate, Caleb stopped. "I think we should split up."

"I'll take Palti." Gaddiel volunteered before Caleb could stick him with Joshua or himself.

Caleb hesitated, but agreed. "It looks like main roads go from the gates to the center. You two go right, we'll go left. We'll meet at the other end of this road."

Gaddiel and Palti set off along the main ring road.

"Look at these houses. They're all exactly the same." Palti waved his hand toward the rows of houses on their left.

"The houses in the delta were all the same."

"Not exactly, and these are of stone, not mud brick. They're bigger than ours, too."

"These people aren't slaves."

They reached another wide road coming from the east gate.

"This is the end of the houses. Looks like this northeast quarter is the trading district." Palti peered toward the center of the market.

Gaddiel looked west with him. "The city seems to run downhill toward the center. Let's follow this road, then we'll sell the grapes and meet the others."

At the center of Arad, a reservoir held rainwater. They dropped their packs and greedily filled their water skins.

Gaddiel upended his skin and squirted the cool water down his throat, then sat back on his heels and surveyed the city. He enjoyed another lengthy draw, then blew out a long breath. "Walls as thick as I am tall, enough water and food for months, towers high enough to see anyone coming from as far away as Egypt... I don't see how we could ever take this city."

"Shhh!" Palti glanced around furtively. "All we have to do is bring back the information. We don't have to plan the attacks. Kamose can help. He's done it before."

Kamose. Gaddiel would have to come up with something before they returned to Kadesh. He would not go back and hand everything over to Kamose. And Joshua. All the planning. All the leading. All the glory.

Six

6 Tammuz

Tirzah settled back against the log. The sun warmed her face and melted away some of the tension in her shoulders. The girls' giggles floated on the air around her and gave her a few moments' peace.

"'Mose! Come here! 'Mose!" The girls ran toward Ahmose, and pulled him by an arm to see their latest discovery.

Tirzah leaned forward, forearms on her knees, amazed at how the twins had taken to the boy.

A shadow fell, covering the spot where she sat. She twisted around to see the tall soldier standing behind her. His nearness made her heart flutter. She shook her head to clear it. She didn't need to be thinking about him like that. Surely he was only checking on Ahmose.

"May I join you?"

She smiled. "Of course."

Kamose sank to the ground, then laid a small cloth on the sand between them and dropped a handful of dates upon it. "Have some."

Tirzah took one of the dates and ripped it open to take out the pit as she watched him from the corner of her eye. He looked so different from Israelite men. His long, straight black hair was tied back, and he wore only a shenti. He was clean-shaven. And she'd never seen any man wear so much leather—belt, dagger sheath, and sandals that laced all the way up to his knees. But on him it looked good. "So how did you end up here with us? Meri said she escaped with Bezalel. What about you?"

He leaned back against the log, arms spread, his hand almost touching her back. "Actually, Meri came with me."

She arched a brow. "What?"

One corner of his mouth pulled up. Almost a smile. "It's not like it sounds. Bezalel wanted her to go with him, but it didn't happen that way. When all of you left, Meri and I were left in the palace. By that time, I knew Ramses was not a god. So instead of chasing you with the army as I was ordered, I found Meri…" He tilted his head and narrowed one eye. "She told you how she came to the palace? Where she ended up?"

"In the harem? Yes." She smiled. He protected Meri's reputation. Was he always so thoughtful?

"So I retrieved a horse, and we caught up with you just before the crossing of the sea."

"So you were part of the army?"

"Not exactly. I worked in the palace." He shifted his weight and looked away.

Apparently that was all she was getting on that subject. She tried something else. "You met Bezalel there, then?"

He tossed a date pit over his shoulder and his gaze met hers again. "He was an artisan to the pharaoh. I met him when he helped Ahmose."

"You seem quite close. How long have you known him?"

"I met him a year before we left, but I've gotten to know him much better this last year."

"Your tent is next to Bezalel and Meri's?"

He nodded. "They're like my family now. Bezalel, Meri, his mother, Rebekah—she spends most of her time with the midwives now. Bezalel's grandfather was killed in the battle of the golden calf."

"I'm sorry. You don't have a family of your own?"

"No."

Once again, a final statement. It was odd for a man his age to have no family. He must have had one at one time. What had happened to them? She tucked her feet under her, turning toward him. "Ahmose is your nephew?"

"My sister, Tia, was lured into the harem. She died in childbirth, and asked me to look after him, but not reveal myself. I only told him who I was a few months ago. Bezalel took him to his home after Pharaoh's magician beat him quite badly, and he stayed there. He escaped with Bezalel."

Ahmose's mother was in the harem? The realization seared her heart. "So, his father is ..."

"Yes, but he doesn't know." Kamose shook his head. "He'll figure it out some day, but doesn't need to know now that the source of all the pain in his life is his own father."

Silence hung between them for several moments. She studied his face as he watched the children. As tall and strong as he was, she saw none of the harshness she'd experienced with Jediel. Jediel needed everyone to know he was in charge, loved to be mean for no other reason than he could be. Kamose seemed to have all his strength firmly under control. It was almost irresistible.

She brought her thoughts back to the present. "What are these? You always wear them." She touched his armband and fingered the row of polished jewels. "What are these stones?"

"Carnelians. The dark red symbolizes the lifeblood of all creation. It's supposed to have healing properties, but of course I no longer believe that."

Her finger slipped and she brushed his warm skin. An unfamiliar sensation moved from her hand through the rest of her body. Her breath caught. She looked up to find his dark eyes fixed on her.

He swallowed. "They are—were—the mark of the captain of the guard."

It took a moment for his comment to take effect. "You were captain of the guard?"

"Yes."

"You lived in the palace."

"Across from the pharaoh. I was his bodyguard."

She let out a deep sigh. "You were captain of the guard and Ramses's bodyguard. Ahmose is his son."

He nodded.

"You share a tent with Joshua, commander of Israel's army. Your tent backs up to Moses's tent. Your closest friend made the tabernacle, and another friend is elder of the tribe of Judah, and Aaron's brother-in-law. Did I leave anything out?"

Kamose grinned. "No, I think you got it all."

Naomi stumbled near. "Imma, I'm hungry." She crawled into Tirzah's lap.

Tirzah stroked the girl's hair. "All right, we'll go back to the tent." She beckoned to Keren.

The smiling girl trotted toward them with a fistful of flowers, Ahmose close behind. Her hair was mussed, and her tunic hung off one shoulder.

Kamose burst into laughter.

Tirzah narrowed her eyes.

He shrugged. "Well, it looks like she had fun."

Tirzah glanced over her daughter head to toe. Her face relaxed. "I guess you're right." She turned to Kamose, and a grin tugged at the corner of her mouth. "Well, well."

"What?"

"You finally laughed. I've never seen you smile, let alone laugh."

A broad smile crept across his face. "Then it must be you."

❧ ❦

Gaddiel and the others stood atop a mountain and surveyed Hebron below. Four massive mountains surrounded the city, which sat nestled in the valley they created.

"Look at those walls and towers! They're higher than Arad's!" Igal wore a worried frown as he paced.

"Maybe they just look taller from up here," Sethur said.

"I don't think so." Gaddiel spat his words.

"We need to go down and get closer to see how we get in." Caleb spoke as if nothing were amiss at all. No towers, no walls.

"Get in? We're not getting in." Gaddiel turned on Caleb.

"You don't know that." Joshua spoke calmly, taking Caleb's side, as usual.

"It's almost dark. We'll climb down while we have light and scout out the city after the gates close." Caleb turned his back on the group and began the hike.

Gaddiel balled his fists. He had no choice but to follow.

At the bottom of the mountain, Gaddiel craned his neck and stared at the looming tower above the main gate. "It's as tall as ten men! At least! There are four more besides." He wheeled and faced Joshua. "There is no possible way we can take Hebron. We might as well go back."

Joshua clenched his teeth. "We are not going back. Moses said we are to go all the way to the north end of the land Yahweh promised us, and Hebron is not the end. If you want to quit, go ahead, but we're not finished with this mission, and we will not stop until we are."

Gaddiel came nose-to-nose with his young leader. He jerked his thumb over his shoulder. "These walls and towers are made of stone blocks bigger and taller than we are. They are wider than the walls at Arad. They cannot be broken. They cannot be climbed. They cannot be burned. I don't even know how they could have moved them." He crossed his arms over his chest. "We cannot take this city."

Joshua's stare drilled into Gaddiel. "You can find your own way back."

Gaddiel took a deep breath. He may have gone too far. At any rate, his position was no longer in doubt. He stomped away from the group, into the olive groves, and slumped against a tree. The gnarled bark was warm on his back, having soaked up the sun's rays all day. The trees around him were massive, stretching to the sky—they must have been hundreds of years old. Vineyards started just beyond the grove and extended out of sight around the wall, with grapes larger than those they had carried to Arad.

The strong, fruity scent of olives surrounded him as he pondered the scene he had just caused. Perhaps he hadn't revealed everything. They now knew he was not the biggest supporter of the mission, but not necessarily that he wanted to take Joshua's place. If he suddenly supported the mission now, it would look suspicious and insincere. But if he continued to defy Joshua, in front of everyone, he would never get the support he needed to become a leader.

He ran his hand over his face. He needed another tactic. But what? He must undermine Joshua's authority, or at least his credibility. He had to shift everyone's trust from Joshua to him. But he couldn't be too obvious.

He may as well join the group for now. Being out of the loop would only hurt him. He pushed himself to his feet and leaned against the olive tree. But just as he was starting to return to the others, they bolted toward him, into the grove.

❧❦

Kamose swallowed the last manna cake of the day and strode toward Tirzah's campsite. He struggled to slow his steps as well as his heartbeat, tamping down a desire to see her so strong it rattled him. Maybe it was due only to the fact that he had nothing better to do. Nothing to do at all, actually. The air cooled as the sun began its slow descent behind the mountains to the west, but dusk was still a couple of hours away.

He neared the spot where he could cut from his row down to hers. Stepping between two tents, he saw her sitting by her fire, combing Naomi's hair, completely lost in the task. Her own hair hung down her back, waves the color of cedar mimicking the curves of her shoulders and waist. The fire brought out red highlights in the brown. He sucked in a breath—what he wouldn't do to bury his hands in that hair, to...

He shook his head as if to loosen those thoughts and toss them out. But as he started to emerge from between the tents, another man approached her. Kamose stilled. His heart beat even faster.

The man, shorter than Tirzah, came too near her for Kamose's comfort. He knelt behind her and placed his hands on her shoulders. Kamose held his breath. Did he even have the right to be jealous? Had he completely missed the signs she had another man in her life? One she preferred to him? His heart dropped to his sandals.

At the stranger's touch, Tirzah jerked away as if she'd been burned. She leaped to her feet.

A small measure of relief washed over Kamose, but it was short-lived as he noticed the fear on her face. Should he step in?

"Tirzah, why do you withdraw from me so?"

She backed away. "Because I despise you, and you have no right to touch me."

Naomi hid behind Tirzah, grasping her tunic. Keren glared up at the intruder, tiny fists at her sides. "Leave Imma alone!"

"Control your daughters, woman." The man spoke with thinly disguised disgust. "They have nothing to do with us." He moved to close the distance between himself and Tirzah.

Kamose ached to grab the man by the neck and squeeze. The thought shocked him. He'd killed often, but only in battle, dispassionately, under orders. He'd never wanted to kill out of pure anger. Until now.

Tirzah fisted her hand in front of her chest. "They have everything to do with us! There will never be anything between us. I will never marry you."

The man shook his head. "You really have no choice. No one else will have you. You are far too much trouble."

Too much trouble?

The man grabbed her arm. "And unless you marry, you will starve. You and your precious daughters."

"I'll find a way to survive. And it won't be by marrying you, Nathaniel. You—you sicken me! Now leave!"

Nathaniel twisted her arm to the side, causing her to contort her body to avoid the pain. "You have no choice! You are as good as mine. I will never release you!"

Blood boiling, Kamose burst from between the tents. He grabbed Nathaniel with both hands and shoved him away from Tirzah. "She asked you to leave."

Nathaniel smirked as he stumbled backward. "Ah, the Egyptian."

Behind Kamose, the girls started crying.

"Whether I am Egyptian or Hebrew does not matter. What does matter is that she does not want you here."

"This is none of your concern. You are the one who must leave."

"I will leave when she asks me to." Kamose took one long step toward the much shorter man and grabbed Nathaniel's arm just as the man had grabbed Tirzah's, then squeezed. "You can go, or I can break every bone in your hand. And I will enjoy doing it." It took every measure of control he had not to snap Nathaniel's arm in two.

Nathaniel winced and nodded, and Kamose released him. He eyed Kamose and then Tirzah, and turned back to Kamose before he left.

Kamose turned to a shivering Tirzah, who stood rubbing her shoulder. He reached for her.

She backed up a step instead.

His heart panged at her rejection. "Tirzah, who was that?"

"Nathaniel," she whispered.

"Who's Nathaniel?"

"My husband's youngest brother."

Another brother? "And why does he say you must marry him?"

She looked away and sighed, her face registering pain, as if she would rather do anything than explain this to him. "In Israel, a widow is required to marry her husband's brother to produce a son, so his name will not die."

All the air left his chest. He couldn't breathe.

"If Gaddiel says no, the responsibility falls to the next brother, until there are no more. In theory I don't have to, but if he does not release me, no one else can or will marry me."

For a moment her words rendered him speechless. He had no idea her situation was so dire. "Tirzah, why didn't you tell me?"

She raised her shoulders. "What would you have done?"

"Why does he say you will starve?"

"Once we reach Canaan, each tribe will be assigned land, which will be divided among the clans, and then among the families." She took a shuddering breath and rubbed her arms. "If I had a son, I would be given some land in Jediel's name, to hold until my son reached adulthood. As it is, I will receive no land, and will have no way to support myself or the girls."

He shoved his own hurt away, his protective instinct taking over. "What can I do to help you?"

"There is nothing to be done."

No. Not possible. "There must be something."

She shook her head, gave him a sad smile, as if he were a small child.

His heart ached for her, but for once he had no power or wisdom to do anything. He despised feeling helpless.

"I've alienated everyone because I haven't already married Gaddiel. Not that he wants me to. He's happy with the arrangement as it is. But Nathaniel will not let me go. I'm going against hundreds of years of tradition, and the worst part is, I haven't any better idea what to do." She looked north. "I can pretend it's not true as long as I am here in the desert with manna falling every day. If I were alone, it would be one thing. But I can't let my girls starve. As soon as we reach Canaan, I'll have to marry one of them."

∾∾

Gaddiel peered from behind the gnarled old tree. From the vineyards, a handful of fair-complexioned men approached. Gaddiel felt dizzy and grabbed onto the trunk. His breath came faster.

The men were twice as tall as Gaddiel, and had long blond hair tied up on the crowns of their heads. Their thighs were as wide as his entire body, their heads as wide as his chest. Their voices were so deep they caused Gaddiel's bones to rattle. The muscles in his shoulders grew tight, and though he wanted to run, he couldn't bring himself to move.

The shortest—if you could call him short in any sense of the word— and stockiest one led a sheep. As the animal passed Gaddiel, its ear brushed the trunk he leaned upon.

The trio stopped outside the city walls. The stocky one grabbed the sheep, straddled it, and twisted its neck. The animal collapsed in a heap. The giant took out a knife and skinned the creature while the other giants built a fire with a spit. After he skinned it, the man skewered the animal and set it over the flames.

The twelve retreated farther into the grove. Once far enough away to assume the giants could not hear them, Gaddiel wasted no time sharing his opinions. He pointed back toward the fortified city. "Did you see them? Now we know how these walls were built!"

"They're huge. Are they all like that or just the guards?" Sethur peered around a tree, angling for a better view.

"It doesn't matter. As I said, we cannot take this city," Gaddiel said.

"You're right, we can't. But we don't have to. Yahweh will give it to us." Joshua crossed his arms.

Gaddiel scoffed. Did Joshua's confidence know no bounds?

"We'll keep watch until daybreak to see what the other inhabitants look like. We'll watch in shifts." Caleb held up three fingers. "Three at a time."

Once again, Caleb makes a decision single-handedly. Might as well get it over with. "I'll go first. Palti, Shammua, with me." Gaddiel headed toward the edge of the grove.

They stole as close as they dared and watched.

The hulking blond guards drank from an enormous jug stashed by the gate. They stuffed mutton in their huge maws and poured the drink down their seemingly bottomless throats. The longer they sat, the louder they talked. The stocky one must have insulted another, since the pair stood and started throwing punches. They seemed to enjoy fighting, and when they were done, sat again and laughed and drank, slugging each other on the arm.

At the end of their shift, Gaddiel lay down to catch a few hours' sleep. It was a fitful sleep, however, and far from restful.

Gaddiel awoke to Sethur shaking him. Geuel, Ammiel, and Gaddi had returned from their turn keeping watch over the guards. They joined the rest of the group seated in a circle. Though the morning was cool, they dared not start a fire.

"They opened the gates. Only a few people are up yet, but everyone we've seen so far is a giant." Ammiel spoke for his group.

"So, the legends are true. You said they were only myths! You said everything would be all right!" Igal waved his hands in the air, barely able to breathe.

"Igal, be calm." Sethur turned toward Igal and grasped his shoulders.

"They're Nephilim. I thought they were destroyed in the flood. How are they still here?" Nahbi stared down toward the fortress.

"They're not Nephilim." Caleb's voice was firm.

Nahbi jumped to his feet. "They are. They are undefeatable. God sent a flood to rid the world of them because they were so evil." He brought his hands to his head. "How did they get back here?"

Caleb rose and stared down Nahbi. "They are not Nephilim. The Nephilim are gone. They are the sons of Anak, the Anakim. They may be descendants of the Nephilim, but they are only human."

Nahbi glared back, clearly deciding whether to take on Caleb. He must have decided against it, since he sat back down. Too bad. Gaddiel would have helped.

Gaddiel stood. "Nephilim, Anakim, does it matter? Take a good look at them. We can't win. They'll use us as playthings. It's useless to even try!"

Joshua, silent until now, rose. "Yahweh is with us. He parted the waters. He destroyed Pharaoh's army. He defeated the Amalekites. He can defeat the Anakim."

Gaddiel took two long strides toward Joshua. "The Amalekites and the Egyptians were not giants! These people are. They're massive. They love to fight. They fight each other if there's no one else around. They won't even need weapons!"

"Yahweh has given us the land. It is not our decision whether or not to take it." Joshua bent and picked up his spear. "We are done here. Time to move on." He glared at Gaddiel as if daring him to challenge the order, then stormed off.

Joshua was just like Caleb. Make a decision. Make a pronouncement. Brook no opposition.

Gaddiel groaned. He'd had enough. He wasn't sure how, but it was time to make his move.

Seven

8 Tammuz

Kamose knelt behind the broom bush where he'd been for the better part of an hour. His thighs ached, but he ignored the pain. He would gain his reward soon. He scanned the foothills of the mountains northeast of camp. Fingers of light clawed their way into the gray sky, loath to give up their hold on the night.

There it was—a flash of white. A streak of brown. Then nothing. He slowly raised his head and chest above the brush and stared down the length of the arrow. He aimed below and to the right of where the movement had been and lifted his bow. When the Nubian ibex took another step down the rocks, it was his last.

Kamose sent another arrow flying to ensure the animal was dead. He strolled to where the magnificent creature lay at the base of the mountains. He ran his hands down the long, gently curved horns. The tan coat was broken by the dark brown stripe down its back. It would make a warm blanket.

Kamose pulled out his dagger and began to field dress the deer. He removed the inner organs, then carried them a good distance away. The meat would feed several families near their tent. He concentrated on each step to keep Tirzah out of his mind, repeating to himself the instructions, as if training someone next to him.

It worked until it was time to drain the blood from the ibex. He tied the front feet together and hung the beautiful animal from a tree branch, and then all he had to do was sit for a while. His mind returned to her. No matter how many times he tried to shift his thoughts to something else, they always came back to Tirzah. Beautiful Tirzah. Her tinkling laugh had invaded his dreams last night.

He stood and paced, his hands clasped behind his neck.

He'd spent his whole life believing soldiers don't make good husbands.

Then again, he was no longer a soldier, was he? Right now, he was nothing. Not an Israelite. He'd embraced Yahweh, had found a family here. But not everyone accepted him. He wasn't truly one of them. Yet not really an Egyptian. Not anymore. He'd turned his back on his country, his king, his gods.

He wasn't a warrior—he had no army. No longer a bodyguard— he had no one to protect. He wasn't a father or a husband. He was an uncle and a friend. That was about it.

So was he free to think about a woman? What did he have to offer? Not much. But as far as Tirzah was concerned, he was certainly no worse than Gaddiel or Nathaniel. He would never hurt her like Nathaniel had done. Never take her for granted like Gaddiel. No, he would honor her. Treasure her.

Love her.

After the blood drained, he took the carcass and returned to camp. Heading for their tent, he noticed Bezalel, Meri, and Tirzah sitting outside. "I hope you kept the fire going." He lifted the enormous animal from his shoulders and held it by its feet while he shrugged the pelt to the sand several strides from the fire pit.

Meri jumped up and grabbed the skin, calling to Tirzah for help.

Kamose glanced at Tirzah, who sat by Meri's tent with wide eyes and an open mouth. He'd impressed her. A rush went through him and he smiled.

"Tirzah!" Meri's sharp command drew Tirzah's attention and she stood. "Help me spread this out."

The women stretched out the skin, fur side down, and Kamose dropped the carcass onto it. He removed his dagger and sliced off huge cuts of meat. Meri slipped inside her tent and returned with a long knife.

Bezalel rose and took it from her.

Nahshon and Sheerah joined them as well, and the women built up the fire in front of Bezalel's tent while the men carved up the ibex.

"Better watch where you're cutting, or you'll slice off a finger instead of meat." Bezalel grinned at Kamose.

"What are you talking about?"

Nahshon pointed his blade over his shoulder. "You keep looking at her instead of this ibex."

Kamose only grunted.

"Have you kissed her yet?"

"What?" Kamose stopped and pulled himself up to his full height, staring down at Bezalel.

Bezalel didn't flinch. "Have—you—kissed—her—yet?"

Kamose frowned. "I don't know if she wants me to."

Nahshon sputtered in laughter. "Of—" He looked around. "Of course she does. Didn't you see the way she's been staring at you? She watches your every move."

"Just as you watch hers," said Bezalel.

"Shut up." Kamose pointed his dagger at Bezalel.

Bezalel only laughed.

"Not the captain anymore. Can't scare him." Nahshon grinned.

"I noticed." Kamose threw a piece of meat onto the growing pile with more force than necessary.

Hours later, Kamose returned from a walk around the camp. The aroma of roasted meat tickled his nose.

Ahmose skipped into camp with the twins, each carrying a pot full of dates.

Tirzah followed several steps behind. She walked slowly, which did nothing to make her stride any less enticing. She raised her hands and ran them through her hair, piling it upon her head for just a few moments and then letting it fall around her shoulders.

Kamose squeezed his eyes shut. When he opened them, Bezalel was biting his lower lip to hold in a laugh. Kamose glared at him.

With the ibex nearly ready, the women browned manna cakes. The children scooted up next to their mothers around the fire and waited as the bread made its way around the extra large circle. Somehow, when all were seated, the only spot left for Tirzah was next to Kamose.

Kamose detected a plan. He searched for Bezalel and Nahshon, but no one would return his gaze. He tried Sheerah and Meri, but Sheerah was busy handing out dates and Meri only smiled sweetly— and innocently.

Not that he objected. He just didn't want Tirzah forced on him. He never could tell what hid behind her eyes.

She approached with two plates and offered him one.

"Would you care to join me?" He took both and pointed to the empty spot.

"I don't think there's any other choice." She laughed as she sat.

He grinned and handed back her plate, and her hand brushed his as she took it. Her fingers were long and lean, and wonderfully soft against his callused skin.

"Thank you for the meat. It smells wonderful."

"You're welcome."

"I see you got all the blood off." She pointed to his shoulders.

He chuckled. "That must have looked pretty bad."

She took a deep breath. "Not too bad." She gave him a smile that reached all the way to her light brown eyes. Then, as if she thought better of it, pulled her gaze from his and suppressed her smile.

What did that mean? Was she afraid? Or was she just not interested at all?

But her smile—it lit up her face. If only he could see it more often. He knew now what he wanted.

She would have to decide for herself.

❧❧

Kamose leaned back against the log by the stream, for the first time completely comfortable in Tirzah's presence. Yahweh's glowing cloud kept the heat to a reasonable level, and in the shade of the tall, waving date palms, it was even pleasant. Black-headed bulbuls called from their nests in the branches overhead, their melancholy songs overlapping one another.

Tirzah folded her long legs to one side, bumping into him with her shoulder for just a moment. Her tan eyes peered at him from under long, dark lashes as she winced. "I'm sorry."

I'm not. The heat of her touch rushed through him, from his arm to his torso to his feet, and he took a deep breath.

"Hungry?" He stood and walked over to a tree to their left. A branch drooping under the weight of a large bunch of oval-shaped fruit held dozens of ripe dates out of reach. He stepped up onto a large rock that had long ago slammed into the stand of palms and stretched to pull the bunch close enough to pick the dates. His foot slid a sandal's length and he grabbed a lower branch to keep from falling.

Tirzah's gasp gave him a strange and unexpected burst of satisfaction.

He glanced down at her as he righted himself and smiled when she blushed. Grasping a handful of slender, long leaves from the upper branch in each hand, he tied a knot to the branch beneath it, leaving the fruit dangling within reach of the ground. He selected the dates that had matured and tossed them at her feet, enjoying her laugh, before he stepped down and sat next to her again.

The girls chased Ahmose as he led them in a game of follow-me, around the palms, under broom bushes, and over fallen logs and rocks. At first glance, the twins looked almost exactly alike. Keren's hair was slightly straighter and a shade lighter, and Naomi had a tiny mole under the lower lashes of her left eye, but those were the only differences Kamose could see.

In personality, however, the girls were as different as the delta and the desert. Keren was fearless and interminably cheerful. The only time she wasn't laughing was when she was asleep. She was the perfect playmate for Ahmose, ready to do anything he proposed. Naomi was shy, wouldn't try anything until Keren had done so first, and preferred to stay near Tirzah.

Kamose ripped open a dark brown, glossy date, pulled out the stone, and handed the meat to Tirzah.

She bit into the juicy fruit, closing her eyes as she savored it. A piece stuck to her lips, and he reached to wipe it away.

She opened her eyes.

He froze, his thumb on her mouth, his fingers on her cheek. He longed to plunge his hand into her hair, draw her near, and kiss her. He was debating whether he should move closer when Naomi's cry decided for him. He suppressed a sigh as he retracted his arm and focused on the girl. She had tripped, skinning her knee.

Ahmose was beside her in an instant, blowing on the tiny wound and distracting her from the sting. He even got her to laugh. Briefly. She pushed herself off the ground and padded toward Tirzah.

Kamose chuckled. "I think she's giving up for the afternoon."

"She didn't sleep last night. It was an especially bad night." Tirzah stifled a yawn.

"And so you didn't sleep either."

Tirzah shrugged, leaned forward, and wrapped her arms around her daughter. "Sleepy?"

Naomi nodded, rubbing her eyes.

"Sit with me for a while."

"I want *him*." Naomi tipped her head toward Kamose, and before he could say anything, she crawled onto his lap, pulled her knees up, and rested her head on his chest.

Momentarily stunned, his mind blank, his hands out to the side, Kamose gaped at the tiny figure snuggled against him. Her action caught him off-guard as much as any enemy ambush. An overwhelming need to shield and comfort her crept over him, and he wrapped his arms around her.

Tirzah stared at the pair, her eyes as big as the fruit hanging above them. "She has never let anyone hold her but me. Many others have tried to calm her, but she refuses to allow them to even touch her. I can't believe she did that."

Holding a small child in his arms both delighted and shocked Kamose. If he had spent his adult life avoiding falling in love with a woman, he had certainly never even considered children. Ahmose had stolen into his life as his sister's child, first as a vague responsibility, and now as more of a tiny friend. He dearly loved the boy, but this was entirely different. The image of a life with a woman and children hovered in the forefront of his mind. A family—his family.

Could Tirzah and the girls be that for him? Could she be part of his life forever? They needed a man to provide for them, to keep them safe. He needed a purpose.

Not to mention what she did to his pulse every time she looked at him with those honey-colored eyes.

9 Tammuz

A falcon soared overhead. Its incessant chirp drilled into Gaddiel's ears. The sun pounded on his head. The ridge road—the way of the patriarchs, from Bethlehem, through Jerusalem, to Abraham's ancient home in Shechem—was rocky, uneven, and full of holes. He had to watch his feet carefully to keep from stepping into one, or several. Why couldn't this be over with? So he could be safely back in his tent?

For the last several days, as they marched away from the soaring walls of Hebron, all he could think about was its dreadful giants. Their massive arms. Legs. Chests. Fear clutched at his throat, making it hard to draw in a complete breath. His stomach ached. He forced his mind to think of something else.

Joshua. How could Joshua and Caleb so glibly insist they could defeat such monsters? Those giants were not human. They must be children of Lucifer, no matter what Caleb said, and that meant they could never be defeated.

Once again he yanked his thoughts back, intent on keeping them away this time.

Ahead, Palti and Igal trudged on.

Gaddiel stepped up his pace to join them.

"It's not as bad as you say. There were no giants in Jerusalem." Palti swung an arm back toward the city.

Igal spread his hands wide, twisted toward the other two. "That we could see. We didn't go in because there's no way in there!"

Palti huffed. "Yes there is. It's not impossible, it's just difficult. More difficult than we need to endure for a scouting mission."

"Valleys too deep on three sides—there's no way anyone could approach without being seen," said Gaddiel. "We'd be dead before we were halfway down, let alone back up. Giants or no giants, that city is impenetrable."

"Still doesn't affect our mission," said Palti.

"Why do we need to keep going if we already know we can't succeed?" Igal spun around and walked backward. "Why keep walking, day after day, in this heat, up and down mountains, looking out for giants, enemies … all so we can go back to say we can't win?"

So was Igal turning out to be his biggest ally, and not Palti? "He's right." Gaddiel pointed to Igal. "We're wasting time. But as long as Joshua is in charge, there's not a thing we can do about it."

Palti glared at him.

"Well, what do we do abou—" Igal stumbled and his arms flailed. He balanced on one foot for a long moment until he lost his purchase and tipped off of the mountain, limbs waving in all directions.

"Igal!" Gaddiel started forward, then stopped and studied the ground before him. It wouldn't do any good to go tumbling after Igal.

Igal slid to a hard stop on the rocky ground. He lay there a moment, unmoving.

Gaddiel picked his way down the slope, and was relieved to hear his friend moan. He knelt beside him, sliding his hands along Igal's arms and legs, feeling for broken bones. When he touched Igal's left wrist, the man cried out.

Igal pulled himself to sit up, still groaning. "Let go! That hurts." He swatted Gaddiel away and cradled his wrist against his chest. He tried to stand but couldn't rise without using his hands.

"You've sprained it, maybe broken it. Let me help you." Gaddiel grasped Igal under the arms and pulled him up. He helped him back up the slope, and then Igal shook him off.

Gaddiel held out his hand. "Let me see it."

Igal glared, but placed his arm in Gaddiel's palm. Gaddiel gently ran his finger and thumb along the bones in Igal's forearm and down into his hand. "I don't think it's broken, but it's badly sprained. You should put it in a sling and let it rest. Don't use it for a couple of weeks." He motioned to Palti. "Help him make a sling. I'll be back."

Marching up the road toward Joshua, Gaddiel opened and closed his fists and clenched his jaw.

He reached Joshua, grabbed his arm, and spun him around. "Now it's gone too far. People are getting hurt."

"What are you talking about?"

"Igal. He just slipped and fell halfway down the mountain. He nearly broke his wrist."

Joshua jerked his arm away. "How did that happen? Wasn't he watching where he was walking?"

"It happened because we shouldn't be out here at all." Gaddiel breathed harder, he raised his voice, he flailed his arms—he lost control in front of everyone, but he didn't care. "We should have turned around at Arad, or at least at Hebron. We are accomplishing nothing here. We're just wasting time and now it's become dangerous. We need to go back."

Joshua planted his feet. "We are completing the mission Moses sent us to do."

"Are you going to keep on until someone ends up dead?" Gaddiel threw his hands in the air.

"No one will die if we do what we are supposed to do."

Gaddiel took a deep breath and calmed himself. "No one was supposed to get hurt, either."

৵৽ঌ

"I don't understand. Why must she marry her brother-in-law? It makes no sense." Kamose followed Moses as the old shepherd wandered through the flock.

"Kamose, this is an ancient custom, a custom that has kept our society—and many other tribal societies—alive and flourishing for hundreds of years. Survival of the tribe, the clan, the family, is paramount. The point is to ensure the name of the man is not lost, that his family is not ended. It is also meant to protect the woman."

"How so?"

Moses looped his staff over his arm and knelt to caress a lamb nuzzling his feet. "Having a child is, for women, what is most important. This arrangement makes sure she has that child, especially a son. A husband will care for her now, but a son will be there for her in her old age. And since a woman cannot inherit, this assures that she will remain part of the family she married into. Her only other options are to return to her father's family, where she will likely be treated as a burden, or choose a disgraceful profession."

Appalling, revolting images stole into Kamose's mind. He blocked them. "And if she refuses?"

Moses stood, the lamb in his arms. "I don't know. I've never known anyone to refuse. I've never known any man to refuse, either. It's considered extremely dishonorable. To refuse is to cause your own brother's memory and family to be wiped from the earth. But from the little I know, Gaddiel is far from an honorable man."

The lamb stretched his nose toward Kamose, bumping his arm.

Kamose frowned at the mewling animal. "And Nathaniel. He grabbed her, hurt her. I believe he would have struck her."

"Well, normally she couldn't marry anyone else unless Gaddiel and then Nathaniel released her. But if he hurts her ... I must talk to Yahweh about this." Moses put down the lamb and faced Kamose. "Have you decided how you are to tend sheep?"

"You mean what I should do here?"

Moses nodded.

"Not yet."

Moses's gray eyes held his for a long moment, as if he knew Kamose wasn't being completely honest. He reached down to pat the lamb's fluffy head, then strolled away.

Kamose bent and uprooted a stringy desert flower. He picked off the tiny leaves one at a time as he walked.

He had never met a more complicated woman—a more complicated person—in his life. She was not just pretty; she was beautiful. Her eyes could make him forget what he had intended to say. She was tall and slender, and the way she walked made his heart race.

The sash on her tunic always seemed to slip just below her waist, accentuating her curvy hips. ...

A moan escaped his throat. The last time he'd thought about a woman like this he was barely a man himself. He'd admired the physical attributes of many women, but only when they were standing before him. None had ever captivated his mind like this one, keeping his thoughts prisoner even after she'd left him.

He wrapped, unwrapped, rewrapped the leafless stem around his index finger. It wasn't just her beauty that drew him. He admired her willingness to stand up for herself, her refusal to bend to what was expected of her if she found it repugnant. Gaddiel was surly, arrogant and demanding. Little wonder she didn't want to marry him, or Nathaniel. But where did that leave her? How would she survive in the new land? What about the girls? Israel, he was learning, operated very differently than Egypt.

Marriage would have made her life easier, especially since leaving Sinai. Twins at this age must be difficult. She was a strong woman to handle it all alone. Packing up every day, walking, gathering manna, chasing after the girls, cooking, let alone handling Gaddiel's demands. No wonder she appreciated Ahmose's help.

His finger began to throb and he realized he'd wrapped the green stem so tightly the blood was no longer flowing. The tip of his finger was red and swollen. He yanked the string off and shook his hand.

She said there was nothing he could do. He could certainly help her care for the girls. He and Ahmose together. Perhaps that was one of the tasks Yahweh had for him. It wasn't particularly taxing or exciting, and certainly not worthy of his skills as Egypt's captain of the guard, but it was set before him and he was capable. He had nothing better to do.

And since he found her endlessly fascinating as well as unbelievably lovely, it was a task he would definitely enjoy. He wouldn't admit it to Moses, but he had found his task. He would help Tirzah as much as he could.

And he would do everything in his power to make sure Nathaniel never touched her again.

Eight

10 Tammuz

The small contingent stopped on the road a few hours south of Shechem. The midday sun poured out heat, baking Gaddiel as if he were a barley loaf in an earthen oven. In the delta there had always been shade and abundant water. The heat never came close to this degree of agony. Even in the desert, the shimmering cloud had protected them, offering relief from the sun without casting a shadow— Yahweh's mercy in the summer and warmth in the cold.

Until now.

Gaddiel drew the back of his hand across his forehead and shook off the sweat. A drop landed on a blue-headed lizard, which skittered away across the rocks at his feet.

Caleb knelt in the dirt. The others circled around him. "We should reach Shechem by mid-afternoon. It sits between Mount Gerazim and Mount Ebal and is heavily fortified. Or at least it was in Abraham and Jacob's day. I can't imagine it's changed much." He drew two circles and some lines in the dirt. "The ridge road we're on leads us out of the mountains to Shechem. First we reach Mount Gerazim. Shechem is on the northeast side in a valley. Then the road continues to Mount Ebal. Another road goes west and then turns south to Egypt, while yet another road leaves Shechem and goes to Lake Kinnereth."

Near the back of the group, Gaddiel scoffed. "He thinks he knows everything. It's grating."

Palti frowned. "Abraham lived in Shechem. Jacob and his sons, too. Don't you know your own history?"

Gaddiel glowered at Palti. "You know what I mean."

Palti grabbed his arm and pulled him back. "No, I don't. I don't know why you are so irritated. Neither Caleb nor Joshua has done anything to you. Yet you continually behave as if they have offended you in some way."

"They have offended me! I should be leader, not Caleb, and certainly not this child Joshua. They could at least let me help make the decisions instead of ordering me around like everyone else. I am not everyone else."

Shammua shushed them over his shoulder.

"And why just you?" Palti lowered his voice, but his anger came through loudly. If they let you help, they'd have to let everyone in. And you forget, Yahweh told Moses who should lead."

"So he says." Moses, Moses, Moses. Yahweh only talked to Moses.

The rest of the group followed Caleb as he marched down the road.

"That is dangerous talk. I refuse to listen to it." Palti moved forward.

"I'm sorry. I didn't mean that. I'm just angry." Gaddiel couldn't afford to lose Palti's support. He thought quickly. "I heard Moses promise them—Caleb and Joshua—their pick of the best land if we finished the mission successfully and brought back the 'right' information—a way to conquer the land."

Palti turned, frowned. "He did?"

"Why do you think they keep pushing so hard, make sure we keep going, insist we can conquer those giants twice our size? They'll say anything, sacrifice anything... anyone."

Gaddiel walked on and left Palti drowning in the false knowledge he had just thrown him in. He turned around and walked backward a few steps. "Don't say anything, though."

Palti nodded and trudged forward.

Gaddiel spun around and smiled. This was going to work.

Several scorching hours later, atop Mount Gerazim, Gaddiel studied the city below them. Shechem sat in a small valley at the crossroads of the two heavily traveled highways in Canaan. Dreadfully vulnerable in such a position, its inhabitants had centuries before built a formidable double wall featuring a triple gate.

How would they ever get through?

Joshua drew in a deep breath. "I don't think we need to get very far into the city. We can see from here what we need to know."

"Agreed," Caleb said. "We'll just pass through, but look around to make sure we haven't missed anything we need to explore more closely." Caleb caught the eye of each spy and then headed down the mount.

Gaddiel caught Palti's sleeve as he stepped off. "See? No conversation with anyone but themselves."

Palti set his lips in a thin line.

Shammua came up behind them. "What are you talking about?"

Gaddiel raised his brow in a warning, then followed the other nine. After a few steps, he threw a quick look over his shoulder. Palti whispered furiously to Shammua.

Perfect.

At the busy intersection, dust-covered traders arriving from Egypt stood in lines at the enormous triple gate. Some led shaggy camels laden with stacks of linen and papyrus. Other animals carried baskets of gold and silver jewelry. Some unloaded crates of alabaster vases carefully packed in straw. All awaited inspection by the armed guards at the front of the line.

The spies sauntered past the doorkeepers. Gaddiel smiled and shook a pouch on his belt filled with a few coins, but mostly broken pottery to provide something for the coins to clink against. As soon as he was safely inside the door he let out a breath. He would have leaned against a wall for support but too many people were watching. *Keep acting like you know what you're doing.*

More vendors headed back out the gates with Canaan's jugs of wine, scented oil, and date honey. Still more left for points north and south with Shechem's local grapes, olives, wheat, livestock, and widely sought-after pottery.

Gaddiel took stock of the city, like the good spy he was. At least the inhabitants here weren't giants. Those walls, though. He craned his neck. They weren't any smaller than the ones at Hebron or Arad. And there were two of them, one inside the other.

He wandered along pleasant lanes filled with stalls. A young woman held out a bunch of deep purple grapes, fairly bursting with juice. He waved her off, but she smiled at him. He pointed to his pouch and shook his head. She shoved the fruit at him, smiling more broadly. Was she flirting with him?

He reached for the grapes, and she grabbed another bunch and turned her attention to another trader.

Just a free sample. Even better. He ambled on. The aroma of baking bread, hot pistachios, and roasted lamb filled his nostrils and made his mouth water. He pulled out his pouch. Only a few coins, and he wasn't supposed to spend them. They were to be used to prove they were traders.

So said Caleb. But Caleb wasn't there, and Gaddiel was starving. He sniffed the air and headed for the meat.

The vendor was an old man, with thick curly hair all over his face and none on his head. His hands were filthy, but Gaddiel's stomach was rumbling. He glanced down the row, and noticed another stall of roast lamb, this one manned by a young girl with light brown curls tumbling out of a dark blue headscarf. An even younger boy, perhaps her brother, tried to help, but only succeeded in getting in her way, nearly tripping her.

Gaddiel made his way toward the stall and slithered toward the front of the table, waiting until a crowd formed and the girl appeared flustered. When two traders argued with her over a transaction, he contemplated grabbing a chunk of meat and slipping it under his trader's cloak.

Before he could work up the courage, the girl stood before him, holding a fair-sized piece of meat wrapped in cloth. She pointed to the old man and shook her head, curls bouncing, then back to herself and her lamb and nodded. Guess she wanted him to buy her meat, not the other vendor's.

Too late now to try to steal it, with her staring right at him. The few coins he had were supposed to be saved to make sure they could gain entrance to the other cities along the way, but that mutton smelled so good….

Gaddiel looked at the other stall and then at the girl. He shrugged and dug into his pouch, then gave her a coin. She handed over the food and smiled, and then stepped away to tend to other customers.

Other stalls were selling fruit and bread, and he used one more precious coin. He found a spot in the shade and slumped against the wall, then ripped off some meat and ate it with his freshly baked bread. He could barely keep from moaning as he savored the flavors.

He used his sleeve to wipe away the evidence on his mouth on his way back to the front of the city. His heart sank again like a turtle ducking under the Nile at the sight of the foreboding triple gate.

Shechem's inhabitants might be very friendly, but it was still a city they would never conquer.

☙❧

Tirzah dried the pan in which she'd cooked the manna cakes and set it near the fire pit.

"More milk?" she asked, holding up the skin.

"Me, Imma." Keren held out her cup, and Tirzah filled it.

"Ahmose? Naomi?" When no one answered, she replaced the skin in its hole just under the tent and covered it with sand.

"I'm going to milk Sarah and check on Benjamin, and then we can go to the river. Stay here with Ahmose." She raised her eyebrows at the girls until they nodded.

Tirzah strolled to the spring on the south side of camp. The stares and whispers didn't bother her this time. She thought of Kamose. Nothing could ever happen with him; she just enjoyed thinking about him. He treated her well, better than anyone had ever treated her in her life. No man—not her stepfather, not her husband, not her brothers—had made her feel as special, as important, as Kamose did, with only a look.

As she neared the spring, huge, black birds circled lazily above the herds. A twinge of uneasiness washed over her, but she dismissed it. There were thousands of animals. Only one Benjamin.

She found Sarah by the water's edge and led her away to more level ground before filling the goatskin with her milk. Draping the heavy bag over her shoulder by its cord, she made her way through the rest of the sheep and goats, toward the donkeys grouped together at one end. She looked for Benjamin's graying ears. Where was he? He was so old. If he could just make it to Canaan, he would never have to work again. Had something happened? No, that was a foolish thought. He was fine.

A loud braying nearby caused her to release her breath. A smile tugged at the corners of her mouth. That had to be Benjamin. She marched toward the sound, shoving past other donkeys and foals, stumbling over brush. Birds skittered about her feet.

She found the source of the noise, and her heart sank. It was not Benjamin. The braying animal continued to call, and other donkeys faced the same direction. She turned to look toward whatever drew their attention. Something was happening, something unusual.

Something bad? And where was her dear Benjamin? She closed her eyes, drew in a deep breath, and placed one foot in front of the other.

She pushed aside one last donkey. On the ground, covered with carrion birds, an animal lay splayed. Her heart nearly stopped beating; her legs buckled. She grabbed onto a jenny next to her to keep from falling.

Maybe it wasn't Benjamin. There was still a chance. She couldn't tell for sure; the birds wouldn't move out of the way. "Shoo! Move!" She clapped and waved her hands over the body, and the birds fluttered away.

Her pulse pounded in her ears and her breathing quickened. Her treasured Benjamin lay stiff before her, eyes open but unseeing. She fell to her knees as tears blurred her vision. She covered her face with her hands, then dug them into her hair, pressed the heels of her palms into her temples. What would she do without him? He always had a cheery nuzzle for her, no matter how hard the day. He had served her for so many years and never asked for more than a little food and water. Now what? How could she walk and carry everything? And the girls—they could never walk all day without riding on his back.

"Oh, my poor Benjamin." She rocked and cried, and after a moment lowered her hands. "Sweet Benjamin." She reached toward him, hovered her hand over his side, couldn't bring herself to touch him. Would he be cold, stiff? She didn't want to know. Bringing her hand back toward his head, she noticed his neck. She leaned in. A long, bloody slash ran from under his jawbone down to the bottom of his neck.

The bright red of the wound disappeared in her hazy vision. Because all she saw was a lifeless friend—an animal, but the truest friend she'd ever had, nonetheless.

Who would kill Benjamin? Or any donkey? Her stomach rebelled and her throat constricted, and her food threatened to come up. She forced it down. She jumped up and raced back toward camp.

She ran, the world around her spinning. She fell into the hot sand. She pushed herself up and fell again. What would she do when she got back to camp? How would she tell the girls? She had no idea.

There was only one thing she could think of to make this any better.

Kamose.

∂∞∾

Ahmose was playing with the girls when Kamose strolled up to Tirzah's tent. Kamose sat on the sand and crossed his legs.

Naomi padded over, kissed his cheek, and dropped into his lap.

The same warm feeling that filled him the first time he held her returned. He placed a kiss on her head.

He glanced up and saw Tirzah running into camp. Why was she running? He set Naomi beside him and stood, but the beautiful, strong woman he expected was nowhere in sight.

Instead, tears flowed down her cheeks, she stumbled, and blood and dirt covered the bottom of her tunic. His stomach tightened and his pulse sped up as he searched for a wound. *Please, don't let her be hurt.* No blood was flowing, only the stains on the fabric. That meant the injury was probably someone else's. *Thank Yahweh.*

But what could make her so upset? Her girls were obviously safe. She was close to no one else that he knew of.

She neared the campfire and he jogged to catch her. She faltered again and fell into his arms. "Be- Be- Ben…" Her words dissolved into sobs as she slumped to the ground.

He slid down with her and wrapped her in his arms. Her hot tears stung his bare skin. She struggled to catch her breath. His world narrowed to only her. All he wanted was to erase her pain.

His training kicked in. The more distraught she became, the more his thinking cleared. He breathed evenly. His pulse slowed.

He looked to Ahmose.

The boy pointed toward the spring. "She went to check on her donkey."

The donkey? Benjamin. He pulled her face up to his. "Did something happen to Benjamin?"

"S- Someone killed him." She sobbed again. The pain in her eyes pierced his heart like an arrow. He glanced at the girls, their eyes wide, clinging to Ahmose. They didn't need to see their mother like this. "Ahmose, take the girls to our camp and send Meri back."

Ahmose nodded. "Yes, Uncle." He grabbed the girls' hands and hurried away.

"Are you sure he was killed? Are you sure he didn't just die?" That animal was ancient. He probably just died of old age.

"No!" She pounded her fist on his chest. "His throat was slit. Someone ki- killed him. Why? Why would someone ki..." Her words became unintelligible.

She had to be mistaken. Then again, she did have blood on her.

Kamose stroked her head and rubbed circles on her back while he waited for Meri. Her convulsions slowed, and she relaxed against him. He held her close and figured out what to do next. What could he do to ease her pain? He could think of nothing. So he just held her.

When Meri came, he transferred an exhausted and silent Tirzah into her arms. "I'll be back," he whispered.

He raced to the spring. He soon found Benjamin, lying near the water, throat wide open as Tirzah said. He removed his shenti, leaving on only his loincloth, then slid one arm under the animal's neck, and the other under its flank, and carried the corpse to the other side of the spring, beyond a small rise.

He lay Benjamin down and took off his sandal to use it as a shovel. As he dug in the soft sand, he tried to think who would want to kill a donkey. It took quite a while to dig a grave big enough for a donkey.

Time enough for him to come up with, and discard, a number of theories. The only reason that remained was to hurt Tirzah.

He finished burying Benjamin, added rocks to deter wild animals, and walked back to the spring. He was covered with blood and sank into the cool water to wash. According to the law, he was now ceremonially unclean, which meant he had to stay outside of camp until sundown.

࿇

Staying away all day while Tirzah mourned had nearly killed him. He sat on an outcropping studying the sun, willing it to drop faster. Planning ways to slowly, painfully kill whoever had caused her such pain. He hadn't wanted to take vengeance this badly since Michael had killed Bezalel's grandfather at the battle over the golden calf at Sinai.

He'd seen thousands of men die, but this was only the second time he'd seen someone kill just to cause someone else emotional pain. The first time was bad enough. This time was even worse. It was a very good thing he had to stay away for almost an entire day. Gave him a chance to calm down before he did something he'd regret for the rest of his life.

The moment the sun dropped behind the mountains to the west, Kamose returned to camp. He paused at Tirzah's tent, fingering the closed flaps. With no air, it must be stuffy inside. "Meri," he called in a low voice.

Meri crawled out. "She's sleeping," she whispered. She took Kamose's arm and led him to the other side of the fire pit. "She's scared, and angry, and terribly sad. She finally stopped crying and fell asleep. The twins are at our tent with Ahmose and Bezalel."

"She was right. Someone slit Benjamin's throat."

"Her brother-in-law came by. He became very upset when I wouldn't let him see her. But Tirzah seemed afraid of him."

"Nathaniel?"

"I think that was his name. Not too tall?"

"That's him. I'm going to see him. I don't trust him." He walked the few tents down to Nathaniel's. "Nathaniel. Come out."

Nathaniel stuck his head out. "Why?"

"I want to talk to you."

"What do you want?" Nathaniel exited his tent.

"I want you to leave Tirzah alone."

"I don't want to, and I don't have to. Gaddiel doesn't want her. I do. It's my right—my duty—to claim her. You have no rights, Egyptian. In fact, I want *you* to leave her alone."

Kamose eyed the brother-in-law, the man who intended to force Tirzah into a life she did not desire. But there was nothing he could do about the possibility that the woman he was falling desperately in love with—and her daughters—would be at this man's mercy every day of her life.

Nathaniel stood smugly, as if he held a secret. He had his arms crossed, tapping his foot, waiting for Kamose to yield, something Kamose had no intention of doing one moment before it was absolutely necessary.

Then he saw the blood on Nathaniel's sandals. Why would he have blood on his feet? Kamose smiled. "Nathaniel, what have you been doing today?"

"What business is it of yours, Egyptian?"

"You have blood on your shoes."

Nathaniel's features did not change, but his face blanched. He didn't look down, which meant he knew the blood was there, or at least it was possible. He didn't deny it.

"Perhaps we should check your tent for a bloody knife."

Nathaniel stepped back. "You can't come into my tent."

Kamose moved closer, so close that he was toe to toe with the man he had come to hate with all his being. "Perhaps not. But I can make you bring it out. Do it. Now."

"I will not."

Kamose grabbed the neck of Nathaniel's tunic with both hands. It wouldn't take much to lift the shorter man off his feet, but Kamose restrained himself. Barely. "Either you produce the knife—without any blood—or you release Tirzah and tell Moses she is free to marry anyone she wants."

Nathaniel didn't move, but his voice was weakening. "I will do neither."

Kamose lifted the man a hand's breadth and stared down at him. The Israelite's ragged breath brushed across his chin. "You will, or I will help you. And it will not be pleasant." He was nearly shouting. When was the last time he'd shouted? Almost certainly during battle.

The man remained silent a moment longer.

Kamose suddenly became aware of many sets of eyes on the two of them. Good. There would be witnesses, and Nathaniel would be forced to keep his word. "I need your answer now. Do I take you inside your tent to discover a bloody knife, or do you go to Moses to tell him you release Tirzah from her obligation to marry you?" He made sure everyone could hear Nathaniel's choices.

"I will talk to Moses." His voice was barely a squeak.

Kamose dropped the man. "If I hear differently by the time the sun comes up tomorrow, I will come looking for you."

Nathaniel nodded.

Kamose delighted at the fear in his eyes.

He had nearly lost control. He didn't care.

Nathaniel would never harm Tirzah again.

Nine

13 Tammuz

Following the wide river, the band of spies stayed to the west. Gaddiel's ankles ached; walking on this rocky plain was difficult and his sandals had slipped many times. He longed for the grassy fields to the south. Even the desert, though worse in every other respect, was easier to walk on than these rocks.

The river widened to a deep blue lake, bluer than the Nile. Standing on a hill, Gaddiel and the others could see across to the other side. Steep mountains dropped nearly straight down, almost to the water's edge.

Palti let out a deep breath. "I've never seen water so blue. It's incredible."

Sethur nodded. "It's beautiful."

Beauty was irrelevant. "It's about time. I could use some fresh water. And a good wash." Rocks skittered as Gaddiel started down the gentle, rocky slope to the lake.

After a refreshing swim and a somewhat less than comfortable rest on the rocks, the group followed the shore northwest for half a day until the end of the lake was visible. The water lapped on the shore, and a light breeze blew down from the mountains in the northeast.

Gaddiel tossed his pack on the rocks, crossed the beach, and stepped into the lake. The rippling water cooled his feet, and he knelt and scooped a handful into his mouth. He threw more over his head, allowing the soothing liquid to caress the muscles in his neck and back.

He waded farther into the deep blue of the lake. Tiny silvery fish darted about his feet. He removed his lightweight thawb and pulled it through the water, catching a few. Holding it up, he allowed the liquid to drain through the fabric while the fish fluttered wildly.

"I caught some fish!" He laughed, holding up the garment of food.

Sethur waded into the water with him and lowered his own thawb. When he raised his cloak full of flapping fish, he taunted Gaddiel. "I've got twice as much as you. Did you even tr—" He fixed his gaze on the sky to the northeast, mouth hung open.

Ominous, heavy clouds dumped rain, and winds charged down the slopes. Dry gulleys flooded and rushed to the lake.

Gaddiel stood transfixed. Boats pitched on the water, embattled between winds coming from northeast and west. Seamen lowered their sails and rowed furiously toward shore.

"Where did that come from?" Gaddiel shouted over the wind, which raged and gusted into his face. Rain pounded his skin so hard it stung. His hair whipped around and struck him. He held his arms in front of his head to block the storm, but it did little good. He looked back to see the rest of the group.

Palm trees bent nearly sideways under the wind, and leaves and twigs, ripped from branches, flew in circles. He abandoned his fish on the rocks at his feet and watched helplessly as the squall carried his thawb down the beach.

Sethur grabbed him and dragged him back toward the others. Gaddiel struggled to keep his balance as the west wind pushed him backward and the north wind shoved him sideways.

They ducked behind trees, hugging the trunks. The trees kept the deadly brunt of the waves from their faces, but they were still soaked as lake water washed over them repeatedly. Debris from the lake, weighty branches and even dead fish smacked their arms as they hugged the palms that stood between them and the raging waves.

Gaddiel's wet clothes stuck to his skin and made him shiver. He held tightly to the tree, burrowing his fingers into the bark. The rough surface pierced his cheek and scratched his arms. Sand covered his feet as he fought to gain solid footing.

The rushing wind moaned on its ride down the mountains, through the trees, up the slopes, and out of the depression of the lake. Gaddiel closed his eyes. How long would this last? Would he be able to hold on long enough?

After what felt like an eternity the winds subsided. Gaddiel peeked out from behind the tree. The palms stretched themselves back to their full height. The lake was as still and waveless as before. Boats raised their sails, threw out nets. Sailors rowed back to deeper waters.

As if nothing had happened!

From the position of the sun he could see the storm had lasted less than an hour. One of the longest hours Gaddiel had ever lived. First giants, now raging lakes. What else could this land possibly hold?

☙❧

Kamose sat at the fire with only Ahmose for company. Bezalel and Meri had taken a fussy Adi to bed early. Rebekah was with a young mother who had just given birth.

The crackling and popping of the fire soothed Kamose's mind, at least a little. Why hadn't Tirzah joined them for dinner? He knew Moses had informed her that Nathaniel had released her. Was she angry with Kamose for stepping in? Had he gone too far? Did she resent his help? Yes, she was strong, but did she really want to handle everything by herself?

"Uncle Kamose?"

"Yes, habibi?"

"How long have the spies been gone now?" Ahmose poured some goat milk into two cups and offered one to Kamose.

Kamose accepted the drink but set it in the sand beside him. "Almost two weeks."

"Have you ever been to Canaan?"

"No. Egypt has a peace treaty with Canaan now. Her armies have not fought there since before I was born, when Ramses was a very young man."

"Ramses young?" Ahmose made a face, probably trying to imagine the old king as a young ruler.

Kamose chuckled and mussed the boy's hair.

Ahmose scooted closer to Kamose. "What do you think the spies will find?"

Kamose wrapped his arm around his nephew's shoulders. "Nothing Yahweh cannot conquer." At the moment he was far more concerned about the next few days, not what the scouts might encounter in Canaan. Had he misread everything? Taken on a task that was not his? Stepped into a place not meant for him? Should he have remained a soldier with no war to fight, instead of hoping for a life he had no business wishing for? He'd obviously made a mess of things trying to live in her world. Perhaps he should back away while he still could.

At the sound of snapping twigs he looked up. His heart rate tripled as Tirzah stepped out of the dusk toward the campfire. He sighed. There was no way he could walk out of her life.

"Ahmose, I haven't gotten water yet. Could you sit by my tent while I get it? The girls are asleep. I won't be long." Tirzah tucked her hair behind her ears and shifted the bags from one hand to the other.

"Of course." The boy skipped off.

"Thank you." She started in the other direction, toward the smaller spring.

"Wait. You should not go alone in the dark. I'll walk with you." The full moon was out but still … he just wanted an excuse to be with her. He caught up with her in a few quick strides and took the skins from her. "We missed you at dinner."

"Naomi had a bad afternoon. I think her back teeth are coming in. She was crying and whining and slept very late. I hope she doesn't sleep poorly tonight because of it." She groaned as she rolled her shoulders. "The last several nights have been quite difficult, actually."

"You are tired."

"A little."

A little? She's exhausted.

They walked in silence until they reached the spring. He filled one skin and offered her a drink. The smile she gave him in return made his heart skip a beat. With no cup, he held the skin above her head and squirted the water into her mouth. She giggled softly as it dribbled down her chin, and she wiped away the errant drops.

He knelt and filled the other skins just to give himself time to slow his heartbeat and clear his head. He stood and placed his hand on the small of her back to guide her and nearly lost his breath. The unexpected heat from the contact was dizzying.

On the way back from the spring, he steered her away from the path toward a copse of palm trees. "Just a moment." He pointed his chin toward the trees. "I want to talk to you before we go back."

Three trees grouped close together gave him the modicum of privacy he sought without compromising her. He hung the skins from a low branch and turned to face her.

She touched his arm. "First, I need to say something." She paused, as if groping for the right words. "I want to thank you for what you did for Benjamin—for me. It meant so very much."

"You're welcome. I'm sorry that happened. But Nathaniel will not bother you again."

"Moses told me Nathaniel released me." She tilted her head. "I wonder what made him do that." She fixed him with a stare that said she knew he had something to do with it, baiting him to tell her the whole story.

He ignored the prompt. "Yes. Since Gaddiel had already made his lack of interest clear, you are now free to find a proper husband." *Or marry me. But that's probably not the wisest thing for you.*

She shrugged. "What did you want to talk about?"

He pulled his thoughts back to what he had planned to say. "What if Ahmose and I sleep with the girls tonight? You can stay in Gaddiel's tent and get a good night's sleep for once. You'll be close enough if they really need you."

A flash of gratefulness in her eyes melted into disbelief. She shook her head and looked at the ground. "You don't have to do that."

"I want to." He put a finger under her chin and lifted her face. "You need some sleep."

She continued to gaze at him, and her brow furrowed. "Why are you doing this?"

He cupped her face and rubbed her cheeks with his thumbs. "Because I care about you."

"But why?"

"Because you're beautiful. And strong."

She scoffed and tried to look away. "I am not beautiful."

Why was it so hard for this woman to believe anything good about herself? What had her husband done to her? "Yes, beautiful."

His gaze roamed her face. What would it feel like to let go? To take her in his arms and hold her the way he wanted, to feel her skin, to taste her lips? One time couldn't hurt. He locked his eyes on hers. Her eyes, the color of roasted grain, the color of sweet honey. Her eyes, darkened with desire.

Or was it only his own desire he saw reflected there? He lowered his head and brushed her lips. A tingle crept from his mouth down his neck.

A shiver ran through him as her hands touched his bare chest. He cradled the back of her head and covered her mouth with his. His other arm enveloped her waist and drew her closer. Heat coursed through his body and his pulse galloped like a chariot horse.

He had kissed many women in many lands. Never had a kiss affected him like this. At the victory parties there were hundreds of beautiful, young girls, and while he had always enjoyed getting to know them before sampling their pleasures, they were interchangeable. But now he was acutely aware not only of her body pressed tightly to his, but of her entire being. Her tinkling laugh, her cautious eyes, even her inexplicable insecurity. The camp was full of pretty Israelites, but he wouldn't exchange her for a single one.

The feel of her lips on his was heady. He could stay here all night. Better stop now before he was unable. He pulled back and studied her face, tucked a curl behind her ear. What was that in her eyes? Confusion? Regret? Fear?

His breath hitched. He'd gone too far. Or at least too fast. He let go and stepped back. "I'm sorry... I shouldn't have done that. I've offended you."

"No." She shook her head and raised her hand to his cheek, took back the distance he had put between them. "Not at all. It's just ... no one..." Her cheeks colored a delightful pink.

"What is it?"

"No one's ever kissed me like that."

He tilted his head. "But your husband..."

"My husband never kissed me like *that*. My husband rarely kissed me at all."

That didn't make any sense. But he'd leave it alone for now. He trailed the backs of his fingers down the side of her face. He brought his lips close to her ear. "Then your husband was a foolish man."

And he kissed her again.

ॐ∾

Tirzah awoke later than usual. She had slept through the night for the first time in months, and couldn't believe how refreshed she felt. She stretched and sucked air deep into her body. She looked for the girls, afraid for just a moment when she did not find them, but her heart soared when she remembered the night before. She brought her fingers to her lips and allowed herself to remember the heat of Kamose's kiss—his kisses. Jediel's hard, rare kisses had never felt like that. Gentle yet passionate at the same time. How did he do that? She could still feel his strong arms around her, his solid chest, his heart beating under her hand. Never had she felt so safe, so wanted.

But why? Why did he want *her*? A man like him could have any woman. Why would he be interested in an older one, with another man's children, who was so plain, when he could have any number of young, beautiful girls?

A giggle, followed by deep, masculine laughter, demanded her attention. She sat up and ran her hands through her hair. She reached for the water skin, poured a bit in her hand and washed her face. Taking a deep breath, she stepped out of the tent.

With one arm Kamose held Naomi against his chest. Her tiny arms were looped around his neck and weren't about to let go.

He appeared perfectly at ease standing there, holding her daughter. Her stomach did a somersault and she imagined him as her husband, their father… and wanted nothing more at that moment than for him to take her in his arms again and kiss her like he did last night. She shook her head to clear her thoughts. "Did you sleep well? And the girls?"

"We all slept through the night. Naomi didn't wake at all." He stepped closer to her.

She ignored her heart thumping against her chest, the blood pounding in her ears, and rubbed Naomi's back. "Not once?"

"Not once. She curled up next to me and slept soundly."

"How did you do that?"

Kamose chuckled. "I have no idea. If I knew I would tell you." He drew his finger along her jaw. "You're even prettier when you've slept."

His smile made it difficult to think. She should change the subject. "Where's Keren?"

Kamose loosened Naomi's stranglehold. "She went with Ahmose to gather your manna before it melted. The sun's getting higher."

Tirzah's checks heated. "I didn't mean to sleep so late. I'm sor—"

His eyes twinkled as he leaned in toward her, his familiar male scent of leather and earth surrounding—and unsettling—her. "That was the purpose, remember?" He was close enough to kiss her. He wouldn't here in the open, though she wouldn't mind at all.

To her relief, Ahmose appeared with the manna before she had to think of something intelligent to say.

"We got it." He held up her pot, beaming.

She placed her palm on his cheek and accepted the jar from him. "Thank you, Ahmose. That was very sweet of you."

"Why don't you bring it to our camp?" Kamose tilted his head toward Judah. "You can cook with Meri." He and Naomi set off for his tent, and Ahmose scampered behind him, holding Keren's hand.

Tirzah had no choice but to follow.

Meri and Bezalel sat by the fire as they neared the campsite. Meri raised her head at the noise of so many people and smiled broadly. "Tirzah!" She pretended to frown. "Kamose and Ahmose, where were you? We were a bit worried."

Tirzah's eyes darted to Kamose to see what he would say.

"We slept with the twins, so Tirzah could sleep in Gaddiel's tent and get some decent rest."

Meri clasped her hands together. "What a marvelous idea! How are you feeling today, Tirzah?"

"Much better, thank you. More rested than in months, actually."
She glanced at Kamose, then at the sand beneath her feet, then again
at Meri.

Meri narrowed her eyes at Tirzah, then Kamose. "Well, I think
you men should take the children and find some dates while we
make breakfast. Bezalel, Kamose—go." She shooed them away.

The men headed toward the spring. As soon as they were out of
sight, Meri pounced on Tirzah. "He kissed you!"

Tirzah put a hand to her chest. "What?"

"He did, didn't he?" The girl's eyes danced.

Tirzah thought quickly. She obviously couldn't hide anything. A
smile tugged at her mouth. "Maybe."

Meri fixed her with a gaze Tirzah assumed she used on Bezalel
to get what she wanted.

"Yes, he kissed me."

"I knew it! Finally." She laughed as she sat near the fire and gestured to a space next to her.

Tirzah nervously scanned the area as she sat.

"Well?" Meri took the jar of manna from Tirzah and dumped it
into a bowl with hers. A pot of water perched on charred sticks over
the fire softly bubbled.

"Well, what?"

Meri huffed an exaggerated sigh and rolled her eyes. "What do
you think of him?"

A smile slowly took over Tirzah's face as the memory of last night
returned. "He treats me like I am a princess. He loves the girls. He
actually listens when I talk. He compliments me."

"And his kiss?" Meri arched her brows.

"He's a very good kisser." She laughed. "Jediel hardly ever kissed
me, and certainly never like that. He just ordered me around and hit
me when I didn't move fast enough."

"He hit you?" Meri's eyes grew as big as the spoon she held.

"Yes." Tirzah shrugged. "So?"

Meri aimed the spoon at Tirzah. "You never told me about that."

Tirzah waved a hand. "What difference would it have made? I already said I couldn't leave him. Besides, I don't want to talk about him."

"Fine, tell me everything that happened." Meri poured some hot water into the bowl full of manna and stirred it into dough while Tirzah continued.

"I came to ask Ahmose to watch the girls. He walked me to the spring to get water. On the way back, we stopped. He offered to sleep with the girls in my tent, so I could sleep all night for once. When I pressed him to say why he wanted to do that, he said he cared about me. And when I asked him why, he said I was beautiful. Then he kissed me."

Meri sighed. "He is such a sweet man."

Tirzah smoothed her tunic. "Yes, but he is obviously blind. I'm nowhere near beautiful."

Meri stopped stirring and sat back, her hands on her hips. "Tirzah, you are a very beautiful woman. Why would you say such a thing?"

"Because no one, except my mother, has ever said I am pretty, let alone beautiful. If I truly were, I think someone would have mentioned it by now."

Meri frowned. "No one? Ever?"

"No one."

"Well, I can assure you, Kamose has seen thousands of women, and I have never known him to lie. He wouldn't say that if he didn't mean it. He is nothing if not honorable." Meri handed Tirzah half the dough.

Tirzah thought for a moment. "Maybe he was just trying to be helpful." Did she sound as desperate as she felt?

Meri scoffed. "Do you think he kisses everyone he helps? He's never kissed me, and he saved my life. Twice."

Tirzah shaped the dough into cakes. "I know he brought you here after the escape. What was the other time?"

"Bezalel asked him to help ransom me from the harem. Kamose found a way, since I was sold into it, which is illegal. He was going to tell Ramses the magician was sleeping with his concubines if he didn't let me go. But he didn't have to, because we left before he could."

Tirzah thought back to their escape the night the Angel of Death came. It was scary enough to leave with everyone else, with Egypt in chaos after the deaths of the firstborn. She couldn't imagine leaving with only one other person, knowing the army and its chariots were right behind them. "That must have been very frightening."

"It was. We would have been killed if we were caught. I'm sure he could have escaped much more quickly without me, but he never would have left me behind. He and Bezalel were good friends by then, as much as a slave and a palace guard can be friends." She giggled, then grew serious and pointed at Tirzah. "He's a good man. You couldn't do any better."

Tirzah contemplated Meri's words while they finished the cakes, making sure they didn't burn at the last moment. The children raced into camp, Bezalel and Kamose behind them. She handed out manna and dates and cups of milk, and laughter and conversation soon drowned out any chance for her to think further about what Meri had said. But there wasn't much she could do about it anyway. She'd just have to wait and see what Kamose did next.

Ten

Tirzah scrubbed the last bowl with sand, wiped it clean, and stacked it with the others. It had been a long day. The girls were asleep, and she was ready to join them. The setting sun allowed the air to cool just enough to make a difference, and the night birds filled the air with their melodic songs.

As she banked the fire, the back of her neck began to tingle. She felt someone standing behind her and turned her head.

Nathaniel.

She took a moment to control her tongue. "What do you want, Nathaniel?"

Feigning shock, he put a hand to his chest. "I've only come to check on the welfare of my sister-in-law. There is no harm in that, is there?"

She stood to face him. "Of course not, except you never do anything that does not hold some benefit for you. So again, what do you want?"

He clucked his tongue. "You wound me, Tirzah."

"Good."

"You must get quite lonely here now that Gaddiel is gone, all alone, no kinsmen around, only the girls—what are their names again?" His eyes ran up and down her body.

Too bad she didn't have a blanket to hide under. "Naomi and Keren." She spoke through clenched teeth.

"Yes, yes." He put a finger to his chin. "Oh, but then I hear whispers that you have been keeping company with a certain man of, how shall I put it, less than pristine character."

She bristled. How dare he call anyone less than pristine when he was a worm himself? "Who I keep company with is none of your concern."

Nathaniel began to circle her. The smell of days-old sweat swirled about her. "Oh, but it is. Because you will never be able to marry this man, and I don't want your reputation ruined when you eventually come back to me."

Her skin crawled as his light eyes followed her. Between the circling and the smell, she had to suppress a gag. "I've told you many times I would rather starve than marry you."

"Would you rather your girls starve as well?"

She had nothing to say to that.

Nathaniel continued. "I know you are dying to know but are too proud to ask, so I'll tell you what I'm talking about. Your *friend*, we'll call him, was an Egyptian soldier, yes?"

"That's no secret."

He stopped in front of her. "But are you aware of all that means? I have an uncle who worked in the palace before the Hebrew servants were kicked out. There were wild parties every month where soldiers and women we wouldn't spit on would get drunk and pleasure each other." The words slipped out as though they'd been dipped in oil. And Nathaniel obviously relished delivering every one. "Soldiers have more women than Ramses has wives. Not to mention what happened while they lived in other lands. Suffice it to say, your captain is not as perfect as you think he is."

The information rattled Tirzah to her core, but she wouldn't give Nathaniel the satisfaction of knowing she even contemplated believing it. She stuck her finger in his chest. "Perfect or not, he is better than you could ever think of being. And you have no idea what he did in Egypt. Your uncle was there years ago. He didn't know Kamose." She blinked back hot tears. The last thing she wanted to do was cry in front of her conniving brother-in-law.

Nathaniel laughed loudly. He leaned back and swept his hands out to each side. "Surely you cannot expect me to believe, or believe yourself, that your friend is the only pure soldier in all of Egyptian history!"

"What I can expect is for you to stay out of my life!" She shoved him away from her fire.

He stumbled backwards. The laughter disappeared, and his face darkened. His eyes shot daggers. "Well, when you arrive in Canaan, and no one will marry you, and you have no land, and no way to support your girls, just remember I warned you." Now he pointed a finger. "And if you're very lucky, maybe I'll take pity on you, and you can be my servant." He spun on his heel and left.

When she was sure he couldn't hear her, she unleashed the pent-up tears. Could it be true? Was Kamose like all the other soldiers? And did that mean she was just another of his conquests?

She dropped to the sand. Maybe that explained his irresistible charm. He'd perfected it on hundreds of other women. He knew exactly what to say to make her want him, trust him, believe every word that came from his mouth.

Was any of it real? She wrapped her arms around her knees and sobbed until her tears were spent.

Her thoughts calmed, she drew a slow breath. Memories of his smile, his kiss, his touch, danced through her mind. She wasn't ready to give up yet. Meri trusted him, and she did not seem to be a foolish girl. Tirzah had met charmers who had come to court her sister. Her stepfather was one. Even her brothers, to a degree. Kamose did not act like any of them. As charming as they were, there was always a shallowness, a hollowness to them. And they were always impatient. If they didn't get the reaction they wanted soon enough, they moved on to the next girl. None of that was Kamose.

Maybe she should forget Nathaniel had ever said anything, see what happened. If it was real, Kamose would continue to see her. If he was pretending, he would move on.

There was no way to find out tonight. All she could do was try to sleep, and wait until tomorrow. And pray that she hadn't already lost what she'd only begun to hope for.

14 Tammuz

Dread settled on Gaddiel like a cloak. The mound had been visible from the time they left the lake. For two hours it had loomed in front of them. Hazor sat atop a huge hill, like a guardian of all northern Canaan. Walls surrounded it. They couldn't see inside, but the outside was imposing enough. It was as big—or bigger—than Shechem. Much as Shechem controlled a critical junction, anyone traveling between Egypt and Mesopotamia had to go through Hazor, and the city profited immensely.

The scouts veered to meet up with the main east-west road. As they passed the mountainous first level, it became clear that Hazor was bigger than all the cities they had seen so far put together. To the north, a lower level, perhaps three times larger than the upper, cocooned it on three sides.

Gaddiel took in the earthen rampart surrounding the lower city. It was not nearly as high as the walls of Arad or Shechem. Perhaps it could be taken. Why would they leave their walls so low? As they neared, towers on the wall proved to be lookout points with guards inside, guards who could call out reinforcements if needed. From the size of the city, they would have plenty of defenders to draw from.

Even the lower level sat high above the surrounding land. Its height was a distinct advantage. The enemy would be seen before they came anywhere near them. Their army would have plenty of time to ready itself if the attackers did not retreat. They could rain down spears and arrows—and any other projectile they could think of, flaming or not. Gaddiel shuddered.

The spies turned off the main road onto the one leading to the city. Gaddiel lined up behind a caravan of donkeys laden with bags. The smell of sweat, dust, and dung hung heavy in the air.

Gaddiel leaned to the side to see what was happening. The guards apparently knew many of the traders, giving only cursory glances at their packs and nodding.

The line moved at a steady pace until the donkey caravan reached the gate. The sentries questioned the trader at the head of the line.

The leader responded, but the guard continued questioning. He motioned to two more guards, who strode over and searched every pack in their group.

Gaddiel pulled at the neck of his tunic, cracked his knuckles. They had nothing to trade. Would they be allowed in? They had a few coins left. Would it be enough? Or would they be discovered as spies?

The group ahead was waved through, and Caleb stepped toward the guard. "We've come to buy." He shook his pack of coins and shells.

"These are all with you?" The guard responded in Egyptian as he gestured to Gaddiel and the others.

Caleb nodded and the guard waved them through.

Gaddiel let out a breath.

Inside the double walls, the scent of roasting meat floated by on a slight breeze. Gaddiel wandered past stalls with fresh fruit, milk, wine, and cool water lining one side of the road that continued deep into the heart of the city. Across the road, vendors offered baths, shaves, clean clothes, even women—anything a man traveling for weeks could want.

"The food is incredibly inexpensive. They obviously want to keep the traders here a few days, spending their money on other things. Look, there are places to sleep." Caleb gestured toward a building with mats visible through open doors and windows. A young girl stood at the door. Four other traders went inside and dumped their belongings on mats after dropping coins in her hand.

Sleeping inside instead of on the ground. The thought soothed Gaddiel's weary muscles. "Do we have enough coin?"

"Depends on how much it costs. Anyone want to find out?" Caleb asked.

"I'll go." Palti left for the building.

"Let's find some food. I'm tired of grouse." Gaddiel marched back to the stalls offering meats of many kinds.

"Watch your coin. We've a long way to go yet," Joshua called after him.

The spies split up. Gaddiel and Igal bought meat, pomegranates, and watered wine, spending very little coin. Gaddiel filled his bag with more fruit for the next day.

They crossed the road and found a bathhouse. A young girl, wearing not much of anything, watched the door. Gaddiel held out his smallest coin, and gestured to himself and Igal. The girl smiled and nodded, then put her arms around his neck, rubbing up against him, fingering his coin pouch. "No, no!" He pulled her arms away and pointed inside, pretending to wash. She frowned, but held open the curtain to the bathhouse after snatching his coin.

Inside the house, Gaddiel's mouth dropped open as he watched men and women bathing together—actually, there was far more than bathing going on.

Igal grabbed his arm. "Do you see what I am seeing?"

Gaddiel nodded, speechless.

Another girl strolled up to them, wearing nothing but a skimpy towel around her waist.

Igal turned away.

Gaddiel felt heat creep up his neck and shooed her off.

Igal grabbed him again.

Gaddiel spun on his heels. A girl was hanging on a young man, who was dropping several coins into an older man's palm. He whistled. "So that's how they make all their money. The food and beds are cheap, but the women are expensive."

"Let's get clean and get out of here." Igal headed for the nearest open area and stepped into the steaming water.

After changing and leaving their dirty clothes behind to be cleaned, the pair explored the rest of the fascinating city. They walked through rows of vendors, through long streets of houses, and at the edge of the city, built into a corner of the wall but by no means hidden or small, they found a temple.

People entered and exited by three stone steps leading to an open archway.

Igal leaned close. "Seems to be awfully busy, doesn't it?"

Gaddiel nodded.

"Want to go inside?"

"Is it allowed?" Gaddiel stood on his toes to try to get a better view.

"We can try. They'll stop us if we can't go in. Maybe there's a space reserved for foreigners, like in the tabernacle."

The pair passed under the arch and entered an enormous open courtyard. An altar commanded most of the space. Peasants in farm attire—presumably from the fields surrounding the city—brought offerings of crops and laid them at the foot of the table. Kneeling, they raised their hands to the sky and called out in their native tongue.

Not too different from us.

Gaddiel and Igal passed a fire pit, then climbed a longer set of steps and entered the temple. Candlelight threw distorted shadows on the basalt walls. Small rooms with only thin curtains for doors lined either side of the room.

Gaddiel's steps echoed off the stone. He halted outside one of the rooms. His stomach somersaulted at the moans drifting from inside. He shook his head. Couldn't be. He moved forward.

The same noises came from the next room. From the third room, a couple, stripped from the waist up, stumbled out. The man dropped coins into the young girl's hand, then kissed her cheek before he sauntered away. She leaned against the doorframe and waved good-bye.

Gaddiel forced down the bile making its way up his throat. He turned to look at Igal.

Igal's face was pale. "Let's go."

They retraced their steps, leaving the cavernous temple behind them. Gaddiel's heartbeat slowed as he stepped onto the dirt floor of the courtyard. He wiped his hands on his tunic. "I want to get away from here. Let's go find the others."

A woman strode toward the altar from the archway. She carried no crops; a babe wrapped in a cloth rested in her arms.

Gaddiel followed her with his eyes as she halted at the altar where a priest now waited. She drew in ragged breaths and held the child to her chest for a moment. She placed a kiss on his cheek and handed the baby to the priest.

Gaddiel held his breath as the woman retreated a couple of paces and sank to her knees.

What was she doing?

The priest took the baby and placed it on a pile of wood on the altar. The infant cried and flailed its arms. The priest mumbled some words over the infant, then he strode to the fire.

Gaddiel's heart beat triple-time. Blood left his head and he felt woozy. Could that priest possibly be doing what it looked like?

The priest grasped a thick stick from the fire, lit at one end, and carried it back to the altar. The babe was now wailing. The priest raised his arms and chanted.

A crowd formed around the trio.

Gaddiel barely breathed. He shoved his way to the front.

The mother knelt stone-faced, though her hands shook violently.

The crowd joined in the priest's chant and drowned out the child's shrieks.

The priest touched the fire to the wood cradling the baby. Flames jumped from one twig to another, quickly surrounding the child with smoke and fire.

Gaddiel's chest constricted. Could they really be doing this?

The crowd swayed from side to side in unison and the chants grew louder.

Gaddiel's stomach soured, the meat and fruit from earlier turning to stone. He breathed faster and harder as within his chest a battle raged—he should *want* to try to save this child, but he didn't; the crowd surrounding him was nearing a frenzy. What would they do to him if he interrupted their sacrifice?

After all, it wasn't his baby….

But it was a baby….

What should he do? What could he do? He held his head in his hands, muttering, talking to himself, trying to hear himself think over the screams before he realized it was his scream he heard mingling with the high, anguished cries of the baby.

The baby stilled.

Gaddiel's legs gave way and his knees slammed against the ground. He buried his face in his hands for a few moments and sobbed.

He picked himself up and grabbed Igal, then raced for the archway. He ran until he reached the public sleeping room, skidded as he turned in the door and raced down to the end. He leaned his hands on his knees and gasped for air.

Caleb rose from his mat and stood before him, his hands on Gaddiel's shoulders. "What happened?"

Joshua jogged over to Igal.

It took Gaddiel a few more moments to slow his breathing to the point he could speak. "We have to leave here. Now."

Caleb narrowed his eyes. "Why?"

Gaddiel straightened. "We just went to the temple. You would not believe what we saw."

Caleb looked from Gaddiel to Igal and back.

"What?"

"Men and women—in the temple—doing what should only be done in the marriage bed. But that's not the worst part." He rubbed his hand down his face.

"What?" Joshua nearly yelled.

Gaddiel glanced around the room. They were alone. The other four traders must have gone. "There was a baby… a mother brought it… she gave it to the priest…" Gaddiel's stomach rebelled at the memory. At his failure. He couldn't repeat it—Igal would have to explain it. He left the room and vomited.

After taking a few moments to calm down, he returned.

Joshua paced, his hands behind his neck. "They really burned it to death? And no one did anything?"

Igal shook his head. "No. The crowd was chanting along with the priest."

"I've heard about these things, but I'd really hoped they were just stories," Caleb said.

"Well, they're not." Gaddiel grabbed his pack. "We have to leave here. Now."

Joshua shook his head and exhaled a loud breath. "The gates have closed for the night. We can't leave until morning."

"No, no! We have to go." Gaddiel grabbed Joshua's tunic.

"Gaddiel!" Joshua grasped Gaddiel's shoulders. "The gates are closed. They will not let us leave." Joshua stared at him until Gaddiel understood. "I'm sorry, but we just can't leave right now. We'll leave in the morning."

Gaddiel released Joshua, doing his best to hide the tears once again threatening to flow.

Joshua clapped him on the arm. "Try to get some rest. Well leave as soon as they open the gates. I'll go early and watch for the guards to unlock them myself."

Gaddiel nodded, then slumped off toward the mat closest to the wall. He lay down and faced away from everyone, tried to shut the image of the baby out of his mind. When his heart finally slowed to a normal rhythm, the soft mat brought sleep quickly.

Just before dawn, armed soldiers burst in the door. Two held torches.

The girl they had paid for the mats, cowering beside them, pointed toward the spies.

The officers marched to their end of the room, spears in hand, and stopped in front of the scouts. "Up, all of you!" yelled one in Egyptian.

The spies stood and reached for their bags.

"Bring nothing!"

In only his tunic, Gaddiel shivered in the predawn air.

A soldier brought an old woman to the front and spoke in a language unknown to the scouts. She pointed to Palti.

"You are under arrest for the murder of her husband." The officer grabbed Palti's left arm and another grabbed his right.

"When?" asked Caleb.

"Last night."

"But he couldn't have." Gaddiel stepped forward.

"She says she saw him. He got in a fight over money and hit her husband in the head with a rock."

"Impossible!" Caleb pleaded with the guards. "Our God forbids it."

It made no difference. They dragged Palti away. He cast a glance backwards as he turned a corner, his eyes full of terror.

Gaddiel turned on Caleb and Joshua. "What do we do now?"

Joshua shrugged, his eyes wide.

"Pray. Yahweh will take care of this," Caleb said.

Pray? Caleb's calm demeanor was beyond irritating.

Even Joshua had sense enough to be worried.

☙❧

Kamose stood by the largest spring, northeast of camp. It gurgled and bubbled, but no matter how much noise it made, it could not mask the thoughts in his head. Thoughts that had been haunting him, hounding him all night, keeping him from sleep. He'd paced until the sun rose.

He crouched and splashed his face. If only the water could wash away his past as easily as it washed away sweat and dirt. At least part of it. He had always been proud of everything he had accomplished. Until little more than a year ago, he'd been the most trusted soldier in the most powerful nation on earth. That wasn't worth much now.

The birds sang merrily above him, but there was nothing merry in his heart. Try as he might, he could not erase the memory of Tirzah sobbing last night after Nathaniel told her about the life of an Egyptian army officer. Just before he stepped into view he'd heard Nathaniel's voice detailing things he hadn't thought about in years. Tirzah had defended him, but after her brother-in-law left… the tears wouldn't stop.

He sat back and drew his knees to his chest. There was no way around it—he simply was not good enough for her. If he pursued a relationship with her beyond helping her or protecting her, he would only end up hurting her. His past was too sullied, too shameful. There was only one option: stop now before things went any further. His heart throbbed at the idea. To never kiss her again, hold her… to give it up would be heartbreaking. But if he truly cared for her, he had no other choice. Thank Yahweh he'd only kissed her once. She would find someone else easily enough.

But how to help her and protect her from Nathaniel without being near her? That was the immediate problem. Ahmose could continue helping her with the girls. He'd just have to stay away for a while, long enough to get his emotions under control. He'd spent his whole life suppressing his feelings. He could do it again. A few weeks of weakness could be undone, before there was any more damage.

Eleven

16 Tammuz

Palti had been kept from them for two days. They had been allowed to visit him and bring him his clothes. He was fed and treated well, but terrified. The punishment for murder was death.

Gaddiel paced the sleeping room. Palti was the calmest man he knew. He had never seen him lose his temper or even raise his voice. To murder someone? Impossible.

But the woman was insistent. She had not changed her story. And they had no proof. She had a bloody rock and a dead husband.

The spies wandered through the city. Even the smell of food could not interest Gaddiel. They stayed in groups of at least three, lest anyone else be accused. Gaddiel, Sethur, and Igal strolled through the streets of mud brick houses. Children ran and chased each other, women chatted in doorways, young girls snickered and pointed at young men. It reminded him very much of his home in Egypt.

Egypt. Where things were simple. Yes, they were slaves, but there were no questions. You knew exactly how things worked. If you obeyed and did your job, life wasn't so bad.

A child running after another bumped him from behind. The two ran away laughing.

Gaddiel turned out of the residential section back to the vendors. They exited the street into a section of stalls offering women.

The sounds of a scuffle to their right demanded their attention. A young girl crying for help. Even if they couldn't understand the words, her tone was clear. They sprinted toward the noise.

When they reached the girl, a man in an Egyptian thawb was holding the girl against the building. He glanced up and saw them coming, let her go, grabbed another girl, and disappeared into a tent.

He looked very much like Palti.

"Did you see that?" asked Sethur.

"He looked just like Palti. And he has the same kind of cloak." Igal's eyes were wide.

"And the temper to kill. Igal, go find a soldier, one who speaks Egyptian. Do whatever you have to, but bring him here. We don't have much time."

Igal sprinted away.

Gaddiel and Sethur kept watch on the tent the Palti lookalike had ducked into. Sooner than they hoped, he reappeared.

Gaddiel grabbed Sethur's shoulder. "I'll follow him. You wait here for Igal, then find us."

Gaddiel followed the lookalike, trying to stay out of sight.

The man stopped at a food stall, pointed at several items, and waited for the boy to bag the items.

The boy handed over the bag, and the man reached into his pouch for coin.

Gaddiel glanced over his shoulder. Where was Igal with that soldier?

The man continued down the row of stalls.

Gaddiel followed. His heart pounded in his ears. What if they lost him? Palti would die. This horrible land—they'd be lucky if all of them made it back alive.

The man stopped again. He'd apparently dropped off some clothing. He spoke to a woman, who ducked in a tent. He dug his sandals in the sand as he waited.

A touch on his shoulder made Gaddiel jump. He turned to see Igal, Sethur, and one of the soldiers who had arrested Palti. "He's there waiting for clothing." He pointed to the Palti lookalike.

The man glanced their way.

"He does look very much like your friend." The soldier shook his head. "I'll arrest him. Let me call another." He stepped back to the main road and whistled. The pair strode to the man, grabbed him, and marched away.

Gaddiel sank against a pole. Now maybe Palti had a chance.

છ≪

After the girls had fallen asleep, Tirzah joined the circle and sat next to Meri. The fire crackled and popped, and a slight breeze wafted through the camp. The smell of burning driftwood tickled her nose. "Naomi finally stopped whining. I think she missed you tonight, Kamose." She smiled at him across the circle but he only glanced at her. A pain pinched her heart.

Ahmose skipped in.

"And where have you been, habibi?" Meri pulled him close and kissed his cheek.

"Playing by the river."

"You missed supper."

"Not hungry. Did the girls go to sleep already?" He hugged Tirzah.

Meri laughed. "Of course. It's quite late. Time for you to go to bed as well, I think."

"Already?" Ahmose scrunched his face.

"Don't whine." Bezalel's voice was firm. "Go to your tent."

"All right." The boy headed for the tent he shared with Kamose.

"I'm going for water." Tirzah stood and waited a moment to see if Kamose would offer to accompany her. When he rose, her heart skipped a beat and her lips curved into a smile.

Instead, he excused himself and headed the other way.

Her heart sank. She couldn't breathe. He hadn't even looked backwards at her. Tears gathered in her eyes, but she fought to keep them from falling.

"I'll go with you, Tirzah. Let me get our skins." Meri stood and disappeared into her tent.

Tirzah lost her fight with the tears and collapsed onto the sand, where Meri sat next to her. "He's been avoiding me for two days. I have no idea what I've done."

"I'm sure you've done nothing." Meri patted her arm.

Bezalel picked up baby Adi and slipped away from the campfire, leaving them alone.

Tirzah put her head in her hands, her elbows on her knees.

Meri wrapped her arm around her and rubbed her back, letting her cry.

Tirzah raised her head and took a shuddering breath. "Nathaniel said some awful things the other night."

"Such as?"

"He said there had been other women—lots of women. He said all soldiers live wild lives."

Meri blew out a breath. "I don't know about wild. But they would have parties in the palace. It happened all the time. Whenever there was a victory, or just to reward them for being good soldiers. Wine, music, and lots of pretty, young girls. And the women wanted to be there, just like they wanted to be concubines."

"Why would they want to do that?" Tirzah stared at Meri through her tears.

"In Egypt, we looked at things differently. Men and women enjoy each other. They were beautiful women and young, strong soldiers. Egyptians see nothing wrong with it if none of them are married. So Kamose was acting as all his people did. Can you fault him for that?"

Tirzah scoffed. "Well, that's a horrible way to live."

"Yet you were married without any choice to a man who did not love you, who beat you, with no way out unless he died. Which way is better?"

Tirzah wiped her eyes. "I suppose you have a point. It doesn't matter anyway. He changed his mind. He doesn't want me. That's why he's avoiding me. He realized he can do much better."

Meri tilted her head. "Does Kamose know you know about his past?"

"I don't think so. I didn't tell him. I haven't seen him since I saw Nathaniel."

"I think somehow he found out and that's why he's been avoiding you."

"I doubt it." Tirzah shook her head. "I never should have hoped. I should have just concentrated on the girls. That's what my life is now. Hoping for more—that's what got me into trouble. And hoping for someone like him—I never had a chance."

Meri grasped Tirzah's hand. "That's where you're wrong. You still have a chance. I know Kamose far better than you do. And if he thought there was the tiniest chance he would hurt you, he would never have started anything."

Tirzah hugged herself. "Maybe I should leave it this way."

"Then why are you crying?"

More tears flowed. "I don't know."

"I do. Because you love him." Meri hugged her, and let her cry some more.

Tirzah raised her head to look at Meri. "So do you think everything Nathaniel said is true?"

Meri shrugged. "At least some of it. You need to talk to him about it."

"I don't know..."

"You *need* to talk to him. Do you really want to give this up without even giving it a chance?"

She didn't want to give up. But she didn't want to confront Kamose, either. What could he say that would make her feel better? She was terrified of the truth—either finding out everything Nathaniel said was true, or that he didn't want her at all.

No matter what he said, there was no way she could come out of this with what she wanted.

෧‍ᕱ

Back at the sleeping house, Gaddiel waited for word on what would happen now that they had, in their opinion at least, found the real murderer.

Caleb lay on his mat, eyes closed, face peaceful as always.

"How can you lie there so calmly when Palti's life is in danger?" Gaddiel wanted to strangle the man.

Caleb sat up. "I said Yahweh would take care of it, and He has."

"He has done nothing yet!"

"He showed us the man responsible. I am sure the truth will be revealed to the king and Palti will be released. Yahweh will—"

"How do you know Yahweh is even here?" Gaddiel jumped to his feet. "I'm not at all sure He is. Maybe we left Him behind, with the manna and the cloud. That would explain why this land is so full of danger. Even He won't come here."

Caleb stood. "Yahweh is with us, be assured of that. If you cannot see it, you are not looking."

Gaddiel growled and stomped out of the building.

Yahweh could not be here. This land was too brutal, too fearsome. Sacrificed babies. Giants. High mountains that cut the land in half, lakes that almost killed, cities with walls to the sky.

This land could not possibly be blessed by Yahweh.

ক্ষ ক্ষ

Kamose turned at the sound of crunching sand.

"I've found hitting things gets rid of anger far better than staring at them." Bezalel came alongside Kamose, searching the water with him.

Kamose allowed himself a half smile at Bezalel's comment. "Probably. But I choose not to abuse my body as you did for the sake of anger."

Bezalel chuckled as he rubbed the brutal scar down his left arm. "Good point."

Kamose sighed loudly. "What do you want, Bezalel?"

"Well, Tirzah's in her tent with Meri, crying, again, and you're out here staring at waterbirds."

Kamose squeezed his eyes shut. "She's crying?"

"She is convinced you do not want her."

Kamose growled as he rolled his shoulders and stared at the sky. "I take it that's not true."

Kamose exhaled a long breath. "Of course not. It is I who am not worthy of her."

Bezalel let a silent moment pass before he continued. "Why not?"

Kamose studied the sand under his feet. "My past… is not… honorable."

"Kamose, I've known you for two years. You are the most honorable man I know."

"Not when it comes to women."

Bezalel scoffed. "I've never seen you treat a woman with anything less than dignity and respect."

"I do, and always have, respected women. But Egyptians do not regard relationships between men and women as sacred as you.

When I was younger, there were many women. It was part of being a soldier. I cannot possibly expect her to understand that."

Bezalel lifted one shoulder. "Perhaps. You love her, don't you?"

"It doesn't matter. I am not good for her."

"Don't you think that's for her to decide?"

"No. She doesn't have all the facts. I have to make the decision for her."

"But you are no longer that person. Don't you think a relationship should be based on who you are now?"

Kamose remained silent. The thought was so tempting. "How can I ask her to accept everything I am, everything I have done? Is that fair to her?"

"Maybe she'll accept it, maybe she won't." Bezalel turned to face Kamose, and spoke only when he caught his eyes. "I can only say to you what you once told me. Talk to her. She loves you. Or she wouldn't be crying."

As Bezalel retreated, Kamose pondered the sting of having his own words tossed back at him. Was Bezalel right? Was there a chance Tirzah would understand? Forgive him? Even if she did, would that be the best thing for her? Or would she be better off if he left her alone and let her find a good Israelite man to care for her? The questions kept coming, and he had no answers.

He hooked his hands around his neck and raised his eyes to the sky. He paced as he ran through the questions again and again. Moses had said to do whatever Yahweh placed before him. Tend sheep. Well, he tried that. He'd tried to help a widow, and all it had done was bring them both trouble. Actually, it wasn't the helping that had brought him trouble, it was his heart. He should have kept his heart under tighter control.

But every time he closed his eyes he saw her honey-colored ones, felt her thick, wavy hair woven through his fingers, tasted her lips beneath his, and his heart galloped away again.

He'd do anything to keep from hurting her. At least any more than he already had.

❧

The stars shone brightly in the moonless sky as Kamose sat by the spring, trying to figure out how he had let this get into such a mess. His arms rested on his knees, his head on his arms as he thought in the near silence of the desert oasis.

"Kamose?"

He twisted his upper body to see Tirzah approaching. His heart almost stopped beating. He'd have to decide later whether to kill Bezalel or thank him. He rose to meet her.

She stopped an arm's length away. She looked so stiff, afraid to move or speak. She raised her face, her light eyes moist.

He longed to wipe her tears away, but he couldn't trust himself to do only that. Instead he kept his hands locked together behind his back. He searched her face. What was she thinking? "You shouldn't have come out here alone in the dark. It's not safe."

She drew a deep breath. "You have been avoiding me. Have I done something to offend or upset you?" She blinked back tears.

He swallowed hard. "Tirzah, you haven't done anything wrong. I… I am not the man you believe me to be." He ached to touch her face, to wrap his arms around her, to reassure her how much he cared for her, how much he thought of her. He shoved those thoughts aside. He had to tell her. Even though he knew what that meant. "But my past is not… there have been… I was an elite Egyptian soldier. Women were a reward for good service." He closed his eyes as he saw the hurt in hers. "Things were so very different in Egypt. I never mistreated anyone, and I never took anyone by force. But I can't expect you to understand it or to live with it." He was silent as she pondered his words. The sound of the water was deafening.

She glanced down. "So what he said was true." She spoke more to herself than to him.

"Yes."

She jerked her gaze back to him. "You heard him?"

"Yes, I was on my way to see you. I heard him tell you about soldiers in Egypt. I also heard you defend me." He paused. "And I saw you crying."

She swallowed. "Were there many?"

He took a tentative step toward her. "Tirzah, I will tell you everything you want to know. But be sure you really want to know before you ask."

She looked away as the tears slid down her cheeks.

His chest constricted as the struggle played out on her face, and his heart ached for her. He had no hope she would forgive him, let alone accept him, but if he could just soothe her pain. ... "I adore you, Tirzah. And I want more than anything to be with you. But I should never have let anything happen between us. I shouldn't have kissed you. I was selfish. You are so beautiful, so kind, and I've never felt about anyone the way I feel about you. But now I've hurt you, and I would do anything to undo it all. I don't expect you to forgive me. I don't know what to say except I am sorry."

She looked deep into his eyes for what felt like an eternity. Then she spun on her heels and without looking back, returned to camp.

He sank to his knees. At least it was over. His heart had been ripped from his chest, but it was done. It could have been worse. He'd only kissed her once. Her heart would heal. He would keep Nathaniel from her, and she would find someone who would care for her, someone who deserved her love. And now he knew better, and would continue to follow the rule he had always lived by, and never fall in love again. Because soldiers don't make good husbands.

He lay back and stretched out on the warm sand. The stars above twinkled and mocked him. *Told you so, told you so, told you so.*

Twelve

Gaddiel climbed the twenty stairs leading to the upper level. He and the others followed the guards up a ramp through an arch onto a wide, open porch. Its roof was braced by enormous cedar pillars on stone bases on either side of the ramp.

At the end of the porch, they climbed two more steps. Massive carved lions sat on either side of another arched entryway. Palti and his lookalike stood a good ten strides away, each bound hand and foot, before the throne. Gaddiel wanted to run to Palti, cut the bonds, and escape. That was foolish. Eight guards armed with spears lined either side of the room.

Gaddiel swallowed. If he believed Yahweh were with them, he would pray. He doubted it would do any good.

Heavy, decorated basalt stones covered the lower portions of the walls. Cedar was everywhere, permeating the air with its fresh scent. Trays of fruit and wine stood on pedestals near the throne. Masks of gods hung on the walls.

The king entered from a room to the right and sat on his throne.

An older man approached. "My king, we have a problem that only you, as king and god of this city, can solve." He pointed to Palti. "This man was accused by the widow of murdering her husband. His companions say this is most unlike him. Furthermore, they have found this man"—he pointed to the lookalike—"who resembles him greatly and was caught harming a woman of Hazor."

The king looked from Palti to the other and back to Palti. "Thank you, Yassib. Is the widow here?"

Yassib nodded. "She is."

"Bring her."

Yassib beckoned, and a guard escorted the old woman into the throne room. Upon seeing the two accused, she gasped.

The king turned to her. "Woman, can you choose between these two which killed your husband?"

She squinted, stood before each man several times. "No, I can't. They look too much alike."

"Thank you. You may wait in the other room." The king waved his hand, and she was escorted out.

"If she can't name me, you have to let me go!" The other man struggled against his bonds and tried to kick his guard, who yanked upwards on his arms.

The king glared at the man, then turned to Yassib. "Do you have the girl he harmed?"

Yassib beckoned once again, and she was brought out.

"Can you tell which of these men tried to hurt you?"

She looked at both men, and pointed to the Canaanite. "Him. I can tell by his eyes. And the scar on his cheek."

"She's lying! I've never met her!" the man yelled again.

"I have seen all I need to see." The king gestured to Palti. "This one, in the face of death, has remained quiet and still. I do not see him as one who would murder another over money. Release him. Send the other to the prison until I decide his fate. And inform the widow."

The guard loosed the ropes on Palti's wrists and ankles.

As Palti rubbed his wrists, his friends gathered around him. Gaddiel slapped him on the back.

Palti grinned. "I did a lot of praying the last few days."

Gaddiel scoffed. Prayer didn't have anything to do with it.

The scouts started to leave when the king called them back. "I want to make up for the extra time you have been required to stay here." He nodded to the old man. When Yassib approached, he whispered to him.

Yassib drew near with a bag of coin. "Who will take the coin?"

"I will." Caleb stepped forward.

"Your hand, please." The old man poured so many coins into Caleb's hand he had to use both.

"But, sir, this is far more than we have spent."

"The king told me to give you back four times what you must have spent." He turned and left before Caleb could answer.

"Yahweh has freed Palti and given us enough coin for the rest of the journey." Caleb beamed.

Caleb could look at it that way if he wanted. Gaddiel knew they had to get out of here. Fast. This land was dangerous. Its god demanded babies and the king almost killed Palti.

There was no way Gaddiel would live here.

❧

The morning breeze chilled Tirzah as she sat by the fire with Bezalel and Meri. Her whole world had collapsed in on her. She'd never felt so empty. Her chest ached, and her eyes stung from crying. "I told you, I should have been content with the girls. I hoped for too much, and I was punished for it. He admitted it was all true."

Meri's eyes pleaded with her. "Years ago. Not anymore. And he only did what every other soldier did. In Egypt, it was not wrong. He did not know Yahweh then. You can't hold him responsible for that, can you?"

Tirzah pulled her hair behind her ear. "I never told you everything about my husband." She closed her eyes and pushed the memories back. "And I just don't know if I can live with that again."

Bezalel knelt before her and took her hands in his. "But that's the point. You wouldn't be living with it again. I've known Kamose for two years. I've never known anyone, Egyptian or Hebrew, more honorable or caring. He risked his life to bring Meri to me, because I am his friend, and he barely knew her. He'd sacrifice anything, do anything, to protect someone he cares about. He would never hurt you."

Meri touched her shoulder. "Tirzah, you are afraid of what your life *might* be like with him because of what Nathaniel said, and what happened years ago. None of your fears are based on anything that Kamose has actually done. I want you to think about what life might be like with him, and what it might be like without him, and decide which is the better choice."

∾∿

In the dark of the night, Tirzah rolled onto her side. Why couldn't she sleep? Naomi slept beside her peacefully. She hadn't wakened in the night since Kamose had slept next to her. In fact, whenever Kamose was around, Naomi seemed to prefer him to her own mother.

And why not? He adored the girls as much as Tirzah did.

Tirzah thought about every time she'd been around the Egyptian. There were always other women around. In tents next to them, across from them. He might smile politely, if one passed, but she'd never seen him initiate a conversation. Perhaps it was all in his past, as he said.

Tirzah remembered how gentle he was when Benjamin died, how he'd held her as she cried and mumbled, making no sense. He'd even buried the donkey for her, becoming unclean for her sake, remaining outside the camp until the sun set. Would he do that if he didn't really care?

Meri said to think about what her life might be like with him. It could be wonderful, filled with his care and concern for her and her girls. It would be different from any other time of her life, from life with Jediel, or her stepfather… a life she could only imagine.

Or it could be just as difficult as life with Jediel, who rarely came home, flaunted his other women, and hit her if he felt like it.

But Jediel had never looked at her like Kamose did. And for some reason, even if he did have other women in his past, she couldn't see him having other women now. And even if he did, she didn't think he'd flaunt it.

And life without him… meant Nathaniel. A horrible situation at best. Even the worst she could imagine about Kamose was better than the best about Nathaniel.

❧❧

Tirzah found Kamose at the big spring early the next morning. She gasped lightly when she first spotted him—facing away from her, his hair loose and wet, dripping onto his broad, bare back. The sunlight bounced off the water droplets as he moved.

He reached behind his neck and gathered his hair, slicked the water from it. He ran his hand down his muscled arms and shook off the water. His armbands lay in the sand at his feet.

She drew in a deep breath before she approached him. She halted a few steps away. "Kamose?"

He froze for a moment before he turned. His face was wary when he did.

"Kamose, I came to talk to you about… about all the things Nathaniel said."

He crossed his arms and dropped his gaze to his bare feet. "I've already told you they are true. As much as I might want to, I can't change my past."

"I know. I just want you to listen."

He raised his head and nodded. His face was soft—the hardened warrior was gone. She was surprised to find she missed that.

"Jediel... Jediel did a lot more than say cruel things to me. He... there were... he had other women as well. He would go to them and then come home to me. He made sure I knew it, too. Told me their names, how much younger and prettier they were."

She brought her hand to her temple as she remembered his games. "I got pregnant soon after we were married. He hated being around the babies. Hated the crying, hated the fact that I couldn't stop what I was doing to get his meals, hated everything. He came and went as he pleased. I never knew if he would come home from the brickfields or not. Eventually, I prayed he wouldn't."

Kamose closed his eyes and swallowed. When he opened his eyes, they were full of deep pain. "Did he hit you?"

She shrugged. "Sometimes."

He pursed his lips. "So when you left Egypt, and had to live in the same tent with him, it became worse?"

"In some ways. He hit me more often. He still found reasons to stay gone. Being in a tent with us was more than he could handle." She scoffed. "He had no trouble finding someone to attend to his needs."

"And he died..."

"At the battle of Sinai. He was on the wrong side."

"Tirzah, I am so sorry." He ran his hands through his hair. "The last thing I want to do is cause you pain. If I remind you of your husband, I will do my best to stay as far away as I can—"

"No!" She closed the distance between them and laid her hands on his chest.

He stiffened.

"You are as different from him as you can possibly be. You listen to me. You care about me. You compliment me. You actually think of things to do to help me. You have no idea how that feels."

"But—"

"No, you see, just the mention of… what you did in Egypt scared me to death. At first. And I overreacted. I'm sorry."

"You're sorry? I'm the one with the past, and you're sorry?"

"It *is* in your past, right?"

"Tirzah, I would never do anything to hurt you. If I could cut off my arm and make it all go away, I would."

She rubbed her hands up and down his upper arms. "Don't do that. I like your arms. Especially when they are around me."

He placed his hands on her waist and drew in a ragged breath. "I don't know if this will make it better or worse, but I never spent the night with any of them. I never felt for anyone anything even close to what I feel for you." He brushed his lips over hers, then pulled back and gazed at her. "You are so beautiful."

She smacked his arm. "Don't keep saying that."

"Why not?" He kissed her cheek.

"Because if you lie to me about that, I'll start doubting everything else you say."

He frowned. "Why would you think I'm lying?"

"Because you're the first person who has ever said that."

"Really?"

"Well, Meri said I was pretty. But she exaggerates about everything. You are the only one who's said I'm beautiful."

"Do you think your daughters are beautiful?"

"Absolutely."

He chuckled. "You've seen yourself in a mirror, haven't you? You must know they look exactly like you."

She scoffed. "They do not."

"Tomorrow we will go to the other side of camp, or at least to Dan, and ask twenty-five complete strangers if your girls look like you."

"We will not!"

"Then you have to believe me." He lowered his voice. "Your husband was a fool, and your stepfather was blind, and you have to stop believing them. Believe *me*, because I love you."

She gasped. Her eyes slowly widened and then filled with tears. "You do?"

"Yes. Don't tell me no one ever said that before."

"My imma. And the girls."

He arched his dark brows then smiled. "The captain in me likes being first." He lowered his head and she raised hers to meet him. His lips were warm and tender, and his kisses made her melt in his arms.

She looped her arms around his neck, pulling him down to her, and his strong arms wrapped around her even more tightly.

Gaddiel, Nathaniel, providing for the girls in Canaan—all those problems disappeared for the moment. She knew it could never last. The fact that Kamose loved her did not change the fact that she would have no way to support herself in Canaan unless she married Nathaniel. Or Gaddiel. She had always been the practical one, had never been one for fantasy.

But the truth was too horrible.

If only she could make the fantasy last forever.

20 Tammuz

Kamose needed to find Moses. What kind of upset would it cause if he asked Tirzah to marry him? He didn't know. He only knew he wanted her and the girls in his life. Every day.

"He's not here or in the tabernacle. Try the flocks." Aaron pointed south.

"Thank you." Kamose headed through the rows of tents, through Judah, then Zebulon, until he came to the open spaces filled with bleating sheep and goats. He scanned the fields, shading his eyes, until they stopped on a lone figure amongst a group of sheep resting by a small spring. Leave it to Moses to be out with the animals in the hottest part of the day.

"Moses."

Moses looked over his shoulder as Kamose approached. "Captain. What brings you all the way out here among the animals?" He held a small one in his arms, the lamb laying its head on the old man's forearm, half asleep.

Kamose chuckled. "The question is, why are you always all the way out here among them?"

Moses stroked the lamb's head. "Sheep are much simpler than people. They need only a few things to be happy. Still water, something to eat, someone to watch over them. Give them those, and they cause you no trouble. I find it very peaceful out here."

Kamose frowned. "Then you may not like my question."

"What question is that?"

"I want to marry Tirzah."

Moses fixed his gray eyes on Kamose. "Hmmm."

"Is it possible?"

"Anything is possible. The question is, is it wise?"

"And what do you think?"

"If she does not marry Gaddiel or Nathaniel, she will not keep Jediel's property. If she marries you, she still will not. Since you are not Hebrew, you will not be allotted any land in Canaan. Her situation will not improve."

"But if she marries Nathaniel—Gaddiel does not want her—I am certain he will beat her, as did Jediel. I do not want her or the girls to suffer that life again."

"Jediel beat her?"

"He did. He had other women as well."

Moses shrugged. "Well, if you are willing, there are other ways of earning a living. You are a man who will work hard. I know you would not let them starve." He set down the lamb then straightened to face Kamose. "She won't marry Nathaniel, will she?"

"If she didn't have the girls, absolutely not. But for their sakes, I think she'd put up with anything."

"You are an honorable man. You have many friends who will stand by you in this endeavor. If you are both willing to do whatever it takes, knowing neither of you will have an inheritance in the new land, I'd say go ahead. Most brides are waiting until we reach Canaan."

"I don't want to wait. I want her safely away from Nathaniel. Now. He's harmed her once. He killed her donkey."

"Very well. You have my blessing. If you do this now, here, it will be the simplest of ceremonies—betrothal and wedding together, since there is no one to ask permission, no bride price, and her safety is an issue. Will that be acceptable to her?"

Kamose smiled. "I'll ask, but I doubt she'll care. She had a big wedding once. It didn't work out so well."

❧

Kamose stroked Tirzah's hair as they sat alone by the fire. Bezalel and Meri had gone to bed, and Ahmose was in Tirzah's tent. The boy liked to play there with Keren and Naomi after the evening meal, when it was too dark to play outside, and often fell asleep there. When that happened, Tirzah let him stay, and she slept in Gaddiel's tent.

Kamose kissed her temple. "The spies should be back soon. They've been gone over three weeks." Even in the firelight Kamose could see her frown, see her eyes drifting closed. "Don't you want to see the new land?"

"I like it here well enough."

"Why?"

"Here I have friends, manna... you. There I will have to go back to Zebulon... and..."

"And..."

She turned to face him. "I will have to marry Nathaniel. Or Gaddiel."

"I thought Gaddiel didn't want to marry you."

"He doesn't. But he likes having a servant. And he doesn't want Nathaniel to have me. I'll have to marry one of them."

"You don't have to."

"I do if I don't want to starve. No one else will marry me. They won't even talk to me. The women shun me."

"Then marry me." His hand caressed her cheek.

"Marry..." Her brow furrowed.

"Marry *me*."

"But why?"

"Because I love you."

She shook her head. "But how will we live? You will get no land."

He cupped her face in both hands and locked his gaze on hers. "You can live with Nathaniel, who does not love you, and will most likely hit you, on his land, and have food. Or you can live with me, near Bezalel and Nahshon, who will never let us starve. I will work in their fields, or their shops, or with their flocks—I don't care, as long as you and the girls are safe. You will have friends and family, instead of people who won't even talk to you. And, of course, a husband who adores you." He drew her closer and kissed her.

"Is it even possible? You are not of Zebulon, and not Hebrew."

"I've already spoken with Moses. The laws are designed to keep the land within the clan. You just can't inherit."

"And you are willing to raise another man's children?"

"I love Naomi and Keren more than you could possibly understand. When I chose to become a soldier, I gave up any chance to have a family. I expected to be a soldier all my life, to die in battle. I never thought I would have a wife, children."

"Soldiers are not allowed to marry?"

"Yes, of course they are. But I didn't think a man could do both things well. And I chose to be a warrior, not a husband."

"What about Ahmose?"

"He'll be there, too. I love him dearly, and he loves me, but he's very independent, half grown already. It's not the same as when Naomi crawls in my lap. He doesn't… he doesn't *need* me. I don't care if I wasn't there at the beginning. I want to be there now and every day for the rest of their lives, if you'll let me."

She touched his face, and a smile slowly formed on her perfect lips.

"Well?"

"Well, what?" She blinked several times.

"Will you marry me?" His chest tightened. Was she going to say no?

"Yes. Of course I will. Didn't I say that?"

Kamose laughed. "No, you didn't."

She smiled again. "Sorry. I must already have been thinking about what it would be like to be your wife."

"And?"

"And it would be wonderful." She placed her hand on his cheek. "No one has ever treated me like you do. No one has ever talked to me the way you do. I could spend a lifetime listening to your voice."

"And I could spend a lifetime making sure you hear it."

Thirteen

21 Tammuz

Gaddiel kicked away the long brown seeds that had fallen from the tree. They were huge, and some had points that pricked his fingers. How could there be so many? Such messy trees. The branches started too far down. The leaves were skinny and poky. They didn't give any fruit, either. They had a nice scent, though. Still, he much preferred the date palms.

He wandered from the grove of trees toward the spring. Water bubbled up to fill it then spilled over into a river. Farther north the river dropped into a rocky gorge and continued. It looked like the spring back at camp. How could so much be the same, but so different at the same time?

The camp sat in a valley between two mountain ranges. On the slopes grew the massive, valuable cedar trees Egypt imported to build their furniture for the palace—and chariots. Plenty of those lay buried under the Yam Suph now, along with their drivers and Ramses's soldiers. The cedars were as wide as they were tall, and they made a beautiful sight covering the mountainside.

He returned to the pine grove and sat. A small brown animal with a fluffy tail as big as its body ran in front of him and up a tree, chattering as loudly as he could. Another waited in the branches, and together they ran to the top of the tree out of sight.

Was the whole thing worth it? It had been—what? A year and a few months. It felt like an eternity since they had left Egypt. And what had been accomplished? Not enough. Not enough to make it worthwhile. Not for him.

He lay back and tucked his arms under his head. Two battles already—Rephidim and Sinai. How many dead? How many had he killed himself? And now they were supposed to fight giants just so they could build little houses and little farms to try to coax enough food out of the ground to stay alive. Or keep enough sheep and goats healthy to sell milk and buy food. Anyway you looked at it, it would be far more work than back in Egypt. He came home at the same time every night there. So he didn't get to choose a job. Was that so bad? At least he wasn't fighting for his life.

He stared at the strange trees. He didn't like them, but the fallen needles made for a very soft bed. He rolled over, and went to sleep. The questions would have to wait for tomorrow.

ॐ∽

Gaddiel awoke after everyone else. *First time that's happened since the first day out.* He'd been up too late thinking about the trip, the escape, Joshua, everything. The aroma of roasting fish filled his nostrils and his mouth watered. He stretched and stood, then walked to the campfire at the river, plopping down next to Palti.

"This is the end. This is Lebo. We turn back today." Caleb stuffed a bite of fish in his mouth.

Gaddiel exhaled loudly. "This is the end?" The wave of relief that washed over him took him by surprise. It was if he had been holding his breath for the last three and a half weeks.

Caleb chuckled. "We have to go all the way back, but, yes. It should be faster going back, since we won't be exploring or finding our way. But we'll stop at Abraham's grave near Hebron."

What? Is that necessary? Gaddiel barely stopped himself from speaking aloud.

"For today," said Joshua, "we can rest here a day, or head back now. What do you think?"

Joshua asking for their opinions? That was new.

Palti volunteered his thoughts first. "We've had Sabbath rests. I think we should move on."

Sethur, Igal, and Geuel nodded their agreement.

"How long have we been gone?" Palti asked.

Joshua pulled out a parchment with marks on it. "Twenty-two days."

"I wouldn't mind an extra day's rest," said Ammiel.

"Nor I," said Shammua.

"Anyone else?" Joshua looked around at those who had not spoken.

"I'd rather get home." Gaddiel reached for a fish. "Soon."

The others grabbed fish. All were silent for a while as they ate. The spring bubbling, the bulbuls singing, and mouths smacking were the only sounds.

"I think it's been a successful mission." Caleb nodded and stuffed another bite of fish in his mouth.

Gaddiel nearly choked. "Successful?"

"Yes. We've accomplished what Moses asked. We know everything we need to know to conquer this land Yahweh has given us."

Gaddiel threw his fish in the fire. "Conquer? We can never conquer it! It is filled with giants and walled cities and Amalekites. We barely beat them the first time. Do you really want to fight them again? Or the giants?"

"Yahweh said He would fight for us. Like he did when we fought the Amalekites. We beat them. We'll conquer anything we find here." Joshua's voice was calm.

Gaddiel stood. "I barely made it through that battle. I have scars all over my body. I certainly don't want to fight another one."

"So you expect everyone else to fight for the land while you sit and wait, so you can move in without working for it?"

"No …"

Joshua rose and jabbed a long finger at Gaddiel. "Then you don't have any other choice. Now sit down and finish eating. We leave as soon as we're done."

Gaddiel stalked off. There were other options. They didn't have to stay here and fight hopeless battles. They didn't have to stay in the wilderness, either.

Back in Egypt they had food. Meat, vegetables, fruit. Not manna. Meal after meal, day after day, week after week. They lived in houses, not tents. It was cooler on the delta. As long as you did your job, life was bearable.

Life here would be far from tolerable. Always looking over your shoulder, waiting for a giant to come eat your children and steal your wife.

Gaddiel couldn't face any more battles. He just couldn't.

23 Tammuz

Tirzah stood next to Kamose, before Moses at the river where the girls so often played. Where she'd fallen in love with Kamose. Meri, holding Adi, stood next to Bezalel. Nahshon was next to Sheerah, who had Naomi on her hip. Ahmose grasped Keren's little hand in his.

She thought back to her first wedding day. She didn't remember very much of it—she had been so nervous. She'd had no friends with her then, and she barely knew Jediel. She'd gone into that marriage alone, but expecting she would have a husband to share her life with. She'd been wrong.

This time would be different. Wouldn't it? She met Kamose's gaze. His smile told her everything she needed to know.

Moses handed Kamose a skin of water. "In view of the circumstances, and since there is no bride price or betrothal period involved, we will first share the cup. We have no wine, obviously, so we will make do with water."

"Wait." Bezalel produced a gold cup.

Kamose's eyes widened as he reached for it.

"Where did you…" Tirzah began.

"From the palace." Bezalel grinned. "We used it when we married." He linked hands with Meri.

Kamose filled the cup and handed it to Tirzah.

Tirzah took it, keeping her gaze on Kamose. She drank half and handed it back.

Kamose finished it and returned the cup.

"Since by accepting the cup you have accepted his proposal, I shall now bless—and marry—you." Moses raised his hands over the heads of the new couple. "Blessed are You, Yahweh, who has heard our cries and delivered us from Egypt. Blessed are You, El Shaddai, the Creator of the earth and all that is in it. Blessed are You, Yahweh, who has brought together these two people who will love and care for each other as no one else can. Bless them and grant them wisdom and strength to carry out whatever tasks You place before them, to care for their family, to love all those You bring into their lives.

"And to you two, I say, if you dwell in the shelter of Shaddai, He will be your refuge and your fortress. If you say, 'Yahweh is my refuge,' and you make El Shaddai your dwelling, no harm will overtake you, no disaster will come near your tent. If you love Him, He will rescue you; He will protect you, if you acknowledge His name. If you call on Him, He will answer you; He will be with you in trouble; He will deliver you. With long life He will satisfy you and show you His salvation.

"Now may Yahweh bless you and make you fruitful. May He keep you faithful to Him and to each other. May He grant your children a long life in the land He is giving us."

After a simple meal with their friends, Tirzah followed Kamose as he took her hand and led her into her tent in Zebulon. They had chosen to spend their bridal week there, knowing that the girls would be well taken care of by Meri and Sheerah in Judah without having to wonder why they couldn't go into their tent or see their mother for seven days.

Kamose lifted the basket of manna cakes and dates sitting next to skins of water and goat's milk in the corner. "Are you hungry?"

She shook her head.

He reached for the far-too-short wedding robe she had borrowed from Sheerah and slipped it from her shoulders. Draping it over his arm, he rubbed his hands down her arms, and the warmth of his touch traveled all the way to her toes.

She smiled at the robe he wore. Nahshon's, it was so small he hadn't even tried to wear it and had simply draped it over his broad shoulders.

He shrugged it off and tossed both garments in the corner.

She stepped closer to him and rested her cheek against his chest, her arms pulled up by her shoulders. She felt his heartbeat under her ear as he rubbed her back. His steady breathing infused her with calm.

He buried his hands in her hair. His fingers moved softly against her neck, sending shivers of pleasure throughout her body. The warmth and solidity of his frame next to hers made her blood heat and her breath come faster.

She circled his back with her arms, and lifted her face to his.

He smiled, and brushed her lips with his. As he cradled her head with one hand, he brought his other down her back to her waist. He covered her mouth with his, and for several moments she lost herself in his kiss.

She moved her hands from his back to his chest, around his neck.

When he slid his hand from her waist down her hip, she stiffened. Memories—bad memories—washed over her.

He raised his head but still held her close. Confusion filled his eyes. "What's wrong?"

How did she explain it? "Nothing. It's just that … this part … was never very pleasant … before."

He tilted his head and studied her. "Do you like my kisses?"

Her cheeks heated, and she looked away. "I love your kisses." She pulled her gaze back to his. "Your kisses make me forget anyone else exists."

A small but satisfied smile crossed his face. "And are my kisses like Jediel's?"

She frowned, annoyed she should have to explain this again. "Your kisses are nothing like Jediel's. I've told you that."

For a long moment he drew his fingers lightly over her jaw, down her neck, traced the edge of her tunic.

She closed her eyes and sighed, tipped her head back as she delighted in his touch. Her heart raced.

"Then I doubt anything else that happens tonight will be like it was with Jediel, either." He kissed her neck. "In fact, other than being a man, I don't think anything I ever do will remind you of him." He whispered in her ear. "I promise you that. Will you trust me?"

At that moment, with his lips leaving a trail of soft kisses along her neck, she could barely think, let alone speak. But then his mouth found hers again, and she didn't have to. And when his hands again began to caress her, this time she did not resist.

స~ళ

Kamose blinked several times. The tent was bright. How long had he slept? He hadn't slept past dawn in years.

Beside him, Tirzah stirred, her body soft against his. Her head rested on his shoulder, her hand on his chest. His arm was wrapped around her waist, and he drew her closer.

She did not awaken.

He rolled onto his side and encircled her with both arms. She snuggled into his chest. He'd be content to stay this way forever. Even if it meant being a farmer, a shepherd, or a household servant. He'd had enough glory to last a lifetime. He'd done everything he wanted. As long as he could fall asleep next to her, and wake with her in his arms every morning, he'd be content to do anything else all day long.

1 Av

Kamose pushed aside the flaps of the tent. Sunlight poured in as he pulled in a plate, as he had three times a day for the last seven days. Meri and Sheerah had gathered manna for the new couple, cooked it, and delivered it along with dates, milk, and water, to the tent in Zebulon. But this was the last time. Their bridal week was over. He sighed. He missed the girls, but he'd very much enjoyed having Tirzah all to himself for a week.

He popped a date in his mouth and set the plate aside, then stuck his hands out once more for another bundle.

"What are you doing?" Tirzah picked up the skin of milk and poured two cups.

He grinned over his shoulder at his new bride, and winked. "One moment." He sat back next to her and shook out an Israelite tunic.

Tirzah's eyes widened. "What's that for?"

"For me."

"But why?" She ran her hand over the fabric lying across his lap.

"I'm no longer an Egyptian soldier. It's time I stopped looking like one. I asked Bezalel to find a tunic for me before we went back to camp. Help me put it on." He rose up on his knees and turned it upside down, fumbling for the bottom hem. He stuffed his arms through and she pulled it down over his head.

She suppressed a smile as she tugged on the short sleeves, drawing them over his shoulders.

"At least it's big enough." He chuckled as he pulled at the garment, straightened it, and then fastened his belt over it around his waist.

"Barely." Giggling, she ran her hands over his shoulders and down his arms.

He gathered her to him and kissed her. Did they have to go back? Reaching into the corner by his sandals, he retrieved the armbands he had not worn all week. He placed them in the small cloth bag delivered with the tunic, tied the string, and set it by the door. Then he grabbed the plate of manna cakes, and settled next to her.

Her eyes glistened with unshed tears.

His chest constricted. What should he do? "Did I do something wrong?" He set the plate down and put his hands on her face.

"Why did you do that?"

"Do what?"

"Put your armbands away."

He looked back at the bag and shrugged. "I-I'm not a captain anymore. I shouldn't be wearing them."

"You've worn them ever since we left. For more than a year."

"Yes, and I didn't need to. I probably shouldn't have. I never thought about it. I simply put them on every morning like I had for years."

She cried harder.

He brushed her tears away with his thumbs. "Habibti, I don't understand why you are crying. You have to explain this to me."

"Did … did I … did I make you give all this up?"

"Give all what up?"

"Being the captain."

He shook his head. "Habibti, I gave that up when I left Egypt."

"Then why are you only now putting on a tunic, taking off your armbands? After you marry me?"

"Because only now am I happy I gave it all up. Now I have something to exchange it for."

She took several shuddering breaths. "Are you sure? Are you sure you won't blame me someday?"

He kissed her cheeks, wet with tears, then drew her close. "Never. I gained far more when I married you than I ever gave up."

After they ate, Kamose held Tirzah's hand as they strolled toward Bezalel and Meri's tent.

Keren's eyes lit up when she saw them and she bolted for them. She ran to Kamose first and jumped into his arms.

Tirzah laughed as Keren slid from Kamose to her. "Imma! I missed you." She gave Tirzah a slobbery kiss and wiggled back down, then ran away.

Kamose noticed Bezalel and Meri, Nahshon and Sheerah—and Rebekah holding baby Adi. How long had it been since Rebekah had been at their fire? She stood and smiled broadly as they approached. "Captain! It is good to see you."

He smiled. "Not Captain. Just Kamose."

"Yes, yes." She handed Adi to Bezalel as she passed him and came to Tirzah, wrapping her in a warm hug. "Tirzah, habibti, come sit with me. I need to get to know you. I had no idea our captain would ever get married, and I must know who could change his mind."

"Uh, all right." Tirzah glanced back at Kamose as she was led to the other side of the fire.

Kamose took a seat by Bezalel.

"I'd have warned you if I knew she was coming." Bezalel laughed as he watched his mother do to Tirzah what she'd done to Meri more than a year ago. "She's doing better than Meri did, though."

"Meri had just ridden across the desert with me and had the army at her back."

"True."

Keren bounded back into camp with Naomi and Ahmose.

"See?" Keren pointed at the couple. "They're home!"

Ahmose ran up to his uncle and wrapped his arms around his neck. "Uncle!"

"Ahmose!" Kamose squeezed him tightly. "Were you a big help?"

"He was a huge help," said Meri. "I don't know what we would have done without him."

Ahmose beamed at Meri, then looked back at Kamose. "I'm glad you're home."

"Me too, habibi." Kamose kissed his nephew's cheek.

Ahmose pulled back as Naomi stepped out of Tirzah's arms.

Kamose held his arms out. "Come here."

She brightened and buried her face in his neck.

He held her close for several moments. "I missed you, habibti."

"I missed you, Abba," she whispered, before she kissed him and ran off after Keren.

His heart nearly exploded. This was a word he never thought he'd hear himself called. Even marrying Tirzah, loving Keren and Naomi as he did, he had not expected them to see him as their abba. He assumed he'd love and care for them, and they'd love him in return, but not this. This was... beyond anything he could ever have hoped for. He closed his eyes and prayed he wouldn't cry in front of everyone.

Bezalel leaned close. "I heard that."

Kamose threw him a sideways glance.

Bezalel smiled. "Adi doesn't talk yet, of course, but she knows I'm her abba. Sometimes in the middle of the night, when she's very fussy and even Meri can't quiet her, I hold her, and she'll rest her head on my chest and grab my tunic in her little fist and be calm." He paused. "It's a little scary, to be so responsible for someone, but the love you get back in return... there's no feeling like it in the world. Feels pretty good, doesn't it?"

Naomi's voice saying "Abba" echoed in Kamose's head. Good didn't even begin to describe it.

Fourteen

2 Av

Gaddiel threw the seed of the fig he'd finished into the dust at his feet. They had been looking for the cave long enough. He didn't see the point to begin with, and now they were wasting valuable time. And they were perilously close to Hebron and its giants. Every time he looked south toward the towering walls, he shuddered.

Caleb frowned. "It's got to be around here somewhere. It's north of Hebron, next to an empty plot of land."

The sun was sailing westward and they were losing light. Joshua climbed up on a hillock and shaded his eyes.

"It doesn't rise up much above the ground. Do you see anything?" Caleb called to Joshua.

Couldn't he be quieter? They were probably far enough away from Hebron, but why take chances? Did they really need to visit the graves of their ancestors?

"Over there." Joshua pointed toward a group of trees to the east.

Gaddiel rolled his eyes and hiked in the direction Joshua pointed, following Caleb. Down off the crest of the mountain ridge, the land was green and full of trees. The air was cooler; it even smelled fresher.

They reached a rounded plot of land, rising to near the height of Caleb's shoulders. Caleb walked all around it, disappearing on the other side for several moments. When he returned, his face was solemn. "I found the entrance." He beckoned them to follow.

They crowded before the small, dark entrance to the cave. The mound of earth, topped with smooth rocks, was unimpressive. Giant trees as old as creation itself surrounded the site like silent sentries. A breeze rustled the leaves above them.

It was impossible to stand before this burial site, this holy ground, and remain unaffected. Even if he thought the rest of the trip was useless, standing before the eternal resting place of Abraham and Sarah, Isaac and Rebekah, Jacob and Leah, connected to a spot in Gaddiel's heart he didn't know existed. His skin tingled, and the other sights and sounds around him seemed to fall away as he concentrated on the spot of land before him.

Caleb's voice broke through his reverie. "… one or two at a time. It slopes down, so be careful." He pointed down into the open mouth of the sepulcher.

Joshua and Shammua went in first.

The stories he had heard all his life echoed in Gaddiel's head. Abraham being called by Yahweh, and Yahweh's promises to him—promises to make his descendants as numerous as the sand on the shore. Isaac on the altar. Jacob and Esau, fighting over the birthright. Jacob working fourteen years for Rachel. Joseph and his coat. Joseph sold to Egypt—which started everything.

Gaddiel envied their faith. In all those stories, they talked to Yahweh, believed every word He said. Abraham ate with angels. Jacob wrestled with God. Joseph believed in the face of overwhelming persecution. Why couldn't Yahweh tell Gaddiel more clearly what to do?

Joshua and Shammua exited, and Gaddiel and Palti went in next. Gaddiel dropped to the ground and followed Palti down a narrow passageway. Pebbles cut into his hands and knees as they crawled. His head bumped the roof several times, raining down a shower of dirt.

The passageway spilled into a room tall enough to rise comfortably off his feet, but not stand up straight.

The smell of cold stone and stale air surrounded him. The silence weighed heavily. On each side lay three bodies placed head to toe on a narrow ledge dug out of the rock. Their names were etched on the stone above them. Gaddiel paused before each one. Careful not to touch the bones, he swept away a cobweb hanging over Abraham. Except for a brief time in Egypt because of a famine, Abraham spent his life in Canaan. Left a comfortable life in Ur and traveled who knows how long to get here because Yahweh said it was good. That kind of faith…

A squeak startled Gaddiel. A tiny white-spotted mouse skittered around a corner. Gaddiel took a step from Abraham to Isaac. Isaac had never lived anywhere else. He lived all one hundred eighty years of life in this land. He couldn't bring himself to marry any of the women here though, and sent his servant far away to find him a wife among his distant kinsmen. Didn't say much for Canaan.

Gaddiel moved over to Jacob. Jacob, too, left Canaan to find a wife. He returned, but left again when famine struck. Didn't seem like the land was able to keep most people fed very well.

Gaddiel placed his hand on the cold rock above his head as he twisted to look at the matriarchs, each one faithfully across from her husband; Sarah, Rebekah, Leah. Jacob's favorite, Rachel, had been buried near Bethlehem after she died birthing Benjamin.

His back ached from slumping and he crawled back out. He stretched, arms high above his head, trying to get the kinks out. An eagle screeched as it soared above him in lazy, ever-widening circles.

He thought about Tirzah and the girls—what were their names again… he couldn't remember. Whether Gaddiel married her—and he definitely didn't want to—or Nathaniel did, they were his brother's children and therefore Gaddiel's responsibility. He needed to make sure they were properly cared for.

He crossed his arms over his chest. Bringing them to this land would be a mistake. Nathaniel would be at war almost immediately and constantly. There were wild animals everywhere. It would take forever to get crops growing—what would they eat until then? They'd have to build houses and villages … and what if famine struck again, as it did for Abraham and Jacob?

He frowned and shook his head. It wasn't safe. This whole trip was a mistake. Maybe the troubles so far had been warnings, and they shouldn't have ignored them. The lack of water, food, the heat, the endless desert …

Joseph left Canaan. Well, he was sold, but when his brothers found him, he had them bring his father and his entire family to Egypt. When they left Canaan, there were only seventy of them. In Egypt, land of abundance, they grew to a great number of people. If they came back here, they would only be defeated again. This place was dangerous. Joseph knew it. Gaddiel knew it.

And he bet that deep down, Joshua and Caleb knew it, too.

6 Av

Gaddiel awoke in a sweat after fitful dreams of giants chasing him and chariots running him down. He sat up and wiped his brow, then put his head in his hands. He exhaled a deep sigh. They were south of Hebron; surely they were almost home.

He smelled grouse cooking over a fire. He was getting about as tired of grouse as he was of manna.

Maybe not. Nothing could be worse than manna.

He packed his bag, then headed toward the fire and filled his stomach with meat.

Joshua stood and addressed the group. "We're getting close to the end of the fertile ground. Tomorrow we'll be in the desert. If we're going to bring home fruit, we need to get it now. Gaddiel, you found the grapes last time. Do you remember where they were?"

Of course I remember. I'm not stupid. Gaddiel had had enough of Joshua, giants, cities—of everything in Canaan altogether. He just wanted to go home and never come back. "They're a little past Arad, in a valley."

"We should be there by tonight. We'll get the grapes and be home in two days."

Two days. The most wonderful words he'd heard in a long time.

As the sun was nearing the western mountaintops, they reached the vineyard. Gaddiel combed the vines for exactly the right branch to cut. He raised his hand to slice one.

"Gaddiel, stop!" Joshua's strident voice caused Gaddiel to jump.

What now? Gaddiel hung his head.

"It's so close to sunset, I think we should wait until morning to keep the fruit as fresh as we can."

"What? Why? There's enough light and the moon is half-full. We can get closer to home before we stop."

"But that's it. Then we have to stop, and put the grapes down one more time. If we leave at first light, and push hard, we only have one night."

Gaddiel sighed heavily. "It took us three days to get here. You think we can make it back in two?"

"It's always faster going downhill. We can be in camp before sunset day after tomorrow."

Gaddiel shoved his knife back into its sheath. "Whatever you say. I'm going to at least determine which are the best grapes to take now, though, even if I don't cut them, to save time in the morning."

"Excellent idea."

Thanks for your approval. Gaddiel returned to the heavy, drooping vines. The grapes had grown in the weeks since they had passed here. He pushed aside tendrils and fruit and looked for the right branches. Even a single bunch would be too much for one man. One bunch weighed a much as a young child and was much longer. And they were traveling farther. They couldn't carry them in their packs, like last time—they'd be bruised and maybe squashed by the time they reached camp. To avoid dragging the ground they'd have to be held almost above their heads, and no one could do that for long.

He growled and plopped down among the trees the vines had overtaken. Tendrils stretched from one branch to another, even from one tree to another, spreading the fruit over an ever-widening area. As he stared at one vine hanging between two trees, its fruit swinging below in the evening breeze, the solution came to him.

He grabbed his knife and searched for the perfect piece he needed.

క్ర

The squawking awoke him. He opened one eye to see a preying kestrel hover over the fields, searching for fleeing mice. The bright sun hadn't completely chased away the night's chill, but it was comfortable.

He'd been up late preparing what they needed, but it didn't matter. He wanted nothing to interfere. He intended to leave on time and arrive tomorrow before sundown.

He retrieved his handiwork and returned to the circle of scouts to address the group. "Here is what we need to do."

Joshua raised an eyebrow but did not interrupt.

Holding a long and fairly straight branch, Gaddiel continued. "I've removed the bark and smoothed this as much as possible, especially near the ends. We carry this between two men, on their shoulders. We drape the bunch over the wood so it doesn't drag the ground. This divides the weight and makes sure the fruit stays out of the dirt and doesn't bruise."

Joshua took the wood from him and ran his hands along the pole, then nodded. "Very nice. Good work and great idea. Let's get some men and cut some grapes."

Gaddiel headed toward the vines while Joshua chose a few men to help him.

Igal and Palti showed up first, and Gaddiel placed the pole on their shoulders. "Someone else will have to carry your packs. Shammua and Ammiel, help me with the cutting." He showed them the bunch he'd picked out last night. They held it high while he grasped his knife and freed it from the rest of the branch. Near the end it began to rip. "Don't let it fall!" They dove to catch it before the grapes smashed to the ground.

The cluster safely in hand, the three of them struggled to lift it over the pole. Igal and Palti squatted to make it a bit easier, and finally the fruit straddled the pole and Gaddiel was certain it would stay there.

Joshua jerked his thumb over his shoulder. "We've got a lot of ground to cover. Let's go."

Geuel and Nahbi strolled over, packs in hand. Geuel frowned. "What about food?"

Gaddiel scoffed and pointed to the vines. "Eat some grapes." Then he set off after Joshua. He wasn't stopping for anything now.

Fifteen

Standing on the hillock north of Dan, Gaddiel shaded his eyes against the bright sunlight. The twelve, along with Moses and Aaron, perched atop it, facing the assembly. The cliffs to the east and the low hills around the rest of the oasis made their voices easy to hear.

They'd dragged themselves into camp to cheers and slaps on the back. It had taken half a day longer than they planned, and they'd arrived just before midday. Before they even had a chance to wash their faces or eat, Moses herded them like so many sheep onto this raised portion of earth to report on their mission. Gaddiel just wanted to eat, sleep, and forget about the whole thing.

That would come later. At least he was home.

Gaddiel's head ached as Caleb droned on. "The land is beautiful. It abounds with grapes, pomegranates, figs, and other fruit we have never even seen. We can grow anything we wish. We brought a sample of the fruit of the land." He signaled to Nahbi and Igal.

The two lanky men emerged from behind the others, hiked down the hill, and waded into the crowd, carrying the pole, now bent under the constant weight of its bouncing, edible load. The crowd parted like the sea did eighteen months earlier. A few reached out to touch the grapes; most backed away, eyes wide, hands over mouths.

Ammiel bumped Gaddiel as he placed a basket full of figs bigger than his fist at Moses's feet.

Gaddiel glared at the younger man, but Ammiel was far too excited to notice.

Sethur and Palti followed with a load of pomegranates the size of small melons.

Gaddiel dug his nails into his fists. All this produce was going to blind everyone to the truth. Yes, there was food. But at what price?

Joshua offered a couple of grapes to Moses while Caleb continued. "Grassy plains for supporting cattle, sheep, and goats are everywhere. Rivers, lakes, a sea to the west. Hills, mountains. Whatever anyone wants to do, it can be done in the land Yahweh has given us."

For several moments the Israelites roared their delight. Men hugged their wives and swung their children in the air. Women cried in relief. Four hundred years of captivity and more than a year of waiting were almost over.

Gaddiel rubbed his forehead as if that would make the pain lessen. This wasn't going well. He needed to say something before it went too far. He had to at least try, even if in the end Caleb and Joshua got their way. The people deserved to know the whole truth, and right now Caleb wasn't telling it.

"Wait!" Gaddiel waved his arms for silence. "Wait! Caleb is not telling you everything."

Embraces fell open, squeals faded, heads turned toward Gaddiel. A hush worked its way through the crowd.

"He is telling you only what you want to hear, the part that makes him look good. He's keeping secrets."

"What are you trying to do?" Joshua stepped forward, his spear tilted toward Gaddiel.

Caleb extended his arm and nudged Joshua aside, closing the distance between himself and Gaddiel. "I am not keeping secrets."

Those closest to the hillock drew nearer, then whispered the conversation to those behind them.

"Let's talk about the cities." Gaddiel spoke through clenched teeth.

Caleb spread his arms and smiled. "Very well, let's talk about the cities."

Gaddiel faced the assembly. "The cities are walled. The walls are high, thick, and impossible to breach. We cannot take them."

Murmurs and whispers rippled through the crowd like a wave on the sea.

A few of the spies moved to stand behind Gaddiel.

Palti joined in. "They have water supplies and are stocked with enough food to last for weeks."

Joshua stepped to the front. "Yahweh has said He will be with us. We can take any city He has given to us. There is nothing to fear."

"Nothing to fear? The people there sacrifice their children! They place babies on an altar of fire to their false gods. They will steal our children as well!" That was a stretch, and totally untrue, but Gaddiel knew it would get a reaction. And it did. From both the crowd and Joshua.

The crowd gasped. Women clutched their babies. Fathers grasped the hands of their children and pulled them closer.

Joshua pointed to Gaddiel. "That's the most ridiculous thing I've ever heard! You're only trying to scare everyone!"

"Then why don't you tell them about the giants? We all saw them." Gaddiel raised his hand far over his head to indicate height. "They tower over us—they were three times our size. They could snap us like twigs. Each one had a long, double-edged knife strapped to his hip. They ripped animals apart with their bare hands and ate the meat raw." Gaddiel glared at Caleb.

Joshua strode toward Gaddiel, fist raised. "You are lying! None of that is true."

Maybe. But it will keep us out of that terrible place. Gaddiel faced the Israelites again. "It's true. They are Nephilim."

Now the women cried, but in fear, not relief. Some fainted. Children who were old enough to understand ran back to the tents.

Caleb held up his hands, palms out, to quiet the people. "Men of Israel, listen to me. They are not Nephilim. Yahweh destroyed the Nephilim. They are the sons of Anak—descendants of Nephilim, and yes, they are large. But Gaddiel exaggerates greatly. They were perhaps twice our height, and they were not carrying weapons of any kind. We can overcome them."

"Caleb speaks the truth." Joshua pointed to Gaddiel. "He lies! They are not Nephilim! They are only Anakim. We will go and take the land. We can defeat them. Yahweh has given us the land. He has already promised it. All we have to do is obey."

The rest of the spies moved to stand behind Gaddiel.

Finally, visible support. Just a few more well-chosen words.... "Obey? We obey, we die! We are like ... like ... grasshoppers to them. They would just as soon stomp on us. We cannot win against them."

Joshua tried once more. "We will not be alone—"

"And they're not the only enemy." Gaddiel paused to let his words sink in. "Caleb makes it sound like the land is ours just by moving in. But the Amalekites dwell in the south, the Hittites and the Amorites live in the mountains, and the Canaanites have claimed the coast."

"You don't know that—we didn't go to those places." Caleb drilled a stare through Gaddiel.

"I heard talk."

"Talk is not always true, as you well know."

Gaddiel turned again to the crowd. Now for the final blow. "This land—this land that *Moses* sent us to—devours its enemies. Our men would be in battle constantly, our women and children in danger. Is this what you want? Is this what we left Egypt for?"

A dark-haired man in the front of the assembly stepped forward. "At least in Egypt we had food! And our wives and children were safe."

Exactly.

Another joined the first. "We should go back. You!" He pointed to Gaddiel. "You want to be our leader?"

The question hit Gaddiel like a punch in the gut. Forty days ago, that was exactly what he wanted. Now, he wasn't so sure. Fear competed with his pride. Did he want to go back to Egypt? Yes. As their leader? Maybe. All he knew for certain was he didn't want to live—let alone fight—in Canaan.

⋞⋟

Kamose's heart was as heavy as one of the rocks the spies now stood on, not because he feared they could not take the land, but because the people had rejected Yahweh's promise.

He'd seen Yahweh push back the Yam Suph, destroy Pharaoh's army, defeat the Amalekites, send the manna. So had everyone else. Why couldn't they believe He could do it again?

Maybe because as a soldier, he knew personally how impossible those victories were without Yahweh's help. He'd led the Egyptian army, experienced himself what the Amalekites were capable of, gone hungry and without water in the desert. He'd taken days to go the long way around the Yam Suph because no one had ever crossed it before.

Had the Israelites already taken it all for granted?

He glanced around. The crowd was working itself into a frenzy.

Caleb tried to shout over the crowd. "This is not the land *Moses* sent us to. It is the land *Yahweh* has given us. We only need to obey."

The dark-haired man in front, not overly tall but strong looking, stepped forward again. "Yahweh brought us here just to let the Anakim kill us! We should go back!"

Others joined him. "At least there we had food! I'm sick of manna!"

"We want meat again!"

The man turned and faced the crowd. "Stone them!" He raised his fist in the air.

The crowd joined the chant. "Stone them! Stone them!" Men around Kamose began to search for rocks. Some headed for the low hills to bring back the rocks at their bases.

Naomi grabbed at Tirzah's skirt. Keren reached for Ahmose's hand.

"Get back to the tents. Quick!" Kamose pointed Tirzah and Meri toward their fire. "Go now!"

"This is crazy. How did it all change so fast?" Bezalel shook his head and looked to Kamose for an answer.

But Kamose bolted for the hillock.

Moses and Aaron dropped to their knees, then on their faces, and cried out to Yahweh.

Caleb tore his clothes as he pleaded with the increasingly panicky crowd. "Don't do this! We can take the land. Do not rebel against Yahweh. Remember what he has already done. Remember the Yam Suph. Remember the Amalekites. Remember the water from the rock."

Joshua ripped his tunic. "Do not disobey! Yahweh is with us. He is not with the Canaanites. We will win! Do not listen to Gaddiel!"

"Our wives and children will be taken as slaves! We have to go back. At least in Egypt we were safe." Gaddiel continued to excite the people. His skin was flushed, and he was breathing quickly. He was beyond reasoning with. Although he was acting like a wild man, it did seem as if he truly believed everything he said.

Kamose looked out over the frantic people. It was no use. He'd seen it before. Panic had set in. They couldn't hear anything. There was no stopping them. He placed himself between the crowd and Moses, who was kneeling, head cushioned on his hands. At least Kamose could keep him from harm.

The people continued shouting down Caleb and Joshua. "The Canaanites will kill us!"

"No!" Joshua said. "As long as we have Yahweh with us, they have no chance against us, no matter how big they are."

"But we can't see Yahweh. How can we know He is with us? How can we be sure He will be there?"

Gaddiel had the crowd firmly behind him. Every time Joshua or Caleb tried to speak, the people shouted them down.

Behind the people, back in the center of camp, movement caught Kamose's eye. The ever-present cloud above them, normally a soft white during the day, glowed hotter and brighter. A tail of the cloud dipped toward the tabernacle until it touched the roof, glowing stronger as it grew. It burned from within, yet did not set the tent ablaze.

Although Moses hadn't been watching anything, he somehow knew what had happened. Kamose watched, amazed, as Moses stood, silently left the hillock. and strode toward the Holy Place. Aaron followed.

A hush fell over the people as the brothers passed. Fingers pointed to the sky and to the tent. People who moments ago were ready to throw rocks at him just let their leader pass, untouched. Most sat down, apparently willing to wait until Moses returned from talking to Yahweh.

Kamose breathed a long sigh of relief. Calm had returned, at least for now. And no one had been injured.

Joshua clambered down and stood beside Kamose.

Kamose glanced at him. "What do you think will happen?"

Joshua shrugged. "I have no idea. But I don't think Yahweh is very happy with us." He plopped to the ground. "Why can't they just trust Him?"

Kamose sat beside him. "Joshua, as I've said before, you have a faith that very few have. You can see a future that most men cannot."

"But is it asking too much?"

Kamose thought about that. "No. It is not."

Joshua was silent for a moment, then he turned and stared at Kamose's clothing. "Why are you in a tunic?"

Kamose smiled. "Later."

After more than an hour, the cloud lifted. An aisle appeared in the crowd, and Moses approached the hillock. His face was ashen.

Kamose jumped up to help him ascend. Joshua and Aaron followed.

The old man faced the people.

A hush rippled over the Israelites.

"Yahweh is angry that you do not trust Him, that you do not believe He will go before you into Canaan. After all the signs He performed in Egypt and on the way here, you have treated Him with distrust and contempt."

The Israelites began to murmur. Men rubbed their hands over their faces. Women hugged themselves. Shoulders slumped as sandals dug in the dirt.

"And so this is His judgment: Not one of you who has witnessed His glory, who has disobeyed and tested Him over and over again, not one of you will see the land He promised He would give to you. You will stay here in the wilderness for forty years—one year for every day the scouts spent in Canaan. The very thing you feared, will happen to you—you will die in this wilderness. As for the children you said would be taken as slaves, they will enjoy the land He promised you."

Wails and cries came from the people. Some women fainted, while others dropped to their knees and clasped hands at their chests and begged. "No, we're sorry. We believe now. Give us another chance!"

Moses raised a hand, and the crowd fell silent. "Of the scouts, only Caleb and Joshua, who believed the promises Yahweh made to all of you, will go into Canaan. As for those who refused to believe Yahweh, who came back and lied to you, lied about Yahweh, lied about His land, today will be the last day they will ever draw breath."

ॐॐ

Gaddiel stumbled down the hill. It was difficult to walk straight. He wobbled on his feet. He drew the back of his hand across his forehead and it came away wet. His head spun and his stomach churned. He swallowed back a bit of bile.

Surely he did not hear what he thought he heard. His last day to draw breath? Was what he had done really so bad? All he had wanted to do was keep from fighting those giants.

And get a little glory for himself.

And take some away from Joshua.

Maybe it was that bad.

But he wasn't trying to show any "contempt" for Yahweh.

At least he didn't think so.

His stomach spasmed.

He reached his tent and fell onto his sleeping mat. Maybe he just needed to sleep. It had been a grueling forty days.

ॐॐ

Violent stomach pains jolted him awake. He grabbed his torso and drew his knees up. He groaned.

Tirzah came to the door. "Are you all right?"

Gaddiel tried to speak, but he could only moan. Blistering sweat poured from every part of his body. His clothes were soaked. "H-hot."

She knelt beside him. "Let me take your cloak. You fell asleep with it on." She reached to remove his outer garment, but even the gentlest touch caused excruciating pain. He screamed.

She jerked her arm back. "I'm sorry! Did I hurt you? Are you injured?" The genuine and deep concern on her face shocked him. Had it always been there, or did he only now notice? It was probably there. He just never gave her any credit.

He rolled to one side and tried to pull his sleeve down. She grasped the end and drew it off without causing too much pain. He swayed to the other side and repeated the action.

Tirzah pulled the tent flaps back and tied them open, then did the same on the other side. The cool breeze flowing through felt good on his wet skin, even through his tunic.

Did Yahweh really mean to kill the spies? Except of course for Joshua and Caleb. It wasn't fair. Perfect Joshua. Always wins.

He had told the truth, for the most part. There *were* giants in Canaan. Maybe he exaggerated their size a bit, but he doubted they could win against them. And those cities, those walls. How could they ever breach them?

No, they could never take Canaan.

He was right.

Wasn't he?

He drifted off again.

❧

Once again a wave of pain woke him. Or maybe his own screams, he wasn't sure.

He coughed into his hand. It came away filled with blood. He grasped at his cloak and rubbed the hot liquid onto it. He curled into a ball again, but the pain did not abate. His skin was on fire, like he'd been dropped into an unending flame for which he was the fuel. Pain seared his chest with every cough, and every movement brought new experiences in agony.

Was this what the baby felt like, burning to death in the sacrificial fire in Hazor? Maybe Gaddiel could have tried to save that baby. But there would always be other babies. What good would saving one do?

He could have tried. Should have tried.

Tirzah came in with a large bowl of water and a cloth. She sat beside him and washed his face, then his arms, then his legs. The relief lasted only a few moments, but it calmed him. When she saw it helped, she started all over again.

He lay there, gratefully soaking in the relief. Guilt overwhelmed him. How could she help him after all the cruel things he had said to her? Did to her? Maybe compared to Jediel, his cruelty was easy to endure. Maybe she thought she had no choice. She probably didn't, if she wanted to feed her children.

He didn't even know the names of his nieces. Was he that selfish? Why? What had his wife done to hurt him that much? Nothing he could think of. She actually had tried everything she could to please him. He married because it was expected. He never wanted to be responsible for someone else. He was truly happy when she died giving birth.

He could have been more generous with Jediel's possessions. He could have let Tirzah have it all. It was being done more and more now, letting daughters inherit when there were no sons. He had kept it all because he wanted it, just because he could.

The cloth moved over his face again. The breeze kissed his wet skin and for a moment the pain—only on that part of his body—disappeared.

He opened his eyes and his gaze met hers. He summoned all his energy. "I'm … sorry."

She stopped in midwipe. She stared at him for what felt like forever. She didn't smile. Did he make it worse?

Finally a smile broke across her face. A small one. A sweet one. "It's all right." She took his hand for just a second. It was worth the pain.

გ~ა

Tirzah brought her hand to her mouth. Gaddiel had apologized. She could hardly believe her ears. Was he delirious? He seemed to be sincere. He had no reason to lie any more.

His breathing calmed—he must be asleep again.

She wiped his face once more with the cool cloth, and grabbed the bowl before she stepped outside. Confused and even disparaging stares met her as she exited the tent, and she tried to keep the tears from falling before she left Zebulon and could get back to Judah. Yes, he had been cruel to her, and yes, she had refused to marry him, but did that mean she should withhold from him the most basic of kindnesses as he lay dying? How could his own people—once her own people—judge her for that? She was grateful she was no longer one of them.

Kamose waited for her at their tent. He did not question her tears for another man, a man who had refused to allow her to keep the things she had owned as his brother's wife, who had made her life as a widow even more miserable. She loved Kamose for that, because she wasn't sure she could explain her sorrow.

"Gaddiel is dying," she whispered.

"I know."

"I didn't like him, but I don't want him to die. I don't want anyone to die." She brushed away a tear. "All the spies are dying?"

"So I hear. All but Joshua and Caleb." He put his arm around her shoulders and pulled her close. "You are very kind to tend to him."

"He said he was sorry."

Kamose remained silent.

"I don't know what that means."

Kamose breathed deeply. "I expect that now that he is dying, he realizes he has made a lot of mistakes, and one of them is the way he treated you. Whether he wanted to marry you or not, he could have done better by you. Men tend to stop lying to themselves when they know they are about to die."

૭✌✍

He must have fallen asleep again. The barest amount of pink light showed in the western sky. The ache was gone. But since Gaddiel could not move a single muscle, that could not possibly be a good sign.

He closed his eyes for the last time. The day was over and he was dying. Yahweh had punished him for giving a false report about the mission. And he deserved it. He knew very well he lied when he stood there and said what he had said. Oh, it was true there were giants in the land. He also knew they could have taken any of those cities with Yahweh behind them. But his fear, his lust for power, and his desire to take down Joshua had blinded him to any truth other than the one he had created in his own mind.

And that had cost him his life.

Sixteen

The despondent wailing was relentless. The night had come and was nearly gone, and still the crying continued.

In their tent, Tirzah slid next to Kamose, and he drew her closer. She shut her eyes tight against the unsettling noise. The warm, solid feel of his body next to hers was usually reassuring, but tonight it seemed to have little effect. "Forty years," she whispered. "We will never see Canaan."

He turned toward her and wrapped his other arm around her. "Your children will." He placed a gentle kiss on her forehead.

"At least we won't have to worry about not inheriting any land." She laughed dryly.

"Your daughters will marry and live on their husbands' land and be well taken care of. You don't need to worry about anything. Besides, I thought you said you liked it here, with the manna, and your new friends, and"—he chuckled and kissed her neck— "me." He rolled onto his back.

"I did say that, didn't I?"

"Um hmm."

He rubbed her back a few times, then his breathing slowed. The soft, regular sound soothed her, and she was almost asleep when a new thought jarred her awake. She pushed up on one elbow. "What if we have a child?"

Kamose opened one eye. "Maybe it will be a girl as well."

"What if it's not?"

"Why don't we worry about that later?"

"But he will not be given land. Where will he live?"

He turned his head to fully face her, and with his other hand lifted her chin. "Tirzah, you cared for Gaddiel all day, and it is now more than halfway into the night. You are tired, and when you are tired, you worry."

"I do?"

"Yes, you do. You need to sleep." He slid a hand behind her neck and pulled her back down against his chest. "If Yahweh gives us children, He will provide for them. For now, get some sleep. I fear tomorrow will be a very long day."

She settled her head on his shoulder, but her thoughts continued to stir. Sleep did not come easily.

৵ৡ

Kamose woke early and slipped out of the tent. The camp was awakening slowly, as most of the Israelites had been up deep into the night. He knelt at the fire pit and stirred the embers to a bright red glow.

A droning from the tabernacle drew his attention. He stepped between his tent and the one Ahmose now shared with Rebekah, whenever she stayed in their camp. Joshua's and Moses's tent, behind Kamose's, faced the tabernacle, and Joshua was already awake when Kamose drew near.

"What's the noise about?" Kamose pointed toward the courtyard.

Joshua shrugged one shoulder. "Not sure. We're going to see."

Moses exited the tent. Kamose and Joshua fell in behind him as the old man marched to the center of camp.

A sizable and restless crowd of men already waited. Before Moses could speak, one man stepped forward. "We are ready to go now."

Twin creases appeared between Moses's brows. "Go where?"

A younger man with curly, light brown hair muscled his way forward from the second row. "To Canaan. We are sorry we did not trust Yahweh yesterday, but we realize our error, and we are ready to fight."

Moses shook his head. "I'm sorry, but it doesn't work that way. Your decision was made; now Yahweh has made His."

"But we know we were wrong. We want to fix it."

Moses approached the young man. "What is your name?" he asked gently.

"Lamech."

"Lamech, you are doing the same thing all over again. You are disobeying Yahweh. He said we are to stay."

Lamech folded his arms over his chest. "We're going."

"I can't stop you. But Yahweh will not be with you. You will not succeed; you will be defeated. The Amalekites and the Canaanites will be waiting. Because you have turned away from Yahweh, He will not be with you, and many of you will fall by the sword."

Lamech glared at Moses a long moment, his eyes narrowed. Then his face hardened. "I don't think so. I think we'll win. We've had plenty of practice in battle." He turned and stormed away.

Moses shook his head. "They'll never learn." He headed into the courtyard.

Kamose and Joshua strolled toward their tents. As they neared Joshua's tent, he knelt in front of it. "Give me a moment." He reached inside and brought out a basket of some of the grapes they'd brought back.

They returned to Kamose's fire pit and sat. Joshua grabbed a grape as he eyed Kamose. "So, care to explain the tunic?"

"I'm not an Egyptian soldier anymore."

"You haven't been for over a year. Why now?"

Kamose opened his mouth, but before he could answer, Tirzah emerged from their tent.

Joshua's eyes grew as wide as the grape in his mouth.

She smiled at Kamose. "I'm going to collect the manna. Shall I get yours, Joshua?"

Joshua managed a nod.

After she left, Joshua punched Kamose in the arm. "She's why. Isn't she?"

"Partly."

"You married her? I'm gone less than six weeks and you get married? Who is she? You didn't even know her when I left."

Kamose could not stop the smile that took over his face. "Long story. She had to marry someone. She was a widow. Her brother-in-law was Gaddiel."

Joshua let out a long breath. "Oh-h-h-h. I understand. No woman would want to marry him."

"Well, he didn't want her, either. A younger brother did, though. But he hurt her. I married her to keep her safe."

Joshua smirked. "To keep her safe? That the only reason?"

"Maybe not the only reason." Kamose chuckled as his neck heated.

Naomi and Keren tumbled out of the tent.

Keren wandered into Rebekah's tent, looking for Ahmose. Naomi padded to Kamose and wrapped her arms around his neck. "Morning, Abba." She dropped into Kamose's lap and snuggled against his chest.

"*Abba?*" Joshua laughed. "Oh, this just gets better and better."

Kamose kissed Naomi's head. "Yes, it does."

16 Av

Seven days later, Tirzah knelt at the largest spring north of camp. A fresh breeze blew across the water and she lifted her face. Loose strands of hair blew around her shoulders. Instead of filling her water skins at the stream closer to their camp, today she had chosen to walk in the cooler air and had come all the way to the largest and most beautiful spring, the one where Kamose had first told her he loved her.

She plunged one bag beneath the water, holding it under as the liquid bubbled and gurgled until it filled the skin. She closed it up and laid it aside. As she reached for a second, a cloud of dust to the northwest caught her eye. Returning her attention to her task, she filled the second bag and started on the third, but glanced up several times as she did. The cloud grew larger, louder. She stood and shaded her eyes.

The ball materialized into individual men. They trudged toward camp.

Her chest constricted and she could barely breathe. The water bag slipped from her fingers.

Were they being attacked? Amalekites? Canaanites? The dread squeezed even tighter—the giants Gaddiel had warned them of?

She studied the figures. They weren't big enough to be giants. They didn't carry the long spears of the Amalekites. She glanced over her shoulder at the tents of Issachar and Dan. Women emerged, taking tentative steps toward the foreboding desert, gaping at the approaching men.

One woman put her hands to her face and bolted for the group. She screamed and then headed straight for one of the men and embraced him. Other women followed.

The stragglers were Israelites, the returning fighters who had defied Moses and attacked Canaan. They did not appear triumphant.

Tirzah grabbed her skins and ran for her tent. She nearly skidded into the fire pit. Thank Yahweh it had been banked. "They're back." She dropped the water bags and rested her hands on her knees, gasping for air.

Kamose's face remained unresponsive, but Bezalel's eyes widened. "How do they look?"

"They were quiet, walking slowly. I'm not sure." She shrugged. "They didn't look like the men who came back to their tents after the Amalekite battle."

Kamose retrieved the skins from the ground. "I am sure Moses will call at least their leaders to the tabernacle gates." He tossed the skins in their tent, kissed her cheek, and strode toward the center of camp.

❧⁓

A bedraggled and bloody group of men stood at the gates when Kamose, Bezalel, and Joshua arrived.

Kamose quickly surveyed the men. All were dirty, sweaty, exhausted, and most likely hungry and thirsty. At least half had removed their tunics to wrap spear wounds, or bind injured limbs and feet. The most seriously injured limped in as the rest waited, supported by others.

It was easy to see they had lost the fervor they had marched out with seven days ago, but Kamose's experience told him they had lost faith in their leaders as well. There was no unity left.

Moses stepped out from the courtyard and waited for the leaders to speak.

Lamech spoke first, barely making eye contact. "They were waiting for us. As soon as we entered Canaan, they attacked. Men from Arad, other Canaanites, and Amalekites from even farther west. We tried our best, but there were too many of them, and they were obviously much more experienced in battle." He grimaced as he held his left arm, bound in a blood-spattered sling.

"Did you all return?" Moses asked.

Most of the makeshift soldiers stared at the sand as Lamech spoke. "No. We left many bodies in the desert."

Another added, "We had no chance to bury them. The enemy was still attacking us."

Moses nodded.

Kamose spoke from behind Moses. "Did you leave any wounded behind?"

Lamech stared at Kamose, but would not answer.

Moses moved closer to Lamech. "Answer him."

Lamech narrowed his eyes, and spoke to Moses. "Yes. I am afraid we did. As we got closer to camp, some of the most seriously injured could no longer keep up. Some broken bones, some deep wounds, some too weak to walk. And we had no more men able to help them, and no way to carry them."

"So you just *left* them there?" Kamose had a hard time keeping himself from punching this so-called leader. Had Lamech been one of his commanders, Kamose would have thrown every conceivable punishment he had at him.

"Someone can go get them. They're a couple days' hike away."

Kamose stepped up nose to nose with Lamech. "No. *You* can go get them. You left them."

Lamech huffed. "Not likely."

Kamose took several deep breaths while he convinced himself not to harm Lamech. "How many?"

Lamech stepped around Kamose, and again spoke to Moses. "I'm not sure. Ten. Fifteen." He stared a moment at Moses, then walked away.

Kamose fisted his hands and suppressed a growl. He would never have left his men behind, not even one. What kind of leader did that? Lamech was no leader, that much was certain. He was barely a man.

ॐ✥

Tirzah stared at the bowl of manna in her hand. Two weeks ago, life was wonderful. Kamose had made her his wife. She lived in Judah, with people who loved her, instead of judged her. Naomi was sleeping through the night, every night. The spies were due back with news of Canaan. And even though life would be hard with no land of their own, she looked forward to a new start in a new land.

Then the spies came back and everything changed. Gaddiel was dead. None of them—at least none of the adults—would see Canaan, which wasn't what it seemed, anyway. And as much as spending her life with Kamose here in Kadesh didn't seem so bad, it wasn't the promise they'd left Egypt for.

And now this. A good portion of the camp defying Moses. Some even going off to fight, and coming back defeated. Was the next forty years going to be filled with constant conflict? She could accept Yahweh's judgment. Her children would forge new lives in Canaan and that was enough for her. But she could not take decades of Israel striving with Yahweh.

She jumped at a hand on her arm.

"Tirzah? Are you all right?" Meri's voice was soft and her eyes filled with compassion.

"I'm fine. Just worried. I don't know what will happen next. I don't like that feeling."

Meri's eyes twinkled. "Sometimes that's when good things happen."

Tirzah sighed. "Meri…"

"It's true. The last time things were so uncertain, you ended up married to Kamose. You can't tell me you aren't happy with how that turned out." She handed Tirzah a spoon. "Now eat. Ahmose and the girls are with Bezalel at the stream."

Meri's reasoning was infuriatingly difficult to argue with. And she refused to see anything but the bright side of a situation.

"Yes, you're right." Tirzah smiled, and Meri wandered off, leaving Tirzah alone with her dark thoughts again. She stuffed a spoonful of manna in her mouth and forced it down. She finished the rest and set the bowl aside.

Kamose's hand touched her shoulder, instantly calming her.

"What happened?"

"As you thought, they were ambushed, defeated. As Moses predicted." Kamose sat beside her and drew her to his side. "They lost over half their men. Left the most seriously wounded on the field." He huffed. "Fools. They should have listened. They were unprepared. They didn't have enough information, enough weapons, supplies, experience—they didn't have enough of anything. And they were slaughtered."

"Are they going back?" Tirzah asked.

"No. They're ready to stay here. Things should calm down now."

Tirzah let out a breath she hadn't realized she'd been holding. It was over.

ॐ✦

The smoky aroma of burning wood from thousands of fires mingled with the sweet scent of manna and wafted through the camp. Kamose swallowed the last of his manna cake and washed it down with goat's milk. He stretched his arms over his head and glanced at the sky. Hawks and falcons returned to their nests on the hills, screeching as they flew over camp.

Naomi crawled onto Kamose's lap after the evening meal. He laid his cheek on her head, wrapped his arms around her. The air had cooled a bit, and Keren scampered off to play with Ahmose a little longer by the river, but Naomi chose to stay with Kamose. And he loved it.

Tirzah sat beside him, resting her head against his arm. Bezalel and Meri, along with Sheerah and Nahshon, sat around the fire as well.

"It's getting darker much earlier now. I hope Ahmose doesn't keep Keren out too long." Tirzah gazed toward the palm trees.

"Will he keep her out, or will she keep him out?" Bezalel laughed.

"I think it's a little of both," said Meri.

"What's a little of both?"

All heads turned at the new voice.

"Imma." Bezalel jumped up and hugged his mother. "No babies right now?"

"No babies to deliver or new mothers to help. And I missed mine. Where is she?"

"Here." Meri lifted her arms, baby Adi asleep within them.

Rebekah sat next to her and Meri slipped the baby into her arms. "Oh, I have missed her so much." She placed kisses on the babe's cheeks.

"Thanks," said Bezalel as he reclaimed his seat.

Rebekah smiled. "You will always be my only son. You're just not as cute anymore."

Kamose chuckled. "My mother always ignored my brothers when they brought their children around, too."

"And I'm sure my mother will do the same thing next spring." Nahshon grinned broadly.

Meri squealed as she nearly pounced on Sheerah. "A baby?"

Sheerah's face pinked as she nodded. She looked to Rebekah. "You'll be here, won't you? My mother isn't here anymore."

"Of course, habibti." Rebekah reached to touch Sheerah's arm and smiled reassuringly. She stroked Adi's cheek. "We may be stuck here, but we are all safe and together. Everyone is home."

The men left behind flashed through Kamose's mind. *Almost everyone.*

"At least the fighting is over. Waiting is better than war." Tirzah snuggled closer.

Meri nodded in agreement. "I'd rather be bored than scared."

"I'm sure we'll have plenty to keep us busy here," Nahshon added.

Moses appeared at the fire, followed by Caleb and Joshua. "Kamose, I need to ask you something. Could you come with us?"

Kamose placed Naomi in Tirzah's lap, then rose and fell in step with Joshua as they strolled away from the tents. "What do you need?"

"I think I'll let Moses explain." Caleb pointed to the older man.

Once out of earshot of their tent, Moses stopped and turned to Kamose. "I'd like to ask you to go with Caleb and Joshua, and some others, and bring back the wounded."

Kamose took a slow, deep breath. "I am no longer a soldier."

"You haven't forgotten everything you know, have you?" Joshua chuckled dryly.

"No." Kamose met Moses's gaze. "I just married her. You want me to leave her?"

"You'll be back."

"You don't know that. That's why I never married as a soldier."

"It shouldn't be too dangerous," said Joshua. "It will be clear we are only rescuing wounded. We'll only carry daggers, no swords or spears. We go in, get them, get back."

Kamose crossed his arms over his chest. "You can't do this without me? Joshua and Caleb know the terrain. I don't."

Caleb touched his arm. "You know how to take care of the wounds. You can keep us out of sight as long as possible, and you know how to deal with the enemy if need be."

"I'll teach you."

"You won't come?" asked Joshua.

Kamose closed his eyes. "I cannot." *This is not my responsibility.*

Joshua raised his hand, palm up. "But—"

Moses placed a hand on Joshua's arm, quieting him. "This is our job, not his. He has already done enough for Israel."

Kamose stared at his feet. The sound of sandaled footsteps faded away.

His stomach clenched; he balled his hands into fists. They shouldn't have left wounded men there. They'd been there already—what did Lamech say? Two days? Three?

It wasn't his job. Let someone younger do it. He'd fought enough wars.

It was someone else's turn.

Seventeen

Only Tirzah remained at the fire when Kamose returned, his gait slower than usual, his countenance clouded.

She studied him. "What did they want?"

He shook his head. "It does not matter."

He was keeping things from her. Important things. She didn't like it. She fixed him with a stare she hoped told him she would not abide secrets. "Kamose, what did they want?"

He paused only a moment before answering. "They wanted me to go with a group of men to rescue the wounded."

Icy fingers gripped Tirzah's heart as her throat threatened to close. She wrapped her arms around her middle.

He smiled and caressed her cheek. "I am not going. I promised I wouldn't leave you. I am staying with you." He embraced her as he whispered in her ear. "That part of my life is over. I am your husband, not their soldier."

The frozen fingers loosened their hold. The steady rise and fall of his chest calmed her and she breathed deeply. That Kamose was staying was reassuring, but for some reason the discomfort did not go away.

"I'm going to find Keren and Ahmose. It's getting dark." He strolled off in the direction of the palm trees by the river.

She smiled as he walked away. Yahweh had given her a husband, a father for her girls. He was a good man, not like Nathaniel. Not like Jediel.

Her stomach tightened. All little girls—and boys—deserved their fathers. And some of those fathers were stuck in the desert. Wounded. Unable to come home.

She frowned. But they disobeyed. It was their own fault. Why should she have to give up her husband because they were stupid? Moses had told them not to go, told them they would be defeated, and they went anyway. It wasn't her problem.

Thoughts raced through her mind, chasing one another around and around. She tried to shut them out, but they refused to stay away. She reached for the dishes from the evening meal. She scrubbed the pot with sand and wiped it clean, then washed the bowls. Then she cleaned them again.

Giggles drew her attention away from the task.

Kamose strolled up with Keren in his arms, Ahmose trotting along behind. He knelt and set the little girl down next to her sister. "Time to go to sleep."

The girls kissed him on the cheek and slipped into the tent.

Tirzah crawled in after them. She pulled off their sandals, washed their faces with a wet cloth, then reached for the comb and pulled it through Keren's hair. By the time she finished, Naomi had already fallen asleep.

Tirzah kissed Naomi's peaceful face. Naomi hadn't awakened once since Kamose had slept in the tent with them that first time, even though he didn't marry her and live with them for another two weeks after that. Just spending time with him during the day seemed to be enough to bring something into her life she had apparently desperately needed.

How many little girls are crying for their abbas tonight?

Tirzah emerged from the tent and eased down onto the sand next to Kamose.

"Girls asleep?"

"Yes. Naomi went fast."

Kamose chuckled.

"Kamose?"

"Hmmm?" He pulled her back against his chest and wrapped his arm around her waist.

"They left men out there?"

"Apparently. Ten or fifteen. The leader, if you can call him that, wasn't sure."

She suppressed a moan. "He wasn't sure how many men he left behind?"

"I don't think he knew how many he left with, so it would be impossible to know how many were killed or wounded. That's why Egyptian armies are arranged as they are. Every commander knows exactly how many men he is responsible for."

Tirzah's stomach ached. How could she let him go?

How could she not?

She turned to face him. "I think you have to go."

"Go where?"

"Go after the wounded men."

He shook his head. "I already told them no."

Tears gathered behind her eyes, and her throat burned. Her stomach ached.

He grasped her shoulders. "Habibti, I told them I wouldn't go."

She placed her hands on his cheeks. "I know, and I love you for it. Believe me, I don't want you to go. But I think you have to."

"I don't understand. You're not making sense."

Tears streamed down her cheeks. "I keep thinking about their children."

"Whose children?"

"The children of the men still out there. If they have a chance to come home, you have to make sure they do."

He wiped her tears away. "Joshua and Caleb can do that. They don't need me."

"I'm sure they are very capable. But if you can help, you must."

"I promised I would stay with you."

"You have to bring them home," she whispered.

He stared at her, shook his head. "Are you sure?"

Hot tears rolled down her cheeks. She called up the picture of crying children one more time. "Yes. I am."

ॐ∙ॐ

Kamose lay awake for several hours, then, after making sure Tirzah was sound asleep, grabbed a small bag from the corner of his tent, slipped out, and made his way to Joshua and Moses's tent. "Moses?"

No response.

"Moses?"

Joshua poked his head out. "Kamose?" He exited and stood outside the doorway, rubbing his eyes. "What do you want?"

"I have decided to go with you tomorrow."

"You have? What changed your mind?"

"Tirzah."

Joshua smiled. "Really? I must get to know her better. But Moses isn't here. I think he went to the tabernacle."

"Has he been gone long?"

"A good while. He should be back soon, but you know him. ..."

Kamose nodded. "I'll try later."

He ambled back toward his tent. Outside Bezalel's tent, he called for his friend.

Bezalel peeked out. "Kamose?" He emerged, then motioned Kamose away from the tent opening. "It's very late. What's wrong?"

"Moses asked me to help bring back some of the injured the group left behind. At first I said no, but Tirzah convinced me to go. I leave in the morning."

"Well, we'll take good care of her and the girls. You don't have to worry about them."

"I know you will. That's not why I'm here."

Bezalel furrowed his brow. "Then what do you need?"

"Tirzah never had the proper bridal jewelry. Her stepfather didn't see to it, and of course when she married me..." Kamose reached into the bag and pulled out his armbands. "If I don't come back..." He swallowed.

Bezalel shook his head. "Kamose—"

Kamose held up his hand. "If I don't come back, I want you to make her something beautiful from these. I know what you are capable of. I want your best for her."

"She'll have it. But you'll be back."

"Create something worthy of her, then keep the rest for when the girls need it." He placed the bag in Bezalel's hand and closed his fingers over it. "Unless Tirzah finds someone else to marry—and I doubt she'd trust anyone again—I want your word you'll make sure the girls find husbands who worship Yahweh and will treat them well. Just as you would for Adi."

"Kamose, if not for you, I would not have Meri, or Adi. I owe you my life, in many ways. I promise I will make sure Tirzah is safe, and take care of the girls as my own."

Kamose released a long breath. "This is why I never married. I can't do these two things at once. I have to figure out how to concentrate on the mission, or I'll put us all in danger."

"Yahweh will watch over you, I am sure." Bezalel paused. "When Sabba died, and then Yahweh asked me to build the tabernacle, I couldn't understand how He could ask something so important of me after such a huge loss. You remember how angry I was."

Kamose nodded. "You were quite a sight after your night on the mountain."

"What I learned was that Yahweh has His reasons, no matter how hard they are for us to understand. I still don't know why He took Sabba from me. I don't know why you should go on this mission. But I know that if you believe He has asked you to do this, you have to trust Him. It's much better than fighting Him."

Kamose wandered toward the tabernacle. Much better than fighting Him? Bezalel should know. He'd struggled with Yahweh a long time. Kamose had never really had anything to argue with Yahweh about, only trying to live as He wanted him to for less than a year—only several months, really. He was used to following orders, but he'd never had one order compete with another. Until now. How was he to care for Tirzah, and leave her alone at the same time?

Moses halted when he noticed Kamose headed for him, and listened carefully as Kamose explained. "And why did you change your mind?"

"Tirzah did not want any wives or children without their men if it was possible to bring them home."

"She was willing to risk you in order for that to happen?"

"After many tears, yes."

"She is a brave and wise woman. You already told Joshua you were going; why did you want to talk to me?"

Kamose stared at the distance, not wanting to look Moses in the eye. "Because I don't want to go. I am only going because she wants me to. I put being a soldier behind me and I was happy with that decision. You told me to look for the task Yahweh had given me. I thought I found it, found a new purpose. Now I am right back to where I was before, and I am not ready for this. I haven't been a soldier in over a year. You all look at me like I'm the expert, but I don't think I'm any better than the rest of you. I don't think I'll be any more help than Joshua or Caleb. I feel as much at a loss as I did right after the spies left." Blowing out a deep breath, he finally met the older man's gaze.

Moses smiled, and then laughed.

Kamose stared at him as he worked the muscle in his jaw. What was so funny? He'd always been able to talk to Moses, trust him. Why was he laughing at him?

"I don't think I've heard you talk so much at once ... ever."

Kamose had to admit the old man had a point. He chuckled. "I'm sure I don't make much sense. I've never made decisions to please anyone else before. But I couldn't tell her no." He dug his sandal in the sand. "Besides, she's probably right."

"If I tell you I also think you made the right decision, does that help?"

"It does. A little."

"I think you would eventually regret it if you didn't go."

"Probably."

"You don't sound completely at ease."

"I'm worried I won't be able to keep my mind from being back here, and that I will make mistakes, and get myself—or worse, someone else—hurt or killed. That is a danger I have never before faced. And I am ashamed to say it scares me."

"That sounds like a helpful fear." Moses put his hand on Kamose's shoulder. "I will pray for you—all of you—while you are gone. And Yahweh will be with you. Remember that."

Kamose nodded.

Moses jerked his chin toward the tents. "Go to your wife. You have a long day ahead of you."

17 Av

The feeble sun tried to nudge its way between the tent flaps. Tirzah sat on her mat in the dim morning light, watching silently as Kamose tied his hair behind his neck, laced up his sandals, strapped his dagger to his hip.

"Don't you need your armbands?"

He shook his head. "They don't serve any purpose in battle." He reached down to pull her to him.

She ran her hands over his bare chest. "Back to no tunic?" She smiled.

He gave her a weak grin. "It's hard to move in that thing." He laid his cheek on her head. "I'm so sorry," he whispered.

"It was my idea." She locked her arms around him. "Don't worry about us. We have plenty of people to watch out for us. We'll be fine." She wasn't sure about that, but he had to be able to concentrate on bringing the men home.

He stroked her hair. "The girls don't know I'm leaving. They went to bed before I changed my mind."

"I'll explain."

"Kiss them good-bye for me?"

"I will." She pulled back and studied him. His dark eyes, his strong jaw, his broad shoulders. "I love you."

"I love you, too." He buried his hands in her hair and kissed her.

She hugged him more tightly, breathed in his earthy scent, tried not to think that this might be the last kiss she might have from him. From anyone. Because if he didn't come back, there wouldn't be anyone else. Ever.

She broke the kiss. "Bring them home," she whispered.

"I'll do my best."

He kissed her cheek and slipped out of the tent.

"And bring yourself home, too." She brushed away a tear, and tried to fight the feeling of dread that threatened to overtake her.

She didn't succeed.

❧❧

Ahmose stood waiting when Kamose stepped outside. His throat tightened, and he knelt before his nephew.

"Are you going to bring home the men who are hurt?"

"Yes, habibi."

Ahmose thought a moment. "That's good. They shouldn't have left them alone in the desert."

"You're right."

"You'll be back, right?"

"I plan to."

"You haven't been gone since we left Egypt."

"I know."

"I'll miss you."

"I'll miss you, too." He took Ahmose's little hand in his. "Will you do something for me?"

"Of course. What?"

"Help Aunt Tirzah with the girls?"

"I already do that. I helped her before you knew her."

Kamose smiled. "I know. But it's especially important now, because I don't want her to worry about me while I'm gone. So I want you to help her all you can. And make her laugh."

"Make her laugh?"

"At least smile."

"I'll try." Ahmose pursed his lips. "She didn't smile until she met you."

Kamose's heart panged like an arrow had pierced it. "Just try." He pulled Ahmose close and hugged him. "I'll miss you."

Kamose rose and left camp without looking back, feeling like he'd left half of himself behind.

19 Av

"Are we getting close?" Kamose wiped his brow with the back of his hand and glowered over his shoulder at Lamech, trying to keep his loathing in check.

"I think so. I'm not really sure."

Kamose closed the distance between them in a few long strides and glared at the former leader as he towered over him. "You need to be sure. Lives depend on how sure you are."

Lamech pointed. "I think it's over that way. There are some caves. We hoped that would shelter them from the heat."

"You *think?*"

Lamech shrank back. "It's over there."

About half an hour later, Kamose entered the shallow cave first. Seven men lay on the floor, barely moving. A few moaned. Hot, fetid air filled the small space. Kamose's head nearly reached the top of the cave, but it was wide enough for the men to lie down without touching each other. He knelt beside the one nearest the entrance and placed his hand on his forehead. The man's skin was warm but dry, his breathing rapid. Kamose pinched some skin between his fingers; when he let go, it stayed pinched.

He stood and surveyed the others. Two more appeared to be in the same condition. "These men need water. Soon. There are springs all over these deserts. We need to find one."

"Let's send a few of us to look for water, and the rest will tend to these men." Caleb gestured to a few near him. "Um … Levi, Asher, Joel, Rafael—search for water. Go in pairs—we don't need anyone else hurt or lost."

The four of them left.

Kamose moved past the first man to those behind him. The second man had obviously died from an injury caused by a sword. A bandage soaked in blood wound around his thigh. Kamose peeked under the cloth. The cut wasn't bad in itself, and had it been treated properly and promptly in the field, he would have survived. But it wasn't attended to, and the long hours of walking caused him to lose too much blood.

One more had died of his wounds. A couple more had the heat

sickness, and two had broken legs and had been left behind because they could not keep up.

Kamose stood and strode to the front of the cave where Lamech waited. How he would love to strangle this man about now. He took a deep breath instead. "Lamech, where are the other men?"

"Right over here." Lamech stepped back and pointed to the right.

Caleb walked toward Lamech and peeked around the edge. "I'll go."

Kamose nodded. "I'll get them started here, then I'll join you. Where are the splints we brought?"

One of the men handed Kamose a bag of wood pieces.

Kamose beckoned to Lamech. Lamech left these men here; he could face the consequences of his actions now. "It's a good time to immobilize the bones. They won't feel too much pain in their current condition. I'll show you how."

"Can't someone else do this? I really don't want—"

"You're helping." Kamose again knelt before the injured man, whose lower leg bent at an abnormal angle. "Grab his leg tight, just below the knee. And you"—he pointed to another man—"who are you?"

"Micah."

"Hold his chest. Keep him absolutely still." Kamose grasped the injured man's heel and pulled with slow but steady pressure.

The man groaned and tried to arch his back, but Micah held him down. Lamech's face lost nearly all its color.

The deformed leg slowly straightened out, returning to its original shape.

"Good. Now, get a couple of those pieces of wood, and wrap them in the bigger linen pieces. Then lay them on each side of his leg, and tie them on with the strips of linen above and below the break." Kamose kept the pressure on while Lamech and Micah applied the splint. "Good, good. There's one more."

They set the other broken leg, then Kamose marched outside and found the other cave. He taught the other men to set breaks there as well before he called Caleb outside. "They haven't come back with water yet. Maybe I should go look, too."

"Give them some time. They'll be here."

Kamose peered inside the cave. "These men need water or they will die. The sun's high in the sky and they can't wait much longer. Which way did the others go?"

"One pair went east, one went west."

"Then I'll go north."

"I'll go with you." Caleb picked up the dagger he'd set by the mouth of the cave and strapped it around his waist.

Kamose grabbed several skins and tied them to his belt. He removed his knife from its sheath and ran his finger down the blade—nice and sharp. Should be; he always kept it that way. Some habits remained. He stuck his hand in a bag and grabbed a handful of dates.

They worked a path north, eating dates and picking their way through the rocks. Kamose placed his feet carefully. He didn't need to break his leg like those men in the cave. Of course, they didn't know what they were doing. Probably weren't watching where they were going. Where they were running. Running from an enemy they never should have been fighting in the first place.

A sparkle to his right caught his eye. It couldn't be this easy, could it? He changed direction and headed for the shimmering pool. Minutes later, they stood at a dry depression in the rock. He shook his head. How had he let that happen? He knew better. He knew how heat acted on hot stone, knew about the waves that rose above the ground posing as water.

What kind of soldier was he?

That was the problem—he was no longer a soldier. He was a husband. Exactly what he feared would happen, had happened. Tirzah had been in the back of his thoughts since he left, and she had apparently kept him from thinking clearly.

That wasn't fair. It wasn't her fault. She had let him go—told him to go. If thoughts of her were compromising his thinking, it was his fault, not hers. He'd been a soldier far longer than he'd been a family man, and he could control his mind. With Yahweh's help.

Yahweh, take care of Tirzah and the girls for me so I can take care of these men.

A lizard skittered over the rocks. There had to be water somewhere near. He glanced at the sky. Hawks circled farther north.

He jabbed a finger toward the movement. "There. Those birds are hovering over either a carcass or water." He left the rocks and entered a flat area. The birds still circled. A dry wadi appeared before him. He dropped to his knees and dug. Caleb wandered farther down the sandy bed before he knelt and was hidden behind a broom bush. After a few moments, Kamose found water. A bit longer, and there was enough to begin filling his skins.

He filled one, and laid it aside. He grabbed the second, and leaned over the hole. As he sat back on his heels, he felt the hot blade of a knife under his chin.

"Don't move, or I'll slit your throat."

Eighteen

Tirzah stirred the manna into the boiling water. Kamose had been gone only three days, but she could not shake the sense of dread that had settled over her the moment he left with Caleb and the others. It had not dissipated, and this afternoon, it felt even heavier.

"Tirzah!"

Meri's voice shook her from her reverie. "What?"

"Your manna is about to boil dry. Why are you boiling it in the middle of the day, anyway?"

Tirzah shrugged. "I didn't have the energy to make cakes. So I just boiled it."

"I'll add some more water and it will be fine." Meri reached for a skin and poured the liquid into Tirzah's pot, then stirred the thick mess into something edible. "There. Perfect."

"I'm sorry. I wasn't paying attention."

"It's all right. I know you're worried about Kamose, but they'll be back soon. You'll see. I think it's wonderful that you let him go bring back the others."

"Let him go? I practically begged him to go."

"You did? Why? You've haven't been married a month."

"I know. I kept thinking about the children who may have fathers left out there." Tirzah brushed tears off her cheeks. "Maybe I made a mistake. Or maybe I'm being selfish. I don't know."

Meri wrapped an arm around her. "Why don't you take a walk by the river? You'll feel much better. I'll feed the girls, and we'll be sure to save you some manna."

Tirzah drew in a shuddering breath, and sniffled. "If you say so. I just can't help thinking something horrible is going to happen."

Meri rubbed her back. "Don't be silly. Go take your walk. Everything will be just fine."

Tirzah stood and headed for their spot by the river, guarded by the date palms. But the cloud of fear came with her.

❧❧

Kamose stood up slowly to keep the hot metal from piercing his skin.

His assailant tied Kamose's hands behind him.

"Are you alone?" he asked in badly-accented Hebrew.

He thinks I'm an Israelite.

Kamose wasn't going to tell him otherwise. "Yes. I am." But no sooner had the words left his mouth than another Canaanite appeared with a bound Caleb.

His guard continued to hold the knife to Kamose's throat, his eyes blazing. "You lie! How many others?"

Yahweh, give me the words. "Only a few. We only came to gather our wounded."

His captor glared at him, obviously deciding whether to believe him. He spoke to his partner in an unfamiliar tongue, then turned back to Kamose.

"As I told you, we only came to gather our wounded. We are no threat. You can let us go."

The guard looked from Kamose to Caleb. "Not all can go. I only need one. You choose."

Caleb stepped toward Kamose. "Kamose, you should go home. Let me go. What about Tirzah?" he whispered.

"I will be more valuable. I know strategy. I can figure out what they are planning. I'll let them question me and then I am sure I can convince them to let me go."

"What if you can't?"

"Maybe this is what Yahweh has planned for me all along."

"Enough!" the Canaanite roared. "Who goes?"

"I will." Kamose turned to Caleb. "Just get the men home. Or it means nothing."

ೋ✥ら

Kamose trudged through the scorching sand and rocks, his chest and his legs burning. Kamose had slept little the past two nights, hiking for two solid days, pushing hard to find the men and get back home as swiftly as possible.

Home. The word hit him like a punch in the gut. Would he ever be home again? It was odd that home now was not so much a place as a feeling, a person. Home had always been a small room with his few practical and necessary belongings, a dwelling that never moved, to which he returned after a battle or a long day. Now, he wouldn't care if it were a different place every night, as long as Tirzah was there.

He stumbled, coughed, tried to talk. His throat ached. He managed to ask for water. The guard seemed excessively annoyed, but stopped and removed one of the skins from Kamose's belt, lifted it, and squirted water into Kamose's mouth. The warm liquid slid over his tongue, and he gulped several mouthfuls.

The guard drank some himself, though he had his own bag, and retied the skin onto the belt around Kamose's waist. He poked his blade into Kamose's side and grunted.

Four other guards caught up with them a few hours later. After a hushed conversation, the first one shoved Kamose into a cave, and followed him in. The four others lined up at the entrance.

His captor, now apparently his personal guard, lay down and appeared to sleep. Kamose tried to do the same, but it was difficult to relax when trussed up like a bird ready to be roasted.

21 Av

Kamose plodded on. The brutal sun pounded heat into his reddened skin and sweat dripped from his brow and his shoulders. They'd been hiking for two days, steadily north and steadily climbing. The last half-day the ground had flattened and was less sandy. Lush grass fed cattle, sheep, and goats. Further ahead grass grew even more abundantly, and wheat, barley, beans, and olive orchards surrounded the city. A walled city, this close to the edge of Canaan—had to be Arad.

As they neared the city, the ground began to rise again. Soaring walls circled the city like oversized protecting arms. Towers stood atop the massive barriers, but Kamose was too far away to see if watchmen stood guard within the strongholds.

Reaching the top of the hill, he gazed at two open, huge, wooden double doors, giving a clear view of the main road cutting through the city. His captor propelled him through. Another guard joined them on the other side. They each grasped a forearm and half dragged him along the street. Several times he fell, his knees scraping raw on the pebbles.

Another half hour brought them to the palace complex in the northwest quadrant of the city, and a second set of massive wooden doors, these closed. On either side thinner, lower walls—but still high over Kamose's head—stretched to the city's outer wall.

Guards stationed on either side of the doorway rushed to the center, grabbed at huge bronze rings, and grunted as they pulled at the heavy doors. The hinges groaned at the weight, and the wood scraped along the ground as it reached the end of its arc.

The trio entered. The temperature dropped immediately inside the long tiled hallway with its stone floors. Small torches set aflame hung in stands along the way, casting peculiar shadows along with the minimal light. Open doors revealed dim storerooms, opulent bedrooms, large bathing areas.

An archway at the end of the hall opened into a large room with two golden thrones against the far wall. Not nearly as ornate as Egypt's capital, it was nonetheless impressive for a city of its small size. Hand-smoothed wooden beams supported a high ceiling, and niches built into tiled walls held art—Kamose recognized vases and sculpture from Egypt and Canaan and beyond. He'd seen similar pieces in the palace in Pi-Ramses. Servants bustled in and out of doors built into three of the four walls. The far wall, facing west, had to be on the outside wall of the city, for all along its length tall windows set high allowed the rich golden light of day's end to pour into the room.

In the center sat a stone, two figures inscribed on it, their heads stalks of wheat. One stood with its arms raised, the other lay on the ground. Grain lay scattered before it as if in offering. Could the rock be one of their gods?

The guards dragged Kamose near the thrones and shoved him to his knees.

A young man rose from the smaller of the golden chairs. A plumed helmet sat atop his head, and a silver belt adorned the shenti around his waist. He looked more like a warrior than a king— perhaps a prince.

He strutted toward Kamose, stopped before him, and puffed out his chest. "I am Keret, son of Ibiranu, king of Arad." He, too, spoke in broken Hebrew. In fact, it was so bad, Kamose had to reveal his identity.

"My name is Kamose. I am Egyptian."

Keret caught his breath and his mouth dropped open. He closed it quickly and crossed his arms. "Why are you traveling with the

Hebrews?" His Egyptian was much better than his Hebrew, but still carried a strong accent.

"That is none of your concern."

"I decide what is my concern!" The prince's cheeks flamed red. He slapped Kamose across the face.

Kamose had struck a nerve. And he intended to keep poking. He refused to deal with this impulsive child. He would wait for the king.

"When are the Hebrews coming into Canaan?"

"They are not."

Keret sputtered, his eyes flashing. Obviously not the answer he was expecting. "Of course they are. Why wouldn't they?"

Kamose bit back a smile. "They are being punished for disobedience."

"Disobedience? To whom?"

"To their God. He is making them wait."

Keret paced, hands on his hips, muttering to himself. "So, how long—next year? Two?"

"Forty."

The prince wheeled around. "Forty?" He scoffed, walked away. Returned. "Forty? How can they wait forty years? They'll die in that desert."

That's the point. Kamose shrugged.

Keret strode away again, muttering. He faced the throne. His hands fisted, the muscles in his neck tightened. "Either you are lying, or you are still serving Pharaoh, and spying on us to seek out our weaknesses. Whichever is the truth, you will tell me soon enough." He signaled to the officers behind Kamose. "Put him in a cell."

22 Av

Tirzah knelt beside Naomi and Keren as she tucked the blanket around the girls.

"Imma, when is Abba coming back?" Naomi reached for Tirzah's cheek.

"I am sure they will be back soon. Maybe tomorrow. Give me a kiss." She leaned over for her kisses, then stood and closed the fabric between the sections of the tent.

Tirzah emerged and raised her face to the setting sun. The pinks and oranges splashed across the tops of the mountains reflected the light in her heart. An owl skimmed by overhead, calling as it started its evening hunt. The breeze wafted gently through the rows of tents.

The rescue team had been gone six days. Two days there, one day to find the men, two days back. One day for any problems. They should be home tonight, tomorrow by dawn at the latest. She hugged herself, wishing for Kamose's strong arms around her instead.

She moved toward the fire and sat, enjoying the quiet.

Ahmose padded up to her, smile on his face, a batch of wildflowers in his hand. He snuggled beside her, staying quiet, just sitting near her.

She kissed his head and wrapped her arm around him.

Caleb trudged into camp, covered in grime, shoulders slumped. She looked behind him, searching for Kamose, but saw only Joshua. When she didn't see him, she stood, walked several paces beyond him, then turned to the older man, brows furrowed. "Where is he?"

Caleb paused before answering, as if searching for the right words. "When we found the men, they were in dire need of water and food. We had brought food, so after we tended to their wounds, we fed them while we sent four others to find springs. When they didn't come back soon enough for Kamose, he went to look himself. I accompanied him, but we were captured by men I can only assume were Canaanite. Probably from Arad, the nearest city."

Tirzah's knees began to buckle. Her greatest fears were coming true. Was he never to come home? She reminded herself to listen to the rest of Caleb's story.

222   ★   Carole Towriss

"They wanted… they wanted one of us to go with them, probably to be questioned about our movements here. I tried to go, but Kamose insisted. He said as a soldier he would be more effective. He told me to bring the wounded home." He touched her shoulder, and gave her a tender smile. "I'm so sorry. But he seemed quite confident he would only be there a day or two. I'm sure he will be back soon."

Tirzah felt dizzy as the blood drained from her head. She locked her knees and forced her breathing to slow. There was no reason to worry. He would be back soon—Caleb said so. He was just a little late. Everything would be all right.

Joshua stepped forward. "Can I do anything for you in the meantime?"

"No, I'll be fine. Thank you."

Caleb bent to address Ahmose. "Don't worry about your uncle. Yahweh will take care of him." He patted Ahmose's cheek and then stood and waited to catch her gaze. "He'll be here soon. I'm sure."

"I know." She said it to ease Ahmose's mind, but she knew nothing of the sort.

The men turned to go.

"Caleb?"

He spun around. "Yes?"

"Did he help?"

"Your husband?"

"Yes. Did he help bring back the men?"

Caleb drew nearer and smiled. "He was invaluable. He was the only one who knew how to set their broken bones properly. He was the one who realized how badly they needed water. I won't say we couldn't have done it without him, but I am sure we would have lost more than we did."

She closed her eyes a moment and swallowed. "Did you bring them all back?"

Caleb winced. "Most of them. We lost a couple."

Unshed tears burned her eyes. "Thank you."

Caleb squeezed her shoulder, then they left.

Meri handed Adi to Bezalel and led Tirzah to the fire. "Let's sit. Do you want some milk?"

Tirzah barely heard the question, but nodded, realizing an answer of some sort was expected. *He'll be fine. He'll be back.* She repeated the sentences over and over.

Ahmose sat next to her. Meri handed her a cup and joined her on the other side. "I'm sure if there were anything to worry about, Caleb would have told you. He'll be here before you wake in the morning, you'll see." Meri patted her hand.

Tirzah forced a smile. "You're right." She sipped the milk and then set the cup aside. She smoothed her tunic, trying to suppress the thoughts that would not go away.

Adi's cries drew Tirzah's attention. "Can I hold her?"

Meri seemed surprised, but gestured to Bezalel, who knelt and slipped the babe into Tirzah's arms.

Tirzah drew the child close to her chest and nuzzled her cheek. The fresh scent of the innocent babe soothed Tirzah, and her warm, soft skin offered an illusion of calm. Adi cooed when Tirzah kissed her.

Tirzah gently rocked Adi for several long moments, hiding her face in the baby's blanket. Finally she drew in a deep breath, gathered her strength, and raised her head with her best smile. "Thank you, Meri." She returned the child to her mother.

Meri rubbed her back. "He'll be back before sunrise."

"Of course." Tirzah nodded.

She ducked into her tent. It wasn't time to sleep yet, but she had no energy for anything else. She lay down on her mat and pulled up the light covering she shared with Kamose, and tried to shake the feeling of dread that followed her, threatened to overtake her, keep her from breathing.

She didn't succeed.

❧❧

Kamose had spent all night and most of the day in a tiny cell on the main floor without food or water. He was exhausted, but hunger and thirst, not to mention unease at what they intended to do with him, made sleep impossible.

He studied the room again. The only light came from under and around the door. It wasn't much, and faded before it reached the far wall. No windows meant not only no light and no fresh air, but no means of escape. He ran his hands along the walls—they were thick, wooden, and impossible to power through, unlike mud brick. He couldn't hear anything, see anything, smell anything.

He forced himself to sit on a tiny bed that wasn't long enough for him to stretch out on in order to give his body a break, even though he felt like a caged animal ready to pounce, ready to destroy something. But even if he could find something to break or smash, that would only waste energy, and he had a horrific feeling he needed to conserve every resource he could marshal for whatever Keret had waiting for him.

Kamose stood as the door pushed into the room. Two new guards, knives on their hips and spears in their hands, moved behind him and ordered him out of the room. At least he assumed that's what they said, since they spoke in Canaanite. Their gestures spoke loudly enough.

One ahead of him and one behind him, he was again led to the throne room.

Keret waited. "Egyptian. Still say you are not coming for forty years?"

"I do."

"You lie! The fact is, you are planning even now to march north!"

Kamose remained silent. How do you argue with someone who refuses to listen to the truth?

"And is it true you now intend to take over my city, in fact, many cities, all the way to Lake Kennerith?"

"Not at this time."

"Not at this time?" Keret waved his arms in the air. "What does that mean?"

"Yahweh had indeed planned to give us this land, but we disobeyed Him. And now we are being punished, and we will remain in the desert for forty years."

"Lies! That's the stupidest lie I have ever heard. You are trying to trick me, to lull me into thinking you are not coming so you can take my city without resistance. It will not work." He raised his finger and two men appeared from the back of the room—carrying whips.

Kamose breathed faster.

Two guards standing near the prince grabbed Kamose's arms and dragged him toward the door. Before they could exit, an older man, dressed in a long robe dyed indigo, blocked the door. He glared at the armed men, who let go of him but stayed nearby. The man barked at Keret, who hurried over to the gathering, yelling back and hands flailing as he marched.

Keret and the newcomer moved to the thrones and continued to argue. The older man had rings on his fingers and a large gold necklace. His robe, and the tunic beneath, appeared to be crafted of fine linen. He shared facial features with Keret, but exuded grace and calm where Keret could not be still and constantly raised his voice. Could this be the king?

The guards moved Kamose toward the center of the room.

Keret paced with his arms across his chest, fuming.

The king spoke to the men with whips, who left the room, then approached Kamose. "I am Ibiranu, King of Arad. I apologize for my son's harsh treatment of you." His Egyptian was accented, but otherwise perfect. "We do not usually treat our guests in such a manner. I understand my son has already spoken to you?"

Kamose nodded.

"And you have told him the Israelites are not marching north?"

Kamose nodded again.

"Not now, and not for forty years."

"That is correct."

The king held his gaze for a moment. "You will now be seen to your room."

"But Father—" The prince spread his arms wide, his brow furrowed.

"The matter is closed." Ibiranu nodded and left.

So the man was indeed the king. And although Kamose was a "guest," he was not allowed to leave.

What next?

Nineteen

Tirzah hated waking up alone. It had only been six days, but it felt like weeks. Until Kamose, she'd never slept with anyone before. Jediel had always used her for his pleasure then left the room—or even the house—when they lived in Egypt. In the tent, he slept as far away from her and the girls as possible for a few weeks, then he stopped coming home at all. Which was fine with her.

She had never loved Jediel. But Kamose was part of her. When he was gone, it was like he took a piece of her heart with him.

She reached for Kamose's tunic and buried her face in it, breathing in his familiar—but fading—scent of leather and earth. How could she miss him this much?

She shook her head. She'd been raising the girls alone for three years, married or not. She could do it again. She washed her face, brushed her hair, pulled on her tunic, and stepped outside.

The sun was barely up, and the cool of the night still lingered. Night birds called to their partners, telling them they were on their way home. A Nubian vulture circled overhead—something hadn't made it through the night. She raised her face to the glowing cloud hovering overhead, reminding her of Yahweh's presence.

She didn't sleep long with Kamose gone, but Naomi did, so even though she rose early, she still rested well. She grabbed her manna pot, caught up with Meri, and collected the day's manna.

"And she actually rolled over last night! When I woke up this morning she was all the way to the edge of the tent. And when I went to pick her up, she laughed at me!"

"Ah." Tirzah couldn't quite work up the level of enthusiasm Meri had. Meri always had. She got excited if the sun rose in the morning.

"She babbles constantly. Whenever she's awake she's trying to talk."

Like her mother.

Meri stood and faced Tirzah. "She's just… I never dreamed I could love anyone else like I love Bezalel. Does that make sense?"

It wasn't Meri's fault. Tirzah had felt the same way when her babies were born, and Jediel didn't care. She remembered how that hurt. She shouldn't do this to Meri. She smiled her biggest smile. "It makes perfect sense. It's amazing how such a tiny person can completely rearrange your life."

Meri giggled, and they headed back.

At the fire, Tirzah stirred the embers.

"Do you want to hold her while I make the manna?" Meri offered the babe to Tirzah.

The memory of holding Adi last night returned. "I do." She reached for her, and Meri placed the baby in her arms. Adi cooed and smiled, as if she knew her job was to comfort and distract Tirzah.

Tirzah ran her fingertips down Adi's soft cheeks, counted her tiny fingers and toes, grinned at the faces she made. Adi kicked her feet and waved her arms. She worked her mouth, trying desperately to talk, unconnected sounds spilling from her little pouty lips.

What would she say if she could? Would she, too, tell Tirzah everything would be fine? Or would she just say she loved her?

Tirzah was vaguely aware of a desire for a baby of her own, hers and Kamose's, far in the depths of her mind, but she shoved it down, hard, and concentrated on the one in her lap.

Adi blew bubbles, and Tirzah chuckled. Not an actual laugh, but enough of one for this morning.

Ahmose and the twins bounced in behind Bezalel with handfuls of sweet dates. "Good morning, Aunt Tirzah." Ahmose drew near and kissed her cheek, then bent and kissed Adi. Nahshon and Sheerah, then Joshua arrived at the fire and soon conversation flowed, and distraction was no longer an issue.

After cleaning up from breakfast, everyone scattered and silence took over for a few moments. Tirzah struggled to control her worrisome thoughts, to keep them focused on Kamose's returning at any time. She looked north. Nothing. She tried to smile.

Ahmose took Tirzah's hand. "Let's go see the big spring. There are these funny birds that hide in the broom bush."

Ahmose was trying to keep her busy. Kamose must have told him to. She grinned at her husband's thoughtfulness. Facing a dangerous mission and still he thought of her. "Why not?" She held the boy's small hand and followed him and the girls to the spring. Wildflowers of purple, yellow, and red dotted the ground as they approached the water. And the warblers did poke their heads in and out of the bushes. Ahmose and the girls tried to catch them, but the birds always won. It wasn't a bad way to spend a morning.

Lunch passed, then a trip to see Sarah and the other sheep, then it was time for the evening meal. Ahmose tried to occupy every moment of her time.

As she came out of the tent after settling the girls for the night, Ahmose appeared before her. "Want to go collect some flowers?" His sweet, expectant face was a joy to watch.

She tousled his hair. "I'm kind of tired, habibi. Why don't you get some for me?"

"Sure!" He nodded and then scampered off toward the river.

Before she climbed back into her tent and lay down next to her girls, Tirzah looked north once again. Nothing. To the west, the sun slipped behind the mountains.

Another day gone and no Kamose. And she was losing daylight as fast as she was losing hope.

∂∽∾

Kamose turned at the sound of keys jingling. He'd been waiting in this room for another day, since being sent here by the king. The door arced open, screeching as it scraped along the floor.

A young guard, dagger on his hip, entered the large, well-furnished room carrying a tray filled with fruits, meat, cheese, and bread in one hand and a pitcher in the other. He was the same guard who'd led him around the day before. Though almost as large as Kamose, he'd not once handled him roughly, and had a kind face, even though he wore his hair down like the rest of the Canaanites, which sometimes made it hard to see his eyes. Perhaps he could be helpful. Did he speak Egyptian?

Kamose moved closer to him. "What's your name?"

"Aqhat." He smiled and winked as he glanced toward the door.

A young girl leaned against the doorway. A gauzy fabric crossed from behind her neck, barely covering her sizeable… assets… before tying behind her waist. The skirt didn't hide much either.

The guard stepped out and locked the door behind her, still grinning.

"I'm Donatiya," she said in Egyptian. Her accent was barely noticeable, even endearing. She moved to the table in the center of the room and drew her fingers over the tray and pitcher upon it, then slinked over to Kamose. She uncrossed his arms and slid her hands along his biceps.

Apparently their tactics had changed. Instead of beating him, they would try to charm the information out of him. Two years ago, maybe even one, he would have played their game, and won. He had no information to give, but he would have invented some, misled them. And enjoyed the girl.

But that was before Yahweh. Before Tirzah. Now the woman before him offered no temptation. At least not to his heart. Or his mind. His body might be another matter.

He sucked in a breath as she ran her hands down his chest. He glanced at the food. "That looks delicious."

She chuckled. "The food? Or me?"

He smiled. "Both. But I'll have more energy if I eat first."

"Energy? Why are you in need of energy?"

"Because I have barely eaten since I arrived here."

"Ah, then you must be under the control of the prince."

The woman had a loose tongue. Perhaps he could learn something. "Why do you say that?"

Donatiya circled him, drawing her fingers across his skin as she talked. "The prince is often more… enthusiastic… than wise when it comes to taking care of his prisoners. The king tries to restrain him, but it's getting harder." She stood facing him, and draped her arms around his neck. An overpowering scent of lilies surrounded them, made his empty stomach roil.

He tipped his head toward the table. "The food?"

She grinned. "If you insist, my love."

"Please?"

She dragged the table toward the low but wide bed, then sat down and patted the space next to her.

For the next hour, he played along. He kept up his part in the conversation, laughed at her jokes, drank the wine. He even allowed her to feed him, which was extremely irritating. He wasn't a toddler. But it kept her occupied, so he accepted the grapes, chunks of bread, and pieces of meat she offered. At least the food tasted good.

The meal consumed, she pushed the table away and placed herself behind him. Her hands massaged his neck, releasing the knots that had gathered there.

He should stop her, but he was exhausted, and it felt so good.

"So, when are you coming to live here?"

Here it comes. "We are not coming."

Her hands slid down to his lower back. "I know you have to tell the prince that. But you can tell me the truth," she whispered in his ear.

More kneading. The physical relief warred with his discomfort at letting another woman touch him. But he wanted to try to find a graceful way out of the situation. If he mishandled this, what would they do next?

She nuzzled his neck. "I want you to come here."

"We're not coming." His breathing came faster. He needed to stop this.

"Come stay with me." Her hands wrapped around his chest and she kissed his cheek. "I'll give you anything you want," she whispered.

He flung her hands away and stood. "I am telling you the truth." He struggled to keep his voice under control. "And no matter what you say or do, it will not change. We—are—not—coming."

Donatiya stood slowly. "Very well, my love." She slithered past him, brushing her body against his as she did. She rapped on the door, and within a moment, Aqhat unlocked the door and let her out.

Kamose stood in the center of the empty room and slowed his breathing. He rubbed his hand down his face.

He couldn't have let her continue. But what would they try next? Would they go back to the whips?

He dropped onto the bed. He'd barely slept for the last several nights. His mind spun. Tirzah. Whips. Lamech. The wounded. A pouty prince.

Whatever they had in mind, it probably wouldn't happen tonight. He couldn't think clearly, and he would need the energy to face whatever it would be. The best thing he could do now was to sleep.

He closed his eyes. Guilt, loneliness, exhaustion, speculation—all combined to keep his head spinning longer than he wanted. But eventually the dark feelings left him, and he settled into a deep sleep, allowing him to prepare for another day.

24 Av

Aqhat pushed open the door and placed a towel and large pitcher of water on the table. He laid a fresh tunic and other necessary items on the bed and closed the door on his way out.

I guess they're not going to beat me. Yet.

Kamose cleaned up and changed his clothes. He combed his hair and retied it. He had to admit, after a delicious meal, a good night's rest, and clean clothes, he felt infinitely better.

It made him wary.

Aqhat and another guard returned and led him to the throne room. No prodding with knives this time, or barked commands. They treated him … with respect.

That, too, raised his suspicion.

In the large, high-ceilinged rom, Kamose knelt before the king.

"This is the Hebrew that was captured outside our gates?"

"Yes, my king," Aqhat answered.

"His name?"

"Kamose."

"Kamose? That is not a Hebrew name." The ruler turned to Kamose. "Explain."

Was the king talking to him or the guard? Unsure, Kamose remained kneeling, silent.

"Explain."

Aqhat touched his shoulder.

Kamose raised his head to the king. "I am Egyptian. I am with the Hebrews now."

"Why?"

"I left Egypt when the Israelite God destroyed it. I have become one of them, and I worship their God as my own."

"Egyptians are a proud people. No Egyptian would take the side of those they have conquered."

"I have seen what their God can do. He is a better God than any of our gods."

The king nodded to Aqhat, who touched Kamose's elbow and helped him to stand.

The king nodded. "Tell me about the Israelites."

"What would you like to know?"

"I hear many stories. Stories I cannot believe. I need to know if they are true."

"Such as?"

"That the Israelites escaped from Egypt and destroyed the army, that they survive in the desert by bread falling from the sky. Water appears from nowhere. Slaves defeat the Amalekites… need I go on?"

"All true, except the Israelites did none of those things on their own. Our God, Yahweh, did them. He drowned the army, defeated the Amalekites, sends the bread every day, and provides water when needed."

"And you now intend to take over all the land of Canaan? How will you do that? You have no chariots, your army is inexperienced. You have only fought desert raiders, not a trained army."

"Again, true. But when it is time, Yahweh will give us victory, just as He did against the Amalekites. You may dismiss the raiders here, but you know they are a brutal force."

The king smiled. "Well done. Now, what does 'when it is time' mean?"

"Yahweh had planned to give us this land, and we would have taken this city. But we disobeyed Him. And now we are being punished, and we will remain in the desert for forty years."

"That is difficult to believe."

"It was difficult to hear."

"How do I know you speak the truth?"

"Surely your spies have seen our camp. Does it look like we are preparing for war, or organizing a settlement?" A twinkle flashed in the king's eyes—he'd finally convinced the old man.

"I can see you are an excellent soldier." The ruler drew nearer. "We could use a man like you. A man who can follow orders no matter what, to the very last." He put his hands on Kamose's shoulders. "Come to our side. I will make you a leader of my people. I will give you a house, riches, women, power—whatever you desire shall be yours. I admire your loyalty and faithfulness to your leaders. I need that kind of honor here."

"And if I left, what would it say about my loyalty then?"

The king chuckled. "I would have been surprised had you answered differently. But I had to try." He beckoned to Aqhat. "Return him to his room. Feed him, then prepare him for his journey home."

A deep sigh escaped Kamose's chest as waves of relief washed over him. The weight lifted from his shoulders. He didn't need food, or sleep. He could run home, all the way. Just show him the door. *Tirzah, Naomi, Keren, Ahmose. Soon. Soon I'll be there.*

Aqhat led him down the hall. He spoke in words Kamose did not understand to a young servant girl as they passed. Within moments of reaching his room, a boy entered with a tray of food. Aqhat thanked the boy and dismissed him. "I'll be back soon with the things you will require for your trip home."

Kamose smiled. "Thank you, Aqhat." He forced himself to remain patient, polite.

Aqhat nodded and left.

The food was delicious, as it was the night before. Kamose ate quickly. He had just taken the last bite of meat and washed it down with juice when two large armed men slammed open his door.

Kamose's blood ran cold. "Where's Aqhat?"

The men each grabbed an arm, yanked him to his feet, and thrust him through the doorway. They led him halfway down the familiar hall, then turned left, down another long hall into a different room, much larger, toward the back of the palace areas, and shoved him to the center.

Pain shot through his shoulders as the guards bound his hands to a metal ring high above his head on a wooden pole, then tied his feet together.

The low ceiling and lack of windows kept the air hot and heavy. The pole at the center of the large room was rough and dug into his chest and his cheek as he looked around the pole at his captors. Both guards had long daggers on their hips. Spears rested against the wall. Rods and rope hung on hooks and six more armed men stood guard at the door. All eight men were sturdy and well muscled.

What happened to going home?

He knew what was coming. He'd never been beaten before; he'd never disobeyed an order and never been captured. He preferred not to use beatings as a punishment himself; other methods were more effective. Still, he'd witnessed enough of them and knew they could be excruciating.

The guards were apparently waiting for something, for someone. They stood silently, unmoving. The two nearest him occasionally glanced at the door.

He forced himself to calm his breathing and his heartbeat. Allowing himself to become agitated would only keep him from thinking clearly and exacerbate the pain. He recited the names of the men under his last command as captain of the guard. It had been well over a year, but he could see each face, remember each man. How many had died when Yahweh sent the Angel of Death?

Not a good distraction. He rehearsed a military drill, one of those he taught to young recruits while still on the field to ready them for battle, executing each exacting move perfectly in his imagination. One finished, he moved to the next. And the next.

After many frustrating moments, the door opened. Kamose raised his head. His mental diversion had worked—his breath was even, his heart beat at a normal pace. His mind was clear and quick. He surveyed the newcomers.

Four slaves, a pair at a time, entered, then moved to each side. Keret, dressed in fine, crimson robes and adorned in jewels, followed. He strolled to the side of the room facing Kamose, yet remained about six long strides away.

The two guards who had accompanied him walked to the wall across from the door, took down whips, and returned to stand on each side of Kamose, slightly behind him.

"Thought you were leaving, did you? My father is old, and easily fooled. I have no intention of letting you go until I learn what I need to know."

Keret spoke a command to the guards and raised a finger.

Kamose heard a whoosh before he felt the stings on his back. He counted twenty lashes, felt the welts rise and fill with blood—not enough yet to run down his skin. Pain shot through each stripe and around his body. He laid his head against the pole, closed his eyes, and breathed deeply through his nose.

"Now, when are they coming?"

Kamose's chest heaved. After several noisy breaths he looked up. "We are not coming. Yahweh is not with us. We will not be back for forty years."

The prince's eyes flashed. Another finger.

Kamose's back blazed with each blow. First one guard, then the other, slammed the thin strips of leather onto his bare back. Blood dribbled from his shoulders to his lower back and onto his shenti. He gritted his teeth against the pain.

"I need an answer. The truth, this time."

"I am telling you the truth."

"You are trying to trick me, to lull me into thinking you are not coming so you can take my city without a fight. It will not work. I will fight to the death. Even if the death begins here."

"We are not coming. We have been defeated. Even if we were, haven't you already proved you can beat us?"

The prince raised his finger again and the lashes rained down.

Flesh ripped from Kamose's body as the leather pulled away. He tried to arch his back, but that only pressed his chest into the raw wood. His body wanted to collapse, but the ropes held him securely, threatening to pull his shoulders from his torso.

"He should think about his answers for a time. Put him back in the cell."

Twenty

Tirzah squatted in front of Sarah, staring at the sheep's thick gray fur. How long had she been here? She'd left the tent this morning to come milk the animal, or at least that's what she'd told everyone. The truth was she couldn't stand to see one more person give her an encouraging smile, couldn't bear to hear one more person say, "He'll be home tonight. Everything will be fine." She told herself that enough. It was starting to sound hollow.

Joshua checked every day to make sure she had everything she needed and to reassure her Kamose would be home later that day. Except lately even he had stopped promising that.

She sat back on the sandy desert floor. The morning sun beat on her head as she rested it on her knees.

She wearied of putting on a smile in front of the girls and Ahmose. It was exhausting, pretending to be calm and content when she was panicking and losing hope.

Hope. What an elusive thing it was. She'd been better off without it. Life was dreary but predictable. Manageable. Then *he* came. And everything changed. He turned her life upside down, and then left. She should have known better than to trust a man.

She kicked a flower at her feet, dug the heel of her sandal into its root until it lay toppled onto the sand, the life draining from it.

She studied the fallen plant. That's how she felt. Rootless, tumbled on her side. Life, purpose, meaning, ebbing away. Why hadn't he left her alone? She was doing just fine without *him*. Why did he have to come and tell her all those beautiful words she didn't need to hear and that meant nothing? And in the end, changed nothing.

Hot, salty tears filled her eyes, and though she tried to fight them, she lost. She pounded the ground at her sides with her fists, while screaming with her mouth closed. She grabbed handfuls of sand, wishing she were still a child and could throw it at something, anything. Instead, she pitched it back at the ground.

Sarah backed away.

Her anger spent, her tears gone, she sat staring at the cloud above her. The cloud that protected her, but no longer protected Kamose. If he were still alive. Which was doubtful.

She was tired. So tired. Every part of her body felt as if it weighed an enormous amount.

Hadn't she felt just like this before Gaddiel had gone on his mission? Wonderful. She'd made no progress at all.

Kamose awoke on cold, hard stone. He tried to move, but his head pounded. Dried blood adhered his back to the floor. He rolled to one side, peeling his back from the stone in prolonged agony, ripping flesh once again. How did he end up on his back? He would never have done that with open, bleeding wounds. He must have lost consciousness and been thrown on the floor by his captors.

He sat up, and blood dribbled down his back. His shoulders ached. His stomach growled. He considered the cell that he feared would be his prison for a long time. This was not the room he'd been kept in before the beating. Light came from a tiny window set at least twice his height above him in the wall. He could see feet shuffling past it.

The sounds of sheep and voices in a language he didn't understand filtered down. He was deep underground.

Crimson stained the stone floor and walls. The hot air in the room refused to move, and settled around him, holding in the stench of sweat and urine. A pile of hay tossed in one corner was someone's feeble attempt at a bed. The ceiling was made of long timbers laid across the walls. His cell must be at least adjacent to the city, perhaps on the outside wall.

They'd taken his sandals and dagger. How long had it been since he'd had anything to eat or drink? When he was younger he could go for days without food, but he was not so strong any more. His age, the lack of water, the loss of blood, the beating… he was getting weaker by the moment.

And of course there was Tirzah.

He fought to control his emotions. Sentiment got in the way. But how could he have possibly foreseen he would need to be so clear-headed at this point in his life? He thought he was past all that, all the soldiering, all the fighting, the need to be insulated, isolated. It was finally safe to fall in love.

Or so he'd thought.

He shook his head. He needed to concentrate. He studied his surroundings again, looked for any way to escape. The only entrance was a massive, wooden door with a narrow opening. At least this one seemed to be at a reasonable height. He rolled onto his knees. The edges of the stones sliced into his skin as he pushed himself up, then he lumbered to the door. He stood with his back toward the door—careful not to lean on it—at one side of the window, and listened for movement. Hearing none, he twisted around and peered out. On the other side, earthen steps led up. The tiniest bit of light shone at the top. He took a step back and his fingers vainly groped for space between the door and the wall; it was well-built. There was half a hand's width at the bottom, but that didn't help.

He ran his hand over the surface of the door. It was worn. He fingered the window, about the width of a small child's head and three times as high. Each edge, inside and out, was smooth as well. He turned and surveyed the floor—also worn and aged. This was a very old prison. Many men had been held here. How many had died here?

He paced. He had to get back to Kadesh. But how?

He thought back to the beginning, when he was caught. *Try to remember everything.* He'd never been captured before, never been on the defensive.

He was not beaten here. Good. That meant they'd take him out of here if they wanted to interrogate—or whip—him yet again. He'd have a better chance of escaping from almost anywhere else. Could he remember where he was before? He squeezed his eyes shut, but all he could remember were the faces of the men who had chained him to the pole so he could be beaten senseless.

Think! He'd been there, he must have seen that room. Think beyond the guards. He'd stared at his feet. The floor. The floor was polished stone, like the palace in Pi-Ramses. He'd been brought before the prince of Arad. He was young, maybe Joshua's age. But he didn't stay in that room. He was led to another room, beyond that one, to be tortured.

The prince. What did he want to know? Yahweh. He wanted to know about Yahweh, kept asking about Yahweh's plans. As if Kamose would know. Yahweh was not going to share his plans with an Egyptian. The prince didn't believe him when he said the Israelites weren't coming. That's what got him punished.

The door opened. The guard set a bowl of food on the floor, then locked the cell again.

At least they were feeding him. Which brought up another question.

How long did they intend to keep him here?

28 Av

Kamose looked at his hands, tied to the ring at the top of the pole again. The air cracked as the whip sliced through it, again and again. After twenty lashes the guards stopped, but the pain did not. One hundred lashes was a common punishment in Egypt. If the guards used a man's entire back—from shoulders to calves—there was plenty of skin to flay and keep a man alive and conscious. More often, however, it took more than one session to reach the total. By his count he was only at sixty, but the strokes had all been to his back, and they were having a profound effect.

The prince drew closer. "When are you coming?"

Kamose stared at the blood dripping onto the floor at his feet while he caught his breath. This time he could not raise his head. He could not speak. He could only shake his head slightly.

The prince stepped back. "Count?"

"Sixty."

"Twenty more."

The blows began again. Kamose held out as long as he could, but somewhere around blow number six, everything went dark.

1 Elul

Tirzah rolled over onto her back. The early morning sun shone through the flap. She should get up. She didn't want to. She'd rather stay in the tent, stay asleep. Maybe then she could forget everything that had happened. She threw one arm over her eyes, then the other, as if trying to block out the memories. It didn't work.

She glanced around the tent. The girls were already up and gone. Again. She dressed, skipped brushing her hair, dragged her exhausted body into the too-bright day. Better hurry before the manna melted. She grabbed the pot and headed outside of camp.

She knelt to gather the precious food, then just dropped onto the sand. It was easy to reach enough of it from her knees. She gathered enough only for two.

She stood and shuffled back to her tent, where she boiled the manna, then scooped some into bowls for Naomi and Keren. After placing the bowls beside the fire, she laid a cloth over them. Everyone else was already finished with the morning meal and had wandered away. She was grateful for the quiet, and sat in front of the fire, staring at the flames that seemed once again to mock her.

Kamose is dead.

She knew it. He had to be. The others had been back over a week now—eleven days. He was either dead or dying. No one else would say it out loud, but she knew it was true. She drew her legs up and hugged them to her chest. She laid her head on her knees and softly cried.

After a while she dried her tears and crawled back into her tent. She curled up on her mat and fell asleep.

Meri shook her gently. "Tirzah?"

Tirzah struggled to break through the fog in her head. How long had she been asleep?

"Tirzah?"

Go away.

"Tirzah, it's time to eat."

She rolled to the other side, facing away from Meri. "I'm not hungry."

"You didn't eat last night or this morning."

"I'm still not hungry."

"Do you want to at least come outside and sit with us? Everyone wants to see you."

I don't want to see them. "No."

"Please?"

Tirzah said nothing.

Meri finally left.

Tirzah sank back into the numbing fog.

A voice woke her once again. How much later was it? She tried to open her eyes, but they would not cooperate for long. It was dark out.

"I'm really worried," the voice whispered. "She's been sleeping all day."

Meri.

"Me, too."

And Sheerah.

"Come here, girls, let's get your sleeping tunics on, and brush your hair," Meri whispered again.

"Is Imma sick?"

That voice was Keren's. *Meri and Sheerah are putting the girls to bed. I can't even do that.*

"In a way. But she'll get better soon. Lie down now." Blankets and mats rustled, and kisses on cheeks smacked, followed by giggles.

"What should we do?" asked Sheerah, as she crawled out of the tent.

"I don't know. But I'm getting very worried."

4 Elul

The tent flaps rustled as Rebekah stepped inside Tirzah's tent. Tirzah didn't much care, though. She didn't much care about anything. The last thing she wanted was to talk.

She watched Rebekah glance around. The girls were already gone, as usual. Clothes, pots, and shoes lay scattered about.

An hour later, Tirzah sat by the fire. Meri and Sheerah had basically dragged her from her tent. She'd hidden there for three days and apparently Meri had had enough.

So what?

Meri had helped her clean herself and Sheerah returned to tidy up the tent. At least they had done it after everyone else had left the fire so she didn't have to face or talk to anyone. Thank Yahweh.

Thank Yahweh? She didn't feel like thanking Him for anything. How could He give her what she needed—though she didn't know she needed it—and then take it away again? She'd been doing fine without Kamose. She'd adjusted to what was expected of her. She didn't like it, but she'd become accustomed to it. The girls had food and a place to live, and that was all that mattered. But then He had to go and give her a taste of what could have been, just so He could yank it out from under her.

She felt rather than saw someone sit next to her. She peeked out from under her lashes and saw Meri and Sheerah by the tent. Had to be Rebekah sitting beside her. A hand landed on her shoulder. Instead of comforting her, the tears began to flow.

"Tirzah, you must eat."

"I'm not hungry."

"I know. You still must eat. You have the girls to think of." She handed Tirzah a bowl of hot manna and a spoon.

Tirzah held the bowl between her hands. The warmth was soothing, moving from her hands through her arms. It felt good against the chilly morning breeze. She picked up the spoon and stirred the porridge.

Rebekah gently lifted Tirzah's hand to her mouth.

The hot, sweet manna slid over her tongue and filled her mouth. She swallowed and dunked the spoon for another bite. Then another… and another. The bowl was emptied quickly.

"I didn't realize how hungry I was."

"I know."

Rebekah handed her another bowl.

"That's the second time you've said I know."

Rebekah nodded. "I was about your age when Bezalel's father died. I know how it feels. How empty your heart, your home, your future feels. But you have to keep going. You have to take care of yourself so you can care for your children. Even if you don't want to right now."

Tirzah shoved the last bite in her mouth. "I'm not sure I can. Not again. It's different this time."

Rebekah shrugged. "How? Alone is alone."

"But before, I was alone even when I was still married. Jediel was a horrible man. I was better off when he was gone. But Kamose ..." The tears began to pour from her eyes and she couldn't stop them.

"You can still do this." Rebekah took the bowl from Tirzah's hands.

"I can't ..." Tirzah raked her hands through her hair, leaving her hands on her neck.

"Yes, you can."

"How do you know?"

"I did it."

She glanced sideways at the older woman. "How?" She wasn't nearly as strong as Rebekah. She'd never make it.

Rebekah shook her head. "You just do it. Every day. You wake up, feed your children, take care of your house, wash the clothes, put the girls to bed, and do it all again the next day." She put her arm around Tirzah. "And you will not be alone. I had Bezalel's grandfather. He did it alone, too."

Tirzah sniffled and wiped her eyes. "He did?"

"Yes. His wife died when Bezalel's father was but a young boy. His family helped him. He helped me. And we will help you. And Yahweh is always with you. Never forget that."

But the weight that had momentarily lifted crashed on her shoulders again. "Maybe it would have been better if I had never known Kamose."

"Oh, no. Never think that." Rebekah pulled her closer and rubbed her back.

"Maybe it wouldn't hurt so much."

"But think of all you have gained, even though you knew him for only a short time. You know what real love is. You have good things to remember, instead of all the things Jediel did to you. Kamose showed you what you are worthy of, what Yahweh thinks of you. Your girls know what an abba's love is like, and they will not settle for someone like Jediel. You have a new family now to be part of. And, most importantly, you are free from Nathaniel. Yes, you have lost a great deal, but you have gained far more than you ever lost."

5 Elul

Kamose lay on the stone floor, and tried to think about anything other than the raging pain of his bleeding back. The cuts from the first two beatings had finally begun to heal when the guards dragged him back to that hated room again last night, and whipped him after he refused to tell Prince Keret that the Israelites were planning an attack on Arad.

He opened his eyes at a noise at the door. A boy came in with a small bowl of food. The boy closed the door behind him and the lock clicked into place.

The boy—a young man, really—held out the bowl and offered it to Kamose. His smile was disarming and he held his other hand palm up to prove he was not armed.

Kamose grimaced as he sat up and took the bowl. He mumbled his thanks in Egyptian.

The boy's eyes grew wide and he backed toward the door, bumping into it. He banged on it and waited for the guard to let him out, then Kamose heard his footsteps race up the stairs.

Now how could he have scared that kid? He could barely move. Surely he did not appear a threat.

Several hours later, the jingling of keys woke Kamose from a light sleep. He must have dozed off. The boy entered the room, this time with a large tray. On it sat two large bowls of hot food, another smaller bowl, and some cloths. He sat on the floor across from Kamose.

"Hello. I am called Danel." He spoke in perfect Egyptian.

Kamose quirked an eyebrow.

Danel chuckled. "We have many Egyptian traders pass through here. I've picked up the language." He handed Kamose one of the steaming bowls.

He'd more than "picked up" the language. He had to have grown up with it—it was flawless, completely unaccented. But Kamose wasn't going to argue with someone bringing him food. He tasted the stew. Lamb, with root vegetables, not all of which he recognized. He ate greedily. It was delicious. Not the stuff they'd brought him the last few days. Obviously the prisoners had a different cook.

"I've never seen anyone eat so fast!" Danel offered his bowl. "Want mine, too?"

Kamose eyed the bowl.

"It's all right. I can get more." Danel chuckled as he pushed it closer to Kamose.

Kamose took it and shoveled the stew into his mouth. "Why did you run away earlier?"

"You shocked me when you spoke in Egyptian. You sounded like…" His face clouded. "I just didn't expect to hear it. We never have Egyptian prisoners. If we captured traders, they'd quit coming here, and we make a lot of coin off of them."

Kamose finished his meal. "What day is it?"

Danel told him the Canaanite name.

"That doesn't help me. I don't know those names." He raked his hand through his hair. "Do you know how many days I've been here?"

Danel moved behind Kamose, dragging the tray with him, and dunked the cloth in the smaller bowl. He gently washed Kamose's back, though he didn't always succeed in avoiding the pieces of hanging flesh or flayed skin. "You've been in this room eight days. You were brought before the prince again last night. You slept all night and until midday. I brought you food at noon, and this is the evening meal."

Kamose added the time in his head. "Fifteen days." And two hiking to get here, and two to get to the injured men. He'd been gone almost three weeks. He arched his back as the liquid stung his wounds. "Is the king going to kill me now?"

"No, the king is done with you. He got the information he wanted. It's the prince you have to worry about."

"Keret?"

"The prince doesn't believe you. But he won't kill you. He likes his prisoners."

"So ... he'll just keep me here, starve me ..."

Danel breathed deeply. "No, he likes his prisoners strong and healthy for when he beats them."

They remained silent for several moments as Danel wiped the dried blood from between Kamose's stripes. Water plopped into the bowl as he wrung out the cloth. A bird hopped on the windowsill above, its chirps barely audible from this distance.

"Are there others?"

"There were."

"What happened to them?"

Danel stacked the bowls, grasped the tray, and strode to the door. "I'll keep bringing you food. You'll be all right. For a while."

Twenty-one

8 Elul

After the midday meal, Tirzah and the children strolled to the river. She sat on the log, in the same spot Kamose sat when he first came to see her. Or rather, to find Ahmose. The breeze had stilled, and the air was heavy. In the heat of the afternoon, even the birds were quiet. Nothing interfered with the memories that surrounded her, overtook her, threatened to drown her. Her stomach ached as she remembered his deep brown eyes, the way he felt, the way he sounded, the way he looked at her. She hugged her arms around herself.

Ahmose found the girls a batch of wildflowers and butterflies, then plodded over to Tirzah. "He's not coming back, is he?" His eyes held a pain she had not noticed before.

She blinked several times. "No, habibi, I don't think he is."

He wrapped his arms around her neck. His tears wet her tunic for several moments. He pulled back and wiped his nose, then sat next to her on the log. "Are you going to die, too?"

She whipped her gaze to him. "Whatever makes you say that?"

He stared at her, his eyes full of concern. The same eyes Kamose had—they made her heart stutter. "You don't eat, and you sleep a lot."

She drew in a ragged breath. "How does that mean I'm going to die?"

He shrugged. "That's what the old people at the palace did just before they died."

She laughed mirthlessly. "Are you saying I'm really old?"

"No." He kicked his heel against the log. "I just don't want you to die, too."

His words hit her like cold water thrown in her face. Had her behavior been that selfish? She put her arm around his shoulder. "Habibi, I do not intend to die."

He kicked a while longer, then hopped off the log and stood in front of her again. He studied her face a few moments, then placed his hand in the middle of her chest. "It hurts here, doesn't it?" Her heart nearly stopped. Until now, she had simply never considered that Kamose's death would affect anyone else as much as it did her. Did Ahmose hurt as much as she did? Kamose was the child's uncle, Bezalel's best friend. He had saved Meri's life. Twice. Yet they had all put their grief aside to help her. She spoke past the lump in her throat. "Yes, it does. It hurts very much."

"I know. It hurt there when Bezalel almost died in Egypt, and it hurt when Sabba died. It hurts now, too." He watched over his shoulder as Naomi and Keren chased butterflies. When he faced her again, his dark lashes were wet as he held back tears. "They don't understand, do they?"

She shook her head. "Not really. They've asked for him, but they don't understand he won't ever be back."

"Will they remember him?"

"I don't know."

"I don't remember my imma."

She placed her arms around his waist and drew him closer. "I'm sorry, habibi."

"It's all right. Yahweh brought other people to love me. He'll bring you other people, too."

She sniffled. He certainly believed that, but she didn't.

He pulled back to look in her eyes. "After Sabba died, for a while I didn't think I'd ever feel like smiling again. But I did. And then Yahweh sent me you. And Naomi and Keren."

Tirzah chuckled. She was sent to Kamose, wasn't she? Or maybe he'd been sent to her. But if Ahmose wanted to believe she was Yahweh's gift to him, that was fine with her.

When the girls finally tired themselves out, they returned to camp. Tirzah laid them down for a nap and joined Rebekah at the fire pit.

Tirzah told her what Ahmose had said at the river. "He believes Yahweh will make everything better, no question. He has such faith. But I'm not sure I do. I'm not sure I want to trust Him anymore."

"Oh, habibti, don't say that. You know, in Egypt, we knew him only as El Shaddai, God Almighty. He made promises and plans and carried them out and we were subject to them. But now, we know him as Yahweh, as the I Am. He dwells with us, in the tabernacle built by my son, who only learned the skills he needed to build that dwelling after being a slave in Pharaoh's palace. Yahweh *dwells with* us, He is with us, all of us, each of us. Do you see the difference?"

"I suppose."

"Remember what Moses said at your wedding? 'If you call on Him, He will answer you; He will be with you in trouble, He will deliver you.' He will be with you in this time of trouble if you let Him."

Tirzah nodded. That might be what Moses said, but the fact remained: Kamose was still dead, and she was in fact, alone. How could Yahweh deliver her from that?

11 Elul

Kamose tried to lift his head, but the incessant, torturous pounding inside it prevented him. No matter, he couldn't see anything even if he could look up. The dark in the room was oppressive. Light only shone in the tiny window about an hour a day, right at sunup.

They had whipped him again last night—the fourth time—until he blacked out. Which took fewer and fewer strokes each time. He'd considered lying and telling them the Israelites were indeed coming, since that seemed to be what they wanted to hear, but then they would only want battle plans, and he had none.

He was beginning to hate Prince Keret of Arad. Actually, he was beyond beginning. He hated him quite soundly now. But nothing pained him as much as the knowledge that Tirzah probably thought him dead. Like every other man in her life, he had let her down. After promising he would be different. Not to mention Naomi and Keren. The sound of "Abba" rang in his ears.

A knock on the door banished his girls' cries from his thoughts. Danel—he assumed it was Danel, since no one else ever came—entered. Kamose opened his eyes to see Danel's familiar feet. The boy placed a tray of cheese and bread on the floor and sat beside Kamose. With his hands on Kamose's biceps, he helped him sit up.

Pain screamed throughout Kamose's body at Danel's touch. He set his jaw and squeezed his eyes tight. Every move was agony, since they had extended the lashes to the backs of his legs the last time as well. Finally he settled into a position he could maintain, with his knees up, forearms rested on his knees.

Kamose wasn't hungry, but he had to eat. As he chewed the piece of bread Danel handed him, he tried to keep the rest of his body as still as possible. His back was stripped raw. The slightest effort caused almost unendurable pain. Even if he could get out of the room again, would he have enough strength to run? Would he have enough energy to even recognize the opportunity?

Danel continued handing pieces of bread to Kamose, forcing him to eat. Somehow he managed to do it without making Kamose feel like a child. He had to be a few years older than Ahmose. His hair and coloring in general were much lighter than his nephew's. His hair was down, but cut off below his ears, like everyone else Kamose had seen. His eyes were a beautiful blue-green. His smile, much like Ahmose's, lit up his whole face.

After the entire loaf and a chunk of cheese were consumed, Danel handed him a large cup of juice. While Kamose downed it, Danel peeked at Kamose's back. "This is looking bad. I've got some honey." He opened a pot and stuck his fingers inside. They came out covered in liquid gold.

The honey soothed Kamose's wounds, and his taut muscles relaxed. Danel talked as he smeared it across each stripe. "Do you have a wife?"

"Her name is Tirzah."

"Children?"

"Twin girls. Naomi and Keren. They're only three."

"I think you must be a good father." Danel pointed to some grapes with his clean hand, but Kamose waved them off. "I'm going to try to get you out of here," Danel whispered.

He had an earnest voice, much like Ahmose.

Oh, he missed his nephew. "How old are you?"

"Thirteen."

"I have a nephew. His parents are … they can't care for him. He's with me now. He's nine. You remind me of him."

"What's his name?"

"Ahmose."

"Ahmose and Kamose. Like the kings?"

Kamose nodded. He'd named his sister's baby after one of Egypt's most powerful pharaohs. At the time he hoped the name's power might somehow protect the child, give him a better life than the one he was sentenced to as a motherless child in the harem. Would Kamose even see him grow up now?

Danel set aside the honey. He knelt before Kamose as he wiped his hands on a cloth. "All right, then, Kamose, you have to eat and get back to him, and to Tirzah and Naomi and Keren. I know you're in bad shape, but you have to try. Finish the cheese and grapes. I'll bring more food tonight. Eat it all. The next time they take you to the chamber, I'm going to get you out."

Kamose's heart beat faster. He could not have anyone else at risk. "No, you mustn't endanger yourself—"

"I won't. My imma and I have been planning this for days. You'll get out, and we'll be safe." He put his hand on Kamose's arm. "You're … you're different. All the other prisoners … they're thieves and murderers and they plot against the king or the prince. The prince may be cruel and crazy, but they still broke the law. You didn't do anything. I don't want you to die here." He closed the pot, gathered up his tray, and left without looking back.

The thought of dying in this room was miserable. The thought of leaving Tirzah alone again was more than he could bear. He'd only married her a few weeks ago.

The wedding. What was it Moses said?

"If you say, 'Yahweh is my refuge,' and you make El Shaddai your dwelling, no harm will overtake you, no disaster will come near your tent."

"No harm will come to you." No harm will come to you? What would you call what had happened to him these last few weeks? He'd been seriously harmed, and only because all those Israelites did not obey. In all his life he'd never once been whipped by a superior, because he'd always obeyed, and now because the Israelite rebels did not listen, he was near death.

"If you love Him, He will rescue you. If you call on Him, He will answer you; He will be with you in trouble, He will deliver you."

He will be with you. Was He here now?

Yahweh, will you deliver me?

13 Elul

Sitting by the dying fire, Tirzah scrubbed the last pot sparkling clean and placed it in the stack outside her empty tent. Rebekah had taken the girls for a walk while Tirzah cleaned up from the evening meal. The setting sun cast long purple streaks across the western sky. Tonight the heavy, dark cloud threatening to suffocate her was a little less ominous, and the pain that was her constant companion a little less sharp. Each pop of the fire seemed to release a tiny bit of tension.

She turned from the tent to find a familiar—and unwelcome—pair of sandals filling her field of vision. She drew her gaze up his legs, his torso, to his disgusting smile.

Nathaniel.

She took several deep breaths before she stood and faced him. "What are you doing here?"

"I came to check on my favorite sister-in-law." His smile made her stomach churn, and it took enormous effort to keep from spewing her food all over him, as attractive an idea as that was.

She glared down at him. "I am no longer your sister-in-law." She clenched her jaw. And her fist. Although she'd do more damage to her hand than to him if she hit him. And be in serious trouble.

"But I hear your precious Egyptian has run off."

"He did not 'run off.' He went to rescue the wounded abandoned on the field by the others."

Nathaniel spread his hands and made a show of looking around. "Then where is he?"

Tirzah's cheeks heated. "He has not returned."

He smirked. "Then perhaps you are no longer married."

Tirzah stepped forward. "If anything, I am *his* widow, not Jediel's. Your obligation is satisfied. You can leave now."

Nathaniel touched his finger to his chin. "Are you sure this marriage was even legal? I mean, he's not an Israelite. ..." Nathaniel scrunched up his face.

From the corner of her eye, Tirzah saw people coming out of their tents. She cringed. What did they want? Were they angry with her for arguing with a man? For creating a scene? Well, she would end this as quickly as possible. "Moses himself gave his permission and married us. I think that's as legal as it can be. You gave up your rights, and Moses said we could marry as long as we realized we would not inherit land in Canaan."

Nathaniel neared Tirzah.

Some of the women came to stand behind her. She sucked in a breath. They were here to support her? That never would have happened in her clan in Zebulon.

Nathaniel eyed the women cautiously. "I gave up my claim on you only because your Egyptian threatened me." He spoke softly.

"You killed Benjamin!" She made no attempt to lower her voice. Every muscle in her body constricted as she fought to restrain her rage. Tears pooled in her eyes, but she willed herself not to cry. Not in front of Nathaniel. He wasn't worth it. She would not cry because of him on the same day she cried for Kamose.

"You have no proof of that." He put his hands on his hips and smiled his horrible smile.

"Kamose found the bloody knife in your tent."

Nathaniel shrugged.

Tirzah drew as close as she dared to her former brother-in-law, and pointed to his feet. "And you still have blood on your sandal." She couldn't help the scorn in her voice.

Men with crossed arms and fisted hands came to Tirzah's side. At nearly the same moment, Bezalel, Joshua, and Nahshon broke through and took their places between her and her tormentor.

"Is there a problem?" Bezalel asked.

"I really hope not." Joshua flicked his thumb over the tip of his spear while he stared down Nathaniel.

"You have no claim on her. Don't *ever* come near her again." Nahshon turned Nathaniel toward Zebulon and gave him a push.

Tirzah caught his eye before he slunk away. Pure defeat. She'd never have to worry about him again. She released a long breath as Bezalel gave her a hug.

"Are you all right?" he asked.

"I am now." She looked at the three of them. "I don't know what to say." Tears rolled down her cheeks.

"There is nothing to say. You're family. We take care of family." Bezalel squeezed her shoulder and stepped away.

Meri grabbed her and wrapped her in one of her all-encompassing hugs. How could she feel so confined by this slip of a girl? But it felt good. Really good.

She watched the crowd disperse. Several of the women smiled or waved as they left. She truly would never be alone.

Perhaps Yahweh knew what He was doing after all.

14 Elul

A key turned in the lock and the door squeaked open on its ancient hinges. The familiar guards entered and grabbed Kamose by the arms. They dragged him out of the cell, up the stairs.

Rescue me, Shaddai.

The pair pulled him into the too-familiar room, dragged him toward the pole, and leaned him against it. He groaned as unbelievable pain surged through every part of his back. The taller soldier grasped his elbow and spun him around, then yanked his arms above his head. His shoulders burned. His vision blurred. His heart pounded in his ears. But as the other guard started to tie his hands to the pole, an intense commotion in the hall drew his attention. A woman screamed. Prince Keret shouted to his men and all went running.

Kamose was left alone. He slumped against the wood.

Though he could barely think, he knew this was his only chance. Though he could hardly stand, he headed for the door. His legs agonizingly objected. He peeked around the opening. Keret argued with the guards while a woman tearfully grabbed at his robes. Kamose glanced the other way; no one was in the hall. It was risky—very risky. He had no idea where to run even if he weren't seen.

Keret continued to quarrel. The words were Canaanite, but the fight was clearly intense, and getting more so.

A guard maneuvered away from the fight just enough for Kamose to see his face.

Aqhat?

The guard winked, then slipped back into the crowd.

This was a setup? It was worth the chance. What more could they do to him? He slipped around the doorframe and bolted away from them down the hall. At the end of the hall he turned right. Danel was waiting for him with a huge smile on his face and a pack on his back. "I knew you'd figure it out. Follow me."

They turned right, then left.

Pounding footsteps signaled the pursuit had begun.

Yahweh, deliver me. I need Your power now.

Energy poured into him from somewhere, he didn't know where. His heart pumped furiously. Sweat ran down his face. His chest burned and his legs begged to stop. He no longer felt the stripes on his back.

The spies had said the palace was in the northeast quadrant of the city. Assuming his cell was on the outside wall, and the room he was beaten in on the edge of the royal dwelling, he should be headed toward the center of town.

The guards would catch him any moment. They were fresh, well-fed, and they knew the layout of the palace. Kamose was weak, injured, malnourished, and unfamiliar with his surroundings. But he was running for his life.

If he didn't get outside soon, he'd be caught again.

One more turn. Left, through a door, into the kitchen. Workers scattered, pots flew. It was a long room. At the end of it, a wooden double door. Danel threw it open.

Kamose rushed for it when his foot caught on something and he went flying. He landed on the floor, his arm hitting a pottery jar and smashing it. Bright red blood poured from the jagged cut onto the dirt floor.

He scrambled to his feet. A young kitchen worker, obviously trying to curry favor with the prince, had tripped him, and stood smirking, ready for a fight. The Canaanite swung his fist but Kamose ducked. Unfortunately he wasn't fast—or alert—enough to duck the other fist, which caught his right eye. Kamose hit back and connected with the young man's nose. The man retaliated with a fist to Kamose's mouth. Whoops and hollers filled the room as the workers cheered for their man.

He didn't have another punch in him. This was it. He'd be captured again and taken back to the torture room, and this time it was doubtful he'd come out alive.

Yahweh, take care of Tirzah and the girls.

Danel stepped in front of him, brandishing a long knife. The worker put his hands out to his side, palms up, and moved aside. Danel motioned Kamose toward the door, then backed to the entrance.

Once outside they picked up the pace. Kamose squinted his eyes against the bright sun, and within several long strides they were through the palace grounds, the outer door, and had lost themselves among the traders in the market. He placed himself behind several men, crouching, and watched the guards tumble out the door in the shorter wall that shut the palace behind him. They spent only a few moments searching for him, then gave up and returned to the palace.

He stood. The noises and smells assaulted him after weeks in the dank and lifeless cell underground. Voices called loudly for others to test their wares. The scents of roasted meat and fresh bread filled the market. People bumped and jostled him as they hurried to buy and sell. Danel handed Kamose a sack. "Here's some food Imma made for you. It should last three days. Or not, depending on how you eat." He laughed. "There's some milk you need to drink right away. Here are two bags of water. I couldn't find your dagger—I'm sure someone has kept it—but here are your sandals, and a cloak to cover your back, at least until you are out of the city. It may sting, but you certainly can't walk around like that."

Kamose's chest heaved as he stared at the boy. "Are you sure you will be in no danger for helping me? They saw you with a knife."

"No, I'll be fine."

"And was that Aqhat?"

Danel laughed. "Yes. And that was my mother, crying in the hallway."

Kamose's chest constricted. How many people had risked their lives for him?

Danel laughed again. "The prince loves my mother's cooking. She's the best cook in the city. No one will touch her, or me. Don't worry." He glanced around. "Put your sandals on. People are staring." Danel slid over to another booth and dropped a few coins into the vendor's hands. The seller wrapped up a large chunk of cooked meat and gave it to the boy, along with a fresh loaf of bread.

Kamose sat on an upturned box and laced up a sandal while he watched Danel. The boy was a younger version of himself. Willing to do anything to counter injustice. Compassionate. Fearless, to a dangerous degree at his age.

Danel returned with the food. "Here's some more. This should give you an extra meal."

Kamose rose and put his hand on Danel's shoulder. "Why would you do all this?"

Danel dug his sandal in the ground a moment before he raised his gaze to Kamose. His face remained impassive but his eyes showed a deep loss. "You remind me of my father. He was Egyptian. He died a couple of years ago. He met my mother on a trading expedition through here and settled in Arad."

Kamose grabbed Danel and hugged him tightly. He could not stop the tears from gathering behind his eyelids. "You are a very brave young man." He pulled back. "Your father must have been proud of you. I'd take you with me, but your imma would not like that much, I'm sure." He chuckled lightly.

Danel laughed through his tears. "No, she'd be very angry."

"You take good care of her then. And give my thanks to Aqhat, too. I pray El Shaddai will protect you and your imma."

"And you as well. Perhaps someday I will learn more about your El Shaddai. Good-bye." He turned and raced back into the palace kitchen.

Now all Kamose had to do was walk out the city gates. He jogged along the street toward the main gate until it was in sight, then he slowed to a respectable walk.

He fell in behind vendors and traders and other visitors leaving Arad. The gatekeepers were more interested in those entering than those leaving and he slipped out easily. Once clear of their view, he pulled off the cloak and headed southwest as fast as his battered body could take him.

15 Elul

Tirzah set the plate of hot manna cakes in her lap. She brought one to her mouth, then set it back down. She looked at the people seated around the fire—her family. Slowly she drew her gaze from one person to the next. She cleared her throat. "I need to apologize to all of you."

Meri blinked at her, a date halfway to her mouth. "For what?"

"I've been incredibly selfish. I was concerned only with myself, with my own pain. I was so angry and scared and hurt at losing something I had never had before, hadn't dared dream of, I didn't realize that all of you were hurting, too. I am deeply sorry."

Her voice broke, and she swiped a tear off her cheek. "And I thank you for taking care of me, and Naomi and Keren, when I couldn't do it myself. I don't know what I would have done without you." She put a hand over her mouth and dropped her head.

Rebekah slid Tirzah's hair behind her shoulder and bent her head to catch Tirzah's eyes. "We've all been in pain, habibti. It's all right. We're family. That's what families do. You didn't lose us when you lost him. It only felt like it."

The back of Tirzah's throat burned with salty tears. Again. "Will I ever stop crying?" She laughed.

"You will, I promise." Rebekah hugged her tightly, then handed her a manna cake. "Now finish your manna."

"Yes, Imma." She chuckled.

Meri giggled.

"Now it's settled." Bezalel laughed. "You're completely ours."

After the meal, Tirzah sat by the big spring where Moses had performed their wedding ceremony. She had faced the truth: Kamose was dead. He was not coming back. Only Yahweh could help her now.

Yahweh, will you be my refuge?

The constant bubbling soothed her thoughts and the breeze blew soft ripples across the water. The evening air cooled her skin, but the sand warmed her hands. She scooped a handful of the soft earth and let it fall between her fingers. No matter how hard she tried to hold onto it, she couldn't keep it from slipping away. Like her life, it changed. Over and over again. Now Kamose was dead, but so was Gaddiel. Nathaniel was no longer a threat. She was free to marry again, assuming anyone would want to marry a twice-widowed woman with two small children who had married an Egyptian. That was unlikely at best. But she had Bezalel and Meri and Rebekah. And Ahmose. She could make it. She would not starve. She had a new family—and a home.

And she no longer believed she was unworthy, unimportant, un-lovable. Kamose had shown her that in his short time with her. She was Yahweh's child. She was as important as any of his people. Just because her stepfather and her first husband had failed to realize that did not make it any less true. Even if no man ever loved her again, Yahweh loved her enough to ransom her from Egypt, bring her to Canaan, and give her a new family—and Kamose, even if just for a while.

Meri was right, after all. Her story did have a better ending. She laughed. A real out-loud laugh. All the times she had scolded Meri for saying that. Maybe there were better times yet to come. Even if there weren't, she'd learned to count on Yahweh. He was with her, would always be with her, and that was enough.

Twenty-two

Kamose slowed to a walk, glanced over his shoulder. He was out, free, safe. He could hardly believe it. If it weren't for Danel...

Yahweh, rescue me... such a simple cry. But Yahweh had answered him. He had delivered him from trouble. And Kamose knew He had been with Tirzah, too.

Oh, Tirzah. He couldn't wait to see her. To touch her skin, bury his hands in her hair, kiss her face. To hear the girls call him Abba.

He found a copse of trees behind a hill far enough away from Arad and collapsed to his knees beneath them. He wanted to sleep so badly. He reached into the bag for the food Danel had bought. He drew out the meat and fresh bread. The meat was still warm and tender, and the bread was soft. He stuffed it in his mouth in huge pieces. He downed the milk. He sat back slowly. The grass was wonderfully soft after the stone floor. The breeze felt good on his wounds. He reached around and gingerly touched his back. He pulled away and checked his fingers—they were tipped with sticky blood. The last time they whipped him was... almost a week ago. His skin was so damaged, though, the lacerations weren't healing properly.

The sun had gone and the air had cooled quickly. Gently, he draped the cloak over his shoulders again and lowered himself onto his stomach. He drifted off quickly. He'd have to rise early to avoid the shepherds.

ॐ⋘

The sounds of sheep bleating pricked at the edges of his consciousness. Words he could not understand. No, go away. He wanted to sleep, needed to sleep. The noises grew louder, more insistent, and sleep was driven from his mind.

Images flitted through his mind. Thoughts slowly came together. Arad. Escape. Were they after him again? He didn't need to sleep; he needed to leave. Now. He raised his head and peered around the trees under which he had slept. Thank Yahweh, they were only shepherds, and they were still far enough away. He grabbed his pack and cloak and loped toward the nearest rise, scurried over the top, and ducked behind. He waited for his breathing to slow, peeked over the crest. No one followed. He relaxed.

He reached into his bag for some bread and cheese. Although the crust was hard, the bread was still soft inside. He gulped it all, followed it with half a skin of water, and headed south.

17 Elul

Kamose stumbled and fell yet again. How long had he been walking?

He'd left Arad two days ago in the evening, walked two solid days, and today until early afternoon. Grabbed some sleep in a cave each night and started again as soon as the sun was up. He wasn't making very good time in his condition—he was much weaker than when he left a month ago.

He'd finished the food Danel had packed yesterday morning, and he had no weapons to kill or catch anything else. The lack of sleep and food was catching up with him, and he had at least another day of walking to go yet.

He dragged himself to his hands and knees. Another cave was close. He pulled himself up and stumbled toward it. He'd have to get more sleep. And food. He needed something substantial to get him home. He was on his last skin of water, too.

He clambered over the boulders toward the darkened entrance. His sandal slid, and his knee slammed against the stone as his hands landed on a nearby rock.

Yahweh, I can't do this. Please don't let me get this close only to fail.

He knelt there, gathering his strength, convincing himself to go forward.

In the distance, thunder rolled.

A thunderstorm? This early in the season? Fresh water. Maybe it would scare some animals into hiding. He glanced around. Some lizards skittered by. They were unclean, and the meat they provided would not be worth the work, anyway. Birds flew south, away from the northwestern wind.

Thunder boomed again. Large drops hit his back. The rain stung, but would probably be good for his wounds. He rose as the rain fell harder, bent over, and let the water sheet off his skin. After a few moments he raised his face to the shower. He opened his mouth and drank in the blessing.

After he was thoroughly wet and somewhat cleaner, he continued toward the cave. He removed his shenti and laid it on a boulder to continue getting doused, then he went inside.

He lay down, though he would have preferred to keep going straight on to Tirzah. Thunder continued to roll. That was good—the noise kept him from thinking. His mind overruled his heart, and he got some desperately needed rest.

✦

The silence awoke him. He crawled out of the cave. The sun hadn't moved far. He'd slept maybe a couple of hours, but the storm had lasted less than that. The rocks were already dry, as was his shenti.

The dirt was less noticeable, but it was still quite bloody. He tied it around his waist.

Water. There must be water collected somewhere. And maybe animals. He crept to the highest boulder and scanned the area. There. A pool. He grabbed his skins and jogged to the puddle.

He halted. The water was surrounded by sandgrouse. He had no arrows. How could he capture one? He went back to the cave and grabbed the cloak he'd discarded, ripped off a narrow length about as long as his arm. He searched for a couple of smooth rocks. He tied a small loop on one end of the cloth, and a large knot in the other.

Placing one of the rocks in the center of the strip, he folded the cloth lengthwise over it then brought the ends together. He put his middle finger in the loop, the knot between his forefinger and thumb, then stood and swung the cloth in the air over his head. His back stung at the motion. The sling whistled as it sped up, until he let go of the knot. The sling opened and the rock flew. It landed to the right of his imaginary target. He tried several more times, adjusting his aim for the inferior material and construction, until it landed where he wanted it every time. Then he jogged back to the pool.

When he neared the water, he climbed up on a nearby rock. He picked out a bird sitting apart from the others while he loaded the sling, then swirled it above his head. He let go and the rock sailed toward the grouse. It hit the bird squarely in the head, and the grouse toppled over.

At least he hadn't lost all his skill. Kamose strode to the bird, picked it up, walked a distance away from the pool, and built a fire. While the bird roasted, he climbed to the highest spot he could find and tried to figure out just how much longer he had to go to reach camp. And Tirzah.

18 Elul

Only a few hours to camp. The hours he thought he would lose to sleep and finding food had helped tremendously. He was out of the mountains, and on flatter ground he made far better time. He glanced west. The sun just touched the mountaintops. If he could keep up the pace he could make it to camp not long after sundown.

His thighs ached and his skin burned. His shoulder had begun to bleed again from using the sling. The softer sand was a welcome relief from the rocky terrain to not only his feet, but his hands and arms as well.

He paused to upend a skin of water. He took a long drink and even spilled some down his back. As he put the stopper in and tied it onto his belt, he squinted into the distance. He blinked and looked again.

His heart beat faster and his chest constricted. Was he really seeing what he thought he saw? The tops of date palm trees? Had he misfigured? He was closer than he thought.

He broke into a jog.

An hour later his chest heaved as he saw his wife sitting on the other side of the spring, her head on her knees. He forced his heart rate to slow as he circled around the water, sneaked behind her, and took a moment to calm his ragged breathing.

He stepped closer to her, still several strides away. Her hair fell in waves down her back, nearly touching the sand. The setting sun reflected off it, bringing out gold and red highlights. So beautiful. So close. If he could just … He drew a deep breath. "I've told you before, you should not be out here in the dark alone. It is not safe."

He watched and waited as she raised her head and remained still for a moment, as if she couldn't believe what she had heard. She slowly looked up over her shoulder, and her face lost its color. "But you're …"

"No, habibti, I'm here." He closed the distance quickly then reached down and pulled her to him.

What little composure she had left, she lost as she fell against him, trembling.

He buried his face in her neck. "I'm here. I love you," he whispered.

She could only cry as she looped her arms around his neck.

Everything else faded from consciousness as he held her—nothing else mattered. He was home, in her arms. He raised his face and held hers, studying it. He'd forgotten how beautiful she was. All he could remember was her kindness, her laughter, her touch. Her touch was what he craved right now. He bent to kiss her. She'd said his kisses melted her, but he was the one who nearly came undone when his lips touched hers. After four and a half weeks of hunger, thirst, and brutality, the tender kiss of his wife was a healing balm, and he didn't ever want to let go.

Though it was the last thing he wanted to do, he pulled away and rested his forehead on hers. "I love you. I dreamed of you every night."

"I can't believe you're here. We all thought... even Caleb and Joshua ..." She raised her hand and caressed his cheek.

"I'm sorry I didn't get here sooner. Bezalel and Nahshon took care of you? The girls are all right? Ahmose?"

"We are fine. Everyone was wonderful to us." She stared at him, and tears began to fall again. "I'm just so glad you're home."

He couldn't take his eyes off her. Was she standing before him? Was he really here? Or would he awaken once again on the cold floor of Keret's prison?

She drew her fingers over his face, touching the swollen eye the cook's assistant had pounded and setting off a shooting pain. The escape was real. He was home.

"We should go to the camp. There are many who will want to know you are safe."

He kissed her once more, then laced his fingers with hers and they started for the camp.

After a step or two, she stopped and pulled on his hand. "What happened? Why were you gone so long?"

"It's a long story. I'll tell everyone at once. Let's just go. Maybe there's some manna left."

Bezalel and Meri, Nahshon and Sheerah, Rebekah and Ahmose were around the fire when they reached their tents.

"Uncle Kamose!" Ahmose ran to greet him first when they were a couple of tents away, wrapping his arms around Kamose's hips, low enough to miss his stripes.

Kamose grunted as he picked him up. "Ahmose, I missed you so much."

Ahmose squeezed him tightly. "I love you, Uncle." His tears wet Kamose's cheek. He leaned back, his face lit up in delight. He laid his hands on Kamose's cheeks. "Yahweh sent you back." He turned to Tirzah, beaming. "He gave him back to you." The boy embraced him again, then kissed Kamose's cheek and hopped down.

The others gathered around the couple. There were a number of frowns and furrowed brows at his appearance. Only then did Kamose realize how bad he must look. His hair was down and tangled, his arms and legs were cut and bruised from the rocky climbs, he'd lost weight, and he was filthy, not to mention his injuries from the palace. Rebekah stepped behind him and gasped.

Tirzah never let go of his arm and never stopped smiling.

"Come sit down, Captain." Rebekah gestured to their fire pit. "Ahmose, get your uncle some manna. There was some left tonight. There never has been before, but there was tonight. Yahweh provided. Tirzah, we need water. Can you go fill all the skins?"

Tirzah furrowed her brow, glancing at Kamose. "But..."

Rebekah touched her arm. "Tirzah, your husband needs water," she said gently. "It will take only a few moments."

Tirzah frowned, but left.

"I'll go with you." Meri gathered her own skins and headed to the spring with her.

Kamose turned to watch her go.

Tirzah looked over her shoulder as she walked away. Her smile sent a rush of warmth through him.

Rebekah pointed to a chair, of sorts. It was smooth and flat on top, the bottom made of tree roots sticking out at all angles. "Bezalel made this for me, since it's getting harder for me to sit on the ground. He made it from a piece of fallen tree he brought from the river. Sit."

"But it's for you—"

"You need it more than I. Besides, I need to reach your back." Kamose sat and Rebekah continued issuing orders. "Nahshon, go to Judith and get some honey. As much as possible. Sheerah, we need olive oil."

Everyone scattered at her commands.

Ahmose sat at Kamose's feet with a plate of manna cakes, a dish of dates, and a skin of fresh sheep's milk.

Rebekah stood before him, hands on her hips. "Now, Captain, what happened to your back?"

"I was beaten." He reached for some manna.

"More than once, I'd say." She shook her head. "I'll tend to it, but disease may already have set in." She laid her hand gently on his wounds.

He stiffened.

"There is no heat. It seems Yahweh has been watching over you."

"I've had honey put on it a couple of times. The rain helped."

Nahshon and Sheerah returned with the honey and oil. Sheerah also brought a large bowl, and immediately began mixing the soothing ointment.

Rebekah smoothed honey on the stripes on his back, and though the wounds were tender, the sting began to disappear, and he relaxed.

A loud cry from behind him drew his attention. He turned to see Tirzah collapse, Meri wrapping her arm around Tirzah's waist, skins scattered on the sand at their feet. He started to go to her, but Rebekah placed her hand on his shoulder and pushed him back down.

"Bezalel." Rebekah pointed her chin to Tirzah.

Bezalel left to attend to Tirzah.

Kamose turned to Rebekah, his thumb over his shoulder. His heart ached—he wanted to tend to his wife. "But what's wrong with her?"

"She saw your back."

"She already saw it."

She offered a sad smile. "No, she didn't."

"Yes, she did. She saw it as she left for the spring. I saw her." He tried to rise again but she pushed him down.

"No, Captain, she only saw you."

"I don't understand." He grunted as Bezalel helped Tirzah stand. It should be *his* job.

Rebekah grasped his chin with her hand and pulled his face to her.

For a moment Kamose felt like a child, being chastised by a teacher.

Then Rebekah's face softened. "She only saw *you*, home, safe, and with her. She did not see your bruised body, your black eye, and certainly not your bloody back."

Kamose munched on manna as Rebekah finished working on his wounds. He answered questions, but he was too tired to say much. Besides, he'd have to tell everything all over again to Moses tomorrow.

"Bezalel, take the captain to the river and help him clean up. But watch his back."

Treated like a child again. He didn't need to be led to the river.

He was perfectly capable of washing himself. Until he tried to stand and nearly toppled over. Bezalel caught him and righted him without making it obvious. They ambled to the river, every movement agony. The cool water restored his energy and soothed his sore feet.

Rebekah had given Bezalel a number of cloths. Kamose reached for one and bent to dip it in the river. He'd lowered himself only a few handbreadths when shooting pain screamed up and down his back. He gasped and balled his hands into fists. Slowly he stood up.

Bezalel dipped some cloths in the river and handed them to Kamose. He washed his arms, chest, and face. Bezalel cleaned his legs. "Your shenti is ruined. Do you have another?"

Kamose remembered having the exact same conversation with Bezalel when he met him coming down from the mountain next to Sinai, after Bezalel had spent the night arguing with Yahweh. Except that time, Bezalel was the one bloody and bruised. "In my tent."

"I'll get it." Bezalel started to jog back to the tent, but Ahmose met him, carrying the clean garment, a brush, and a strip of leather.

Kamose removed the bloody shenti and handed it to Ahmose. "Toss it in the fire when we get back."

Ahmose made a face and nodded as he traded the clean shenti for the dirty one.

Kamose began to brush his tangled hair. His shoulders ached as he lifted them, but he refused to let Bezalel do it. "Perhaps you should have returned the favor and met me and cleaned me before Tirzah saw me."

Bezalel laughed. "Friend, had I known you were coming, I would have gladly done so." He stepped back and looked Kamose over. "I hate to say it, but you look worse than I did."

"At least I didn't do most of it to myself."

"At least you've still got a sense of humor."

Kamose chuckled lightly. It was the first time he'd laughed in weeks. He pulled his hair back and tied it. Then he grasped the length of it, pulled it up, and stuffed it back behind the tie again without pulling it through, to keep it off his sticky, injured back.

Back at the fire, Kamose said final good nights. Nahshon and Sheerah left first, and Bezalel and Meri soon followed, dragging Ahmose behind them.

While Tirzah wouldn't let go of him before, now she wouldn't come near him.

"Let's go inside. I could sleep for a month." He reached for her hand, but she turned and entered the tent without him.

He peeked in on the girls behind the curtain in the back of the tent, their sleeping faces full of innocence. He prayed they would never experience the evil he had known, both here and in Egypt. Resisting waking them up, he turned to face Tirzah.

She stood hugging herself in the corner.

Pain gripped his heart. "Tirzah, are you afraid of me?"

She brought her hand to her mouth and shook her head. "No, I am afraid to hurt you," she whispered.

"Any pain you would cause me would be worth it, habibti. Please don't stay away from me." He drew near to her. "I need you tonight."

She drew in a shaky breath.

"Please."

She came to him and placed her cheek on his chest. She kept her hands balled by her shoulders.

She felt so good next to him. He enfolded her in his arms, and kissed the top of her head, sighing. He wanted to melt into her.

She relaxed against him, and her arms found their way around his neck. She lifted her face to meet his, and kissed him.

Her kiss was delicious, and heated his blood. He pulled her closer. He definitely wanted more, but a kiss was all he could handle right now. He groaned, and pulled away. "I have to lie down," he whispered.

Only one mat lay in their half of the tent.

The reality hit him like an enemy's arrow. "You really thought I wasn't coming back, didn't you?"

She shrugged. "There was nothing else to think. You were gone over a month."

He ran his knuckles down her cheek. "I'm sorry. I promised I would never leave you."

She touched his split lip. "That's not really yours to promise, is it? I know that now." She walked to the corner and unrolled his mat.

As he had for the last twenty-four nights, he lay down on his stomach. Exhaustion filled him. "Come lie next to me."

Tirzah lay next to his elbow.

He opened one eye. "Closer."

She snuggled next to him, her head on his bare bicep. Her hair spilled over his arm onto the mat. Her fresh scent enveloped him, releasing the last of the tension in his body.

"Mmmm. Thank you," he whispered. A deep sigh escaped him. For the first time in weeks, contentment settled over him. Within moments he fell into a peaceful sleep.

ॐ✦⛬

The early eastern light peeked in through the tent and tickled Tirzah awake. She'd stayed awake long after Kamose last night, just watching him sleep. Now she sat up and studied his back. The honey had helped calm the angry skin, but it was still a ragged mess. There was no way to count the number of lashes between his shoulder blades and ankles. Many of them wrapped all the way around his sides. His arms and legs were turning black and blue and green.

She ran her fingers through his hair and pushed it from his back. She bent and kissed his cheek and moved to the back of the tent.

She kissed the twins awake and led them out the rear entrance and back out between the tents. "Imma, what's wrong?"

"Hush. I have a surprise for you. First let's go get our manna."

She led them outside camp. "We have to collect an extra omer today."

"Why?" Keren rubbed her eyes. "Why did we go out backwards?"

"We have to collect an extra portion because Abba came home last night."

Keren jumped up and down and squealed. Naomi's bottom lip quivered. She collapsed on the sand, wrapped her arms around herself, and silently cried.

Tirzah reached for Keren's wrist as she started to run back to the tent.

"Listen first. He came home after you went to bed. He is badly hurt, and he is still sleeping. That's why we went out the back. You must not go in the tent until he wakes up, and that may be a while."

"Not fair!" Keren folded her arms and pouted.

Tirzah grabbed Keren's chin and placed her nose a finger's width from Keren's. "He needs to sleep. Will you promise you will not wake him?"

"I promise," she whispered.

"Keren?"

Keren huffed. "I promise."

"Who hurt him? Why is he hurt?" Naomi wiped tears from her cheeks, but more replaced them.

"Some bad men in the city. But he's home now, and he will get better." Tirzah beckoned to the girl, then wrapped her arm around her waist. "Now, when he wakes, you must be careful with him. He cannot pick you up and hold you here like he used to." Tirzah pointed to her hip. "Or carry you on his shoulders. And when you hug him, you must hug only his neck, not his shoulders or back."

Both nodded.

"Then let's get our manna and make our morning meal. Hug?"

She gave them both a good squeeze and they set to work.

 formula

Tirzah was opening the pot of manna for the noon meal when Kamose crawled stiffly out of the tent. He placed a lingering kiss on her cheek.

Bezalel and Ahmose and the girls returned from collecting dates near the river. Keren dropped her bag of fruit and ran for him. He bent to pick her up as she jumped into his arms—one of hers went around his neck and one around his shoulder.

He grimaced.

Tirzah closed her eyes. So much for her instructions. When she opened them he was moving Keren's little arm higher on his body, above the lash marks.

"I missed you so much, habibti."

"I missed you too, Abba." She kissed his nose, and wiggled out of his embrace.

He set her down and she bounced off.

Meri joined Tirzah and rubbed her back for a moment. Then she slipped the jar of manna from Tirzah's hands and went to the fire.

Kamose bent and reached for Naomi.

She kept her arms to her sides. "Are you sure I won't hurt you?"

He chuckled. "No, I won't let you. Come here." He lifted her to his chest.

She hugged his neck. "I love you, Abba."

"I love you, habibi."

After several moments, Naomi sat back on his arm.

He looked in her eyes. "Did you have any bad dreams while I was gone?"

"No, Ahmose slept with me at first and he prayed for me every night. Then, after a while, he just had to pray for me and I would sleep all night by myself." She smiled proudly.

"Ahmose is a very good cousin, isn't he?"

Naomi's tiny fingers hovered over his swollen eye, then dropped to his lip. "They shouldn't have been so mean to you." She pouted.

"But I'm home now. And I'll get better."

Tirzah's heart swelled as she watched Kamose with her children—his children. Yahweh had indeed blessed her. He'd given her more than she had ever imagined possible. A loving husband, a family of friends, a father for her children. And the knowledge that she was never alone.

Canaan could wait. She had everything she needed right here, by the waters of Kadesh.

Acknowledgments

My unending thanks to:

My mother—my first and biggest fan.

My husband John, and my beautiful, noisy, loving, patient children: Emma, Mira, Dara and Johnny—thank you for letting me do this *again*.

My critique partners and writing buddies, who always encourage me, push me, and inspire me to write my best.

My beta readers—Lynn Rose, Carrol Mercurio, and Dr. Sue Pankratz.

Sandi Rog.

Ellen Tarver—for once again refining my manuscript.

Dan DeGarmo and Nathan Ward—my publishers.

Reuben Rog—for a beautiful cover.

And of course you, my readers.

To learn even more about these characters and their world, as well as the stories to come, visit **www.caroletowriss.com**.

For a full listing of DeWard Publishing Company books, visit our website:

www.deward.com

Lightning Source UK Ltd.
Milton Keynes UK
UKHW012014170620
365176UK00001B/33